The Naga's Journey
A Novel

THE NAGA'S JOURNEY

A Novel

by

Tew Bunnag

Orchid Press

Tew Bunnag
The Naga's Journey: A Novel

ORCHID PRESS
P.O. Box 19,
Yuttitham Post Office,
Bangkok, 10907 Thailand
www.orchidbooks.com

This is a work of fiction. The characters and plot of this story are solely the
product of the author's imagination. Any resemblance to events, locales, the
personality or actions of any person, living or dead, is purely coincidental.

Printed in Thailand

ISBN-10: 974-524-102-4
ISBN-13: 978-974-524-102-2

For my mother, with gratitude.

The cult of the Naga (*Naak*, or *Phaya Naak* in Thai) is a remnant of the animist worships that existed in South East Asia prior to the introduction of Buddhism in that region. With the establishment of the Buddhist culture, which was imported from India and Sri Lanka, the old beliefs and practices were incorporated and absorbed and became part of the new practices and rituals. The Naga is sometimes represented as a serpent with either seven or nine heads. In the Buddhist myth their king, Mukhalinda is supposed to have saved the Buddha from the flood waters sent by Mara who epitomizes the dark forces of the universe. But those who still follow the cult do not merely relate to the outer representation. For them he is not a serpent but the element of water itself with its power to nurture and to destroy.

Peter Kandy, *Journal of Asia-Pacific Studies*, 1968

PART 1

CHAPTER 1

It was 3 a.m. on the last morning of the rainy season retreat being held in Wat Thammacitta in Nongkai province, on the banks of the Mekong River. The storm had finally passed over, leaving the air cool and smelling of wet leaves. The chorus of bullfrogs, which had been deafening during the rain, was now more intermittent and the cicadas in the nearby forest were starting up their rhythmic scratching. The sky was clear again and in it a full moon hung low over the river, making it look like a milky expanse stretching to the horizon. Phra Boontam, as he was then called, a tall, light skinned young man not from those parts, sat cross legged on the floor of his small wooden kuti with the windows wide open, absorbing the light that came streaming in towards him at an angle directly hitting his face. Since he was a child the moon had always evoked in him the feeling of wonder and fascination. Now as he bathed in its glow he could feel its cool radiance wash over him. There was a notebook in his lap above which his right hand was poised holding a pencil, as if waiting for inspiration to begin writing.

Half an hour earlier Phra Boontam had woken up with a start from a dream that was so vivid that it felt as though it had taken place in reality rather than in the dream state. On awakening he was trembling and his body was covered in sweat and for a moment he did not know who or where he was. Then as he recovered his bearings a sense of awe filled him. In the dream he had been transported to some kind of parallel dimension, outside of time and incarnated in another body, not that of a human but of a mythological creature; the seven headed Naga, the water spirit. He had come across the Naga many years before when the spirit spoke to him (at least this was what it felt like at the time). But this was different. It was as if he had undergone an actual metamorphosis and slid back into some primal nature.

A dream, only a dream, he repeated to himself as he eventually calmed down, and he reasoned that given the fact that he had been doing eight hours of meditation a day for the past three weeks and keeping silent for that period except for the brief interviews with his teacher which took place every couple of days, it was not surprising that his mind, removed from dealing with the external world and turned inward on itself, should touch on such an unexpected area of the psyche. Besides, it was not the first time during his five years in the monastery that he had experienced unusual phenomena. Often during the last year in a session of sitting meditation he would have the sensation of being so light that he was hovering above the ground, or of stepping outside his body altogether and standing, watching himself from the corner of the hut. There were also instances when, while wide awake, he had come across things which he could not explain; bands of light hovering above the bamboo thicket behind his kuti, the sound of his old name, which nobody in the area knew, being called out from the opposite bank of the river, the sight of his dead father waving to him from the trees by the gate. Up till then Phra Boontam had always kept these moments to himself knowing that he was not alone in having glimpses of the deeper illusions, as the abbot called them.

His teacher, the abbot who was known as Phra Achaan, was aware that most of the monks got lost now and then in these unfamiliar mindscapes, especially during the periods of intensive practice and he often summoned them to the main sala to teach them about the nature of the mind. In these talks, held as the rain pelted down on the tiled roofs, all but drowning his soft voice, he told them that the meditation practice which was the central activity of their particular monastery generated a strong collective field of psychic energy and as a result the boundaries between normal everyday reality and the more subtle levels were much less distinct. They had to be constantly prepared for the unexpected, the stuff beyond everyday gaze. But all the visions that arose in the course of their practices, however weird and colourful they might be and the phenomena they could encounter from time to time such as the preta ghosts that roamed the grounds and the forest spirits that made their presence felt and the fireballs that shot out of the river were to be treated as nimitti, or hallucinations. They should not be afraid or overwhelmed but maintain their awareness and understand the essential emptiness of all these strange events. Phra Achaan was always solid and reassuring and provided amusing anecdotes to make the point that no one was special in experiencing these phenomena. Sometimes his tone would turn serious and he would warn them against the danger of playing around with psychic energy and becoming attached to them, for in the end they were all various layers of illusion, like the skin of an onion.

The abbot's teaching was for the most part a transmission of the standard, traditional line but he made it interesting and relevant to them every time he gave these discourses because it was clear that, having spent many years journeying through the labyrinths of his own mind, he was still intrigued by the capacity of consciousness to penetrate into the more bewildering aspects of so-called reality. As a young man he had been a writer and a poet as well as a heavy gambler who had, by his own admittance, experimented with various drugs that stimulated the imagination and opened the gates of his perception. Afterwards through meditation practice he explored the same terrain with sober awareness. So, on this subject as well as others, the abbot elicited respect from the monks, because they knew that what Phra Achaan offered to them was not a second-hand opinion. Like a true pilgrim he had himself gone into all the twists and turns and the blind alleys that their chosen path had to offer and had equipped himself with the wisdom that only direct knowledge could bring.

Like his fellow monks Phra Boontam trusted his teacher's advice, which was one of the reasons why he hesitated about mentioning the dream at all to the abbot, who would later that morning visit his kuti for their interview. He already guessed what Phra Achaan would say, and likely as not his dream would probably be added to the list of anecdotes as another example of nimitti. But it was not just that he was afraid of being criticized or ridiculed for giving importance to something he had been taught to dismiss as illusion. It was also because he was embarrassed by the content of the dream and thought that it would sound grandiose and tainted with ego if not downright sacrilegious to the Achaan. Yet for all this he felt the need to share his experience with his teacher because it seemed, oddly, to be the most significant thing that had happened to him during his whole time as a monk.

So that morning before the dawn Phra Boontam remained seated on the floor of his kuti for a long time, waiting for the appropriate moment to begin setting his thoughts to words. He had decided that it would be better to first write down as clearly and truthfully as possible every detail that he could remember, while his memory was still fresh. He wanted to avoid any distortion or later embellishments. This, of course, was more difficult than he thought. He realized, even before beginning his task, that choosing the right words was the problem, and, like many before him, that the gap between remembering a dream and putting it down on paper is the space between two worlds. But when he finally gathered his concentration he wrote the following account in one straight draft by the light of the full moon.

I am the Naga and I have watched him, the Buddha figure, sitting there by the river where I have seen many come and go. But he is different from the rest of them. Not because he can be still for whole days and nights. Many of the Yogis before him were able to do even more impressive things. But it is the quality of his simplicity that sets him apart. There is an absence of denial and self punishment; no pride, no sense of "I've won. I've conquered my body." He is content. His sacredness is of the earth. In the way he accepted the food that was offered by the shepherdess I saw how his quiet generosity blessed the giver.

I knew that he was in trouble as soon as the storm clouds gathered in the southwest corner of the sky. They were not ordinary clouds but bright, metallic ones that cast heavy shadows on a human heart. They could only have been Mara. When I heard that a man had become enlightened under a Bodhi tree after subduing the daughters of Mara, I knew that it was not long before the true test would begin. For Mara comes to those who have seen the light, to remind them of the dark underbelly of existence where earthly life takes place.

The skies are turning black. Fierce winds begin to howl through the trees and lightening flashes overhead. Then with a deafening crack a thunderbolt strikes the earth. Now the rains pour down. I am still watching.

He sits near the bank slightly away from the cover of a giant banyan tree. When a huge branch, struck and torn from its trunk, falls next to him, he shows no outward reaction. His eyes, as always are half closed. His samadhi is firm. He is aware of everything. He can see the waters steadily rising. He knows that Mara is close by. I can tell that he has no fear of what might happen, of what could happen. He is simply watching the storm beginning to rage. At one point when the sky is lit up I see Mara's face for an instant and he is smiling.

The river bank is now crumbling away and the waters have suddenly become a powerful torrent carrying along boulders and tree trunks and between them there are men and women and children being thrown about, struggling to cling on to whatever they can to keep afloat, but failing. All is being destroyed. The Buddha is aware of all this and in his mind the images and thoughts and feelings that are now springing up out of the shadows are just as raw and horrific. He who has cut through his own conditioning and cleansed the poisons from his heart now sees the pain of his loved ones as they fight to survive through times of plague and war, as if they were being tormented there in front of him and he is moved to tears. He can hear the screams of the sick and the tortured and the maimed from the four corners of the universe and he can see the carnage that is taking place all over the earth and there is nothing he can do. He is a helpless witness to the dukkha of pain and sorrow that surrounds and invades him. He knows that he has the mental power to detach himself and treat it all as a play of the mind. This is a possible way out. But he hesitates, feeling that as a man he must open up his heart to the world as it is, and take on all the suffering and hurt of those drowning by jumping into the river, knowing that he will himself drown there. And in doing so what would be achieved? Would the storm cease? For a moment he doubts his path.

This is Mara's test.

I cannot set myself against the inevitable. I have seen others perish not because they were unworthy or unwise but because Mara defeated them. This was their Karma and I have never interfered. It is not my place to do so. I am the Naga, always moving in those shadows that people are afraid of, the unknown waters where the wreckage of hope and ambition sinks. I am not part of the human struggle for truth and redemption. But this time something moves me to act. It is because of the Buddha himself. His confusion and fragility touch me and speak to me, awakening in me something like gentleness. But I know that I cannot help him, that in feeling his pain I have lost my power. I know that this time I cannot lift him above the rising waters. I will let him drown.

CHAPTER 2

At precisely the same time that Phra Boontam was having his Naga dream in a small wooden hut by the Mekong River, far away in Bangkok, Marisa was standing on the balcony of her sixteenth floor apartment looking down at the Chao Phraya River. (They verified this later when they eventually met). A breeze was getting up. Suddenly feeling its chill she hugged the silk dressing gown tighter around herself. But she did not want to go inside just yet. Ever since she was a girl, Marisa could not sleep when the moon was full. For her fortieth birthday, two years earlier, a well known astrologer had presented her with an elaborate updated chart of her stars as a gift. In his hand-written analysis of her personality he told her the reason for her insomnia. But his explanation, which was to do with the conflict between certain planets, was too complicated and obscure for her. Besides, it changed nothing. She had long resigned herself to these sleepless nights and never complained because she enjoyed being awake and alone at an hour when the city was quiet. Then, if the sky was clear, she would sometimes take out the telescope that an old admirer had given her and spend hours looking through it at the moon and marvelling at its delicate, pitted texture. She who was neither artistic nor poetic often derived from this sight what paintings and words never gave her; a sense of wonderment that made her heart leap.

Marisa and her lover, Khun Chai Noi, had come back at half past two from the reception held in the ballroom of the 'Hotel Asiatique' following the premiere of the film they had jointly produced, which was called 'The Sad Killer'. The evening had gone off without a hitch from beginning to end. The film, shown in the newest and most luxurious cinema in Bangkok had been enthusiastically received, drawing a standing ovation from the select audience and afterwards the PR company had done a flawless job in ferrying the guests to the hotel and handling the party, in which the high society and the powerful figures of Bangkok mingled with the celebrities from the media. All of it was the culmination of a year's hard work and, for Marisa, proof that she had managed to make the crossover from actress to producer in a way which left no doubt about her capacities.

The hours of heavy socializing, the alcohol, the interminable speeches and then the dancing afterwards to a salsa band should have made her tired. But on returning home Marisa was as alert as a cat on the prowl.

The moon seemed particularly close and large that night. It had rained earlier. Through the tall, ornate French windows at the hotel they could see the water cascade down. But now the storm had passed and the bright globe was hanging just above the horizon. From her balcony Marisa gazed at the city which was transformed by the liquid sheen that covered it. The leaves of the trees shimmered and the tiles of a temple roof over on the Thonburi side sparkled like gems. In the distance the rough edges of the buildings melted into one another. The jagged, unfinished skyscrapers which were so ugly and skeletal in the daytime now looked mysterious in the moonlight, like futuristic monoliths. And there was the river itself. At this hour it was free from the busy traffic of barges and ferries and the roar of the longtail boats. The light was penetrating the water at an angle that seemed to make it ripple just beneath its surface, so that it looked like a long serpent whose shiny body was winding its way northward towards Ayudhya. The view that spread out before her would, on any other occasion have been enough to uplift her spirits. But as she stood there looking down, Marisa could not shake off the dark mood that had clamped itself on her all evening, spoiling the sense of triumph that she should have been enjoying.

There was no mystery to this. She knew precisely the causes of her unease. It was a remark that had been addressed to her earlier in the hotel ballroom that had set it in motion. She had been talking to a group of people she vaguely knew about her inability to sleep when the moon was full and how she liked to stand in its light, when an up-and-coming film critic, who was walking past, overheard her and stopped. Theatrically raising his eyebrows, he stared at her pointedly and exclaimed loudly that he had just read somewhere that moonlight had the power to rejuvenate the skin. It was meant to be funny and the others, on queue, laughed, but in a rather embarrassed way. Of course she did not show her annoyance at the obvious implication. She did not want to give him the satisfaction of thinking that a trite, bitchy dig like that could upset her.

"Oh really?" she said flatly and turned from him.

But during the celebrations, as guests came up to congratulate her on the success of the film, she kept being annoyed by what he had said. At one point when she saw him with his back to her amusing another group with his jokes she was tempted to throw her glass of wine over his head. And now back in the apartment the stupid comment kept on playing in her mind like a CD that she could not stop. It hurt her to be reminded in public that she was no longer the beautiful, sought-after star that she had once been. But more than the humiliation she realized that despite her efforts to go beyond the shallow waters of vanity and reinvent herself as a serious and creative person she had not really come to terms with the loss of her former glamorous image. She thought that she had accepted that her time as the diva was over and that she did not mind the fact that younger women with a more slender waistline, firmer skin, shinier hair and brighter eyes had taken her place. She thought that she had moved on from the fickle world of public image and stardom to more solid ground. Producing 'The Sad Killer' was meant to prove this to herself and to those who knew her. But the critic's remark had pierced through her self delusion with disturbing ease. She saw how much she still cared and she was angry with herself for it.

The other reason for Marisa's bad mood came in the shape of the dishevelled male figure lying on the bed on the other side of the glass partition, just two feet from where she stood; her princely lover who she no longer wanted to be with. Six months had passed since she had first decided to leave him and still she had not taken the step. During that time she had lit incense and candles at various temples and asked for the courage to confront him but each time an appropriate moment arose she had pulled back. Tonight was to be the very final deadline, the moment of truth after the film was completed and their joint project accomplished. The timing made sense. She had been determined to sort it out with him after they returned from the party and tell him that she did not want things to drag on, that if he wanted to continue their business partnership then it was fine by her, but that she did not want to be in an intimate relationship with him any more. She had rehearsed her speech many times during the last few days as if she was learning the lines for a part in one of the movies she had starred in. She had the inflections and the pitch down to a tee. He would have no choice but to accept her decision.

But once again she had let the opportunity slip away. It was obvious when she saw him wash the pills down with the whiskey in the VIP room at the 'Asiatique' that he would be too far gone by the end of the evening for any conversation. She should have seized the moment and spelt it out to him there and then when he was still sober enough to take it in, instead of tiptoeing around the issue and trotting out the cliché that she had used so many times that she hardly believed any more herself; namely, that she was going to leave him if he carried on hurting himself. That evening she knew even before the words were out of her mouth that it sounded tired, hollow and unconvincing. Khun Chai knew it too and responded in kind. He put on his little boy look, pleading, smiling, then saying gently:

"Please don't do that."

Even before they left the hotel he was barely conscious. When they got back she had asked the night porter to help carry him into the lift. He hardly had the strength left to kick off his shoes before collapsing onto the bed.

Just as the moon disappeared over the horizon, Marisa slid the door open and stepped back into her bedroom. The air had helped to clear her mind. She walked to the side of the bed and looked down at Khun Chai who was laying the whole width of it, in the same position that she had left him earlier, with his head thrown back and both hands crossed on his chest like a corpse waiting to be cremated. In the lamplight the fat beads of sweat on his temple glistened. A trickle of saliva had run down from the corner of his mouth and left a trail across the stubble on his chin. His body exuded the stale, sour mix of cologne and perspiration. For a moment she considered waking him up and telling him to get undressed and take a shower. But she knew it was useless. The cocktail of drugs and alcohol that he had managed to consume that evening was enough to knock out an elephant.

For a while Marisa stood there and again thought about her decision to leave him and her chronic inability to make the final move. As she mentally covered the familiar ground it struck her once more how ironic it was that she should find herself in the position of being the one with the responsibility of trying to end a relationship. Men had always left her to go back to their wives and children or to the countries where they came from. They had wanted her body and her company for a while but in the end they had all found a reason for moving on. She now understood more clearly how hard it must have been for some of them to work up the courage to make the final declaration of intent. For the first time it was she who wanted to leave, she who was in the commanding position with the power to hurt and wound.

Another woman—the character she had played in her second to last movie who had been cheated by both her husband and her lover—might have seized on the opportunity to get her own back and exact some sort of revenge for the way that she had been treated. But that was film stuff. Real feelings were more complicated. Marisa felt no desire for vengeance and she was far from being able to articulate what she had come to feel for Khun Chai. As Marisa watched the figure on the bed breathing heavily, and occasionally letting out a long throaty sigh, the one thing she knew was that she was no nearer to resolving her dilemma.

Finally she decided that she would sleep in the living room, but as she was taking a sheet out of the cupboard, Khun Chai stirred and groaned and muttered some incomprehensible words. Then as if he had been jabbed by a sharp object he sat up abruptly and rubbed his eyes with the backs of his hands. He fumbled for his glasses on the bedside table, put them on and then stared at Marisa with a puzzled expression before flopping back.

"How did you get me back here? Did I make a fool of myself again? Was I gross?" he asked addressing himself to the ceiling.

Marisa nodded, trying not to smile at the ridiculous way that he was expressing the obvious. His words as usual managed to disarm her.

"Yes," she said wearily. "It was one of your best performances to date."

"I'm sorry. I'm really sorry," he put on his sincerely contrite tone. "Sorry I spoilt it for you again. Can you get me some water? Please. I'm so thirsty."

Marisa got up and went to her dressing table, poured him a glass and gave it to him. When he had finished gulping it down Khun Chai looked up towards her, reached out his arms and hugged her clumsily round the waist. Then his voice slurring, he mumbled:

"You're good to me. Don't leave me. Forgive me. You must forgive me. I'm nothing without you. You know that. You've always known that."

She drew back slightly and hesitated before letting herself be pulled onto the bed and enveloped into his groggy embrace.

CHAPTER 3

For almost two decades Marisa's life had been the admiration and benign envy of a whole generation of Thai women, because it was a fairy tale come true. Her fans knew her story by heart. Coming from a humble background in Saraburi she was discovered, at the age of sixteen by an agent who happened to see her one afternoon helping out in her mother's noodle shop. He was so struck by her beauty and her poise that on his return to the capital he persuaded a film studio to take her on and pay for her acting and singing lessons. Their faith in her was rewarded when less than a year later she was given her first role in a romantic musical called 'The Dignity and the Passion' and stole the show from the lead actress. By the time she was in her mid twenties, with a string of films behind her, she was one of Thailand's best known stars. Her smiling face looked out from the magazine covers and advertising billboards all over the country. Her white skin, the angular features that suggested mixed blood, the flowing mane of jet black hair, the flashing teeth, laughing eyes and perfectly proportioned figure became the standard of beauty against which others were judged. She was seen as a home-grown success story. For the next ten years the offers came flooding in. She appeared in everything from Kung Fu movies to love stories and TV soap operas. If a foreign film being made in Thailand needed a local beauty it was usually her they chose. It was said that the only reason that she never achieved international fame was due to her fear of flying, which prohibited her from travelling out of Thailand. But in her own country she was famous enough. If her name was connected with a project it guaranteed a faithful audience.

During these years her public persona gradually came to be established. The fans who accompanied her on her journey from innocent schoolgirl to full time diva saw her as the person who lived out their fantasies and repaid their loyalty many times over. She represented the possibility of success and the rise from poor background to stardom without the sacrifice of integrity. To them she was a woman whose wealth, achieved through hard work, did not change her basic values or spoil her and yet she was also someone who had good business sense and knew exactly where she was going. Her private life was always discreetly withheld from public scrutiny, which added to the allure of mystery and fuelled speculation. It was rumoured at one stage that she was the mistress of an army general who was influential in the opposition party but this was not held against her. All in all the legend that was woven around Marisa was impressive and the more so by being untainted by scandal and invulnerable to the kind of malicious gossip that her fellow stars were prone to. She was very much the national role model. The only ingredient, perhaps, that was missing was the fact that she did not have a family. But, said her camp followers, there was time for everything. For almost twenty years her position in the pantheon of stars was undisputed. Marisa was the queen of the roost.

But it was natural that with the passing of time and the emphasis on youth a new generation would demand their own icon. It was not that her fans deserted her. But they had grown up and become parents whose tastes were mocked by their children. In the new culture, marked by a calculated show of indifference and casualness, Marisa's sharp beauty and glitzy style did not quite fit. She recalled how this was driven home to her one day when she had just turned thirty five and the producers of a ghost film that was about to be made offered the lead role to a twenty three year old starlet and to her the part of the girl's auntie. To add insult to injury her character had a scar across her face. From then on the parts that she played were nearly all as a more mature woman. The TV chat shows now invited her to sit on panels giving out advice on diet and exercise and to share her secrets in maintaining her looks. Newspaper interviews now began to talk about her career as if the golden days were in the past. It all combined to give Marisa the sense that her star was beginning to fade. And this produced a sense of panic in her. Having spent most of her life in the limelight, she did not want to be pushed into the shadows, and yet, having watched other stars before her pathetically failing in their attempt to hold onto youth, she felt that she would never want to end up staying in the public eye at any cost. So little by little she began to think of ways to reinvent herself. She was in her late thirties and still full of energy. The media world was as familiar to her as the contours of her own body. She had been exploited by it since she was in her teens. Now it was time that she took part in controlling it. But before Marisa's plans took solid shape she was deviated into a direction which was new to her.

At a reception held to open a new shopping mall she was introduced to Señor Eduardo B, the Spanish Cultural attaché in Bangkok. A few months earlier her relationship with the general, whose mistress she had been for over three years, had been amicably terminated. Even with the help of Viagra, his interest in sex had evaporated, and he was more interested in spending his retirement playing with his grandchildren and tending the orchids in his garden than in making the effort needed to achieve carnal pleasure. He paid her off with a generous transfer into her bank account and let her keep the Italian sports car and the condo he had bought for her, overlooking the river. Even though she was losing a protector and benefactor Marisa was not upset but secretly relieved that it was all over and that she no longer had to tolerate his old fingers slithering over her body. She had never been attached to anyone. Men had sought and won her with what they could offer. It was part of the unwritten contract. She had realized early on the option she had at her disposal to manipulate and to demand her price in return for the gratification that she would give them. She had always been a survivor.

But with Eduardo B. it was different. Had they met when she was younger Marisa might not have been impressed by him at all. He was, at first, quiet and unassuming and unlike the men she had known. In their initial exchange she did not find him attractive or interesting, just another farang who looked lost and dismayed in Bangkok. And he had nothing to offer her except his passable good looks—graying hair, trim moustache, Mediterranean tan—and his elegant old world manners. But he was obviously struck by her and his subsequent insistent attention flattered her at a time when she felt insecure about herself. Little by little she allowed herself to be seduced by his charms until one morning she woke up to find that she had fallen in love with him. This frightened and pleased her at the same time because despite the romantic roles she had played on film and in television she had never imagined that she would ever experience the exhilaration of being in love first hand.

During the next two years she and Eduardo were inseparable. They were seen as the most elegant couple in the city. Their photos appeared regularly in the social pages of newspapers and life style publications which showed them attending official dinners and private parties that were held in the city and attended by the rich and influential elite of the land. Marisa, who, despite her fame, had been familiar only with the world of media celebrities, was enchanted by this new milieu and quickly adapted to it with Eduardo as her guide. He, in turn, seemed proud to have won such a rare beauty and took her into his bachelor's existence as though she were the one true companion of his life. Together they went on excursions to places where she had never been in Thailand and he told her the history of her own culture. He even managed to persuade her to fly with him to Rangoon and to Tokyo. Everything about Asia seemed to fascinate him, and he shared this enthusiasm generously with her. In Bangkok they spent their time discovering the city together, walking through neighbourhoods in Thonburi which had not been touched by the brash development that marked the other side of the river, wandering through bright markets and into small temples where tourists did not usually go. Eduardo seemed to be at home in the heat and the dazzle of the tropics. Through his eyes Marisa saw a different city, one that was coloured by love. The sights that she had always taken for granted, like the corner of a street in the twilight, a busy intersection, a stretch of overgrown wasteland, even the clashing yellows and pinks of the taxis, acquired a poetic quality that she could not express in words, but which brought her a feeling of magic.

But she knew that, however much Eduardo appreciated the exotic surroundings, he would never be at home there. During the dinners that they shared in discreet, expensive restaurants or on a weekend's leave on an island resort in the south, he would talk to her for hours about the Mediterranean lands, telling her how he wanted one day to show her the places which inspired him in his own country and Italy, and Greece and North Africa. His passionate descriptions brought those towns and landscapes alive for her and made her dizzy, because no one she had known had ever spoken like that to her. And for the first time in her life she, who had built up so many defences on her road to stardom, was foolish enough to let her guard down and allow herself to get carried away by her feelings. As the days went by, she dreamed of living in an apartment overlooking the harbour in Barcelona and sharing the villa on the coast with him. They had not exactly made plans. but it was understood that the intimacy they shared was the foundation of an even brighter future. She even thought for a while that she wanted to have a child with him or, if it was too late, then to adopt a baby that they could love as their own.

Then one afternoon towards the end of the rainy season everything changed. He called her and asked her to come urgently to see him at the embassy. It was something that he had never done before and it was strange

because they were due to meet only a few hours later for dinner. He said
that he could not tell her the reason for wanting to see her over the phone,
which left Marisa in a mildly expectant mood as she made her way through
the traffic to get to his office. She had even thought that he was impatient
to see her because of his desire for her. But when she arrived there and was
shown into a reception room by a prim secretary, she sensed that something
was wrong. Eduardo entered but did not kiss her. Then without warning he
declared, as he stroked his well trimmed beard and paced round the marble
table as though he were under some grave diplomatic pressure. that he could
not be seen with her any more, that he was leaving Bangkok shortly, that she
should remove everything of hers from his residence at once. He said he was
sorry, but gave no reason for his decision. He even offered her an envelope
full of cash, as though she were some high class whore that he had rented for
the duration of his tour of duty, like the farang tourists with their holiday
wives to fill the empty nights. She would have liked to believe that he was
being forced by some higher authority to make the decision to separate, but
her experience of men told her otherwise. In that last painful encounter at
the embassy, she saw in his eyes the panicked expression of a coward who
was cornered. Time had run out on him. He would move on to another
country and another mistress. His words had been like a spell to get her to
comply with his temporary needs. It had made him feel good to have a well
known star on his arm to squire round town. Now her usefulness was over.
Yet again.

CHAPTER 4

When Eduardo dumped her Marisa felt the humiliation of someone who had been thoroughly fooled into thinking that she was the object of a special love and devotion, not just an expensive plaything that had reached its sell-by date. For three years she had been floating in a kind of dreamy state, vaguely preparing herself to eventually leave Bangkok and the world that she had known behind and start a new life in Europe. Not once did she doubt Eduardo's feelings for her. She had turned down parts that she felt were not right and she accepted fewer and fewer invitations to appear on television. Already in her heart she felt she had outgrown the incestuous world of the Thai media. She was ready for a bigger stage. She was looking forward to a new life in a new land and of reinventing herself as anything she cared to be. But with the shock of suddenly finding herself abandoned and alone once more, Marisa fell back down to earth with a hard thump that revealed all the cracks in her defences.

It took her a year to get over the resulting depression. During this time she received help and support not from her old friends, most of whom told her, rather cruelly, that they had seen it coming, but from the elderly psychiatrist from whom she obtained the prescriptions for the tranquilizers she was taking. This was an old Scottish lady affectionately known by everyone as Dr. June, who was the widow of a Thai politician and who had been living in Bangkok since the nineteen fifties.

"Why don't you try to face up to what happened rather than drug yourself into oblivion?" the doctor told Marisa on their third meeting and from that day on they began to talk. It was not formal analysis or psychotherapy that took place, simply an ongoing, two way conversation and over the months they became friends. The doctor, who was by then past retirement age but who carried on in the clinic out of habit, talked of her own life with a candour that permitted Marisa to reveal things that she had never dared to share before, like the abuse she suffered as a little girl and other, though not all unpleasant and painful, moments from her past. The old lady would sit and nod without interrupting and rarely offered any judgment. The openness of her listening permitted Marisa to unburden all the complicated feelings that were associated with her failed love affair with Eduardo; the bitterness and disappointment, the anger at having been betrayed and all the darker shades of emotion when a love affair ends.

What Marisa learned from those conversations with Dr. June not only gave her the strength to put the past behind her but also the means to look forward to a future that seemed more spacious than before. Dr. June quietly showed her what it might be like to make her own choices based on something other than the need to satisfy and to be rewarded in turn.

In the end the knot in her heart gradually unwound and the wounds eventually healed. Moreover Marisa felt transformed by that year of being alone, the first time in her life since she was fifteen when she was not in a sexual relationship with a man or a woman. It was good for her body to rest from being handled and caressed and penetrated. She got into physical training and played tennis and swam every day at the Polo Club so that in a few months her body became fit and lean. Gradually what remained of her affair with Eduardo was a sour aftertaste, but nothing that could now hurt her or stand in the way of her goal. A new confidence had grown in her. She was ready to face the world again.

At the age of forty one, Marisa emerged from her year's sabbatical a changed person, with a new look that was more discreet than before and an attitude that those who knew her could not fail to notice. Despite the face being a little plumper she was still beautiful and could pass for someone in her thirties. Some nasty tongues said that she had been to a clinic to get her breasts firmed up and that her new look was due to a personal stylist from Australia who charged the earth. But it was generally agreed that she had never been more elegant and that the transformation she had undergone in that time was for the better. It was as though the fairy tale-come-true girl next door had grown up. Instead of dresses she now wore well cut trouser suits. Gone were the gold chains and bracelets. She now wore diamonds and then only on special occasions. The sports car was traded in for a more sober model. Her long hair was now cut short to give her the impeccable, springy look of an active woman on the move. Her image had been radically transformed. She was no longer a beautiful object on display but a rare collector's piece for viewing only by private appointment.

Once the news was out that she was back on the scene and looking better than ever, the offers came pouring in once more. The fact that she had been out of the spotlight did not seem to matter because her reputation as an actress still stood and besides there were now many parts for attractive women of her age both in television and in the film industry. But Marisa, while naturally encouraged that there should be such an interest in her, declined them all because she had her own agenda. She wanted to make up for lost time and resume the direction she had visualized before meeting Eduardo. She knew for certain that she no longer wanted to be at the end of the camera being given orders and told how to move and what to do. She was sure that she could do the job just as well if not better than those temperamental prima donnas who called themselves directors. The idea of being an actress, once so glamorous and so full of promise, had long lost its attraction. With the experience she had accumulated she felt she was ready to be creative and to take active part in producing the kind of material that she could chose.

The trouble was that no one in the business was convinced that she had it in her to do so. It was not just that she was a woman, for there were now a few of her sex who, through determination and perseverance, had broken into the industry. But it was hard for those who had known her rise through the ranks, from child star to sex icon to serious thespian to let go of their image of her as a full time performer, an image which she herself had deliberately cultivated over the years. They still saw her as the compliant actress willing to do what was asked of her. It was impossible for them to see her giving out the orders and dealing with all the behind the scenes politics, or navigating through the financial maze that lay behind each production.

But Marisa was determined to go ahead. She felt that with no one to support her and with middle age now on top of her she had no choice but to forge the next stage of her own journey. She could only pray for someone to come along who would see her worth and back the projects that filled her briefcase. And pray she did, to the laakmueng spirit of the city, to the Vishnu shrine at the Erawan intersection, to the goddess at the Hindu temple and to the various Buddharupas in temples upcountry, where she went on short pilgrimages to make merit. With her new-found faith in herself, Marisa was in no doubt that her prayers would be answered. After a few months they were, and for a while it seemed that the fairy tale was entering a new episode.

CHAPTER 5

The benefactor who came into her life like a shining knight offering her anything she desired was, in fact a prince, though only a minor one, a momrajawong from a long line of royals who had served the country in various ministerial posts. Khun Chai Noi was in his late twenties and had been educated in America. After graduating he spent a further two years interning in several film production companies in New York. His ambition was to make films in his own country, where he saw endless possibilities waiting to be tapped; plenty of raw material for the plots he had in mind and an abundance of new talent. He wanted to produce films that were both box office successes as well as being socially relevant. He felt that the Thai film industry, with his help, was about to come of age.

With all the advantages that his family's wealth and social connections offered Khun Chai had reason to feel confident of his future. But when he finally returned to Thailand he found, like Marisa, that the problem lay in getting others to believe that he was capable of delivering. He was new to the scene and, although there was a distant uncle who had become famous for his lengthy epics, by the time Khun Chai returned this man was already disenchanted with the whole business of making films and not only refused him help but even tried his best to dissuade him from going ahead with his decision.

"You have a private income. More money than you can spend in a lifetime. Why work at all? Film people are all vipers. They'll poison you and suck your blood," the old man told him.

Others in the business saw him as a spoilt, rich, privileged brat who was not capable of the hard grind that they had all been through and they did not hesitate in trying to discourage him, sometimes by telling him point blank that he would better off forgetting about being creative and find work as an investment banker instead. So in the end those who he thought might have helped him quickly closed ranks and barred the way forward. Within months of returning to Bangkok, Khun Chai was beginning to give up hope of fulfilling his dream.

Given their circumstances Marisa and Khun Chai were meant for each other. This, at any rate, was what they both agreed on over their first dinner together, as they sipped wine and complained about the people in the Bangkok film world like two conspirators thrown together plotting to overthrow the establishment and usurp power. They had met a few evenings earlier at an extravagant gala held in the Siam Towers to launch a new TV series where they found themselves, champagne in hand standing next to one another during the speech given by the newly appointed director of the company. Afterwards they fell into conversation without any awkward preliminaries. They were surprised that their interests were so similar and their goals were in the same direction. An appointment for their next meeting, in quieter surroundings, was hastily arranged.

The meal went well. They talked about the films that they liked and the film that both wanted to make and soon found that they were united in their ambition. They flirted and took the first tentative steps towards intimacy. Khun Chai was amazed that he should find an ally in such a wonderfully haphazard way. Of course he knew who Marisa was and admitted to her that he had drooled over her in his teens but he had never imagined that she might be the sympathetic ear that he had been waiting for since arriving back in the country. Marisa for her part found the momrajawong charming and refreshingly intelligent and she giggled at his jokes and anecdotes like a girl on her first date. By the end of the evening they had forged a working relationship, which would be sealed a week later by the sexual act which took place in a hotel suite.

There was, of course, no doubt in the minds of the gossip mongers that Marisa had engineered the whole affair. It was obvious that she had used her experience and good looks to snare a tubby, prematurely balding young princeling in order to milk him dry. Beauty and the Beast, they were dubbed behind their backs almost as soon as their affair started. She was lucky, they said, because without him she could well have been back at the bottom of the ladder without a penny to her name, defenseless and, at forty one, too old to have a future in the film industry. These cruel things were put about by people she hardly knew and she learned of them through the usual channel; the servants relating dinner table conversations to each other. Her maid and trusted ally Mae Nee always told her everything she picked up from the others.

Outwardly Marisa took it all in her stride. They were envious, she told herself. But secretly she knew that what they were saying was partly if not wholly true. Even though she had not planned the whole scenario with anything like the kind of ruthless precision with which she had known some starlets to ambush a producer or a casting agent, the meeting with Khun Chai had not been as fortuitous as it was made to look. She had done her research when a friend had told her that there was an extremely wealthy young man just back from the U.S. looking to get started and serious about making films and not just chasing the starlets. She knew the kind of circles he moved in and she had been stalking him until she found the right moment to pounce.

But Marisa justified this scheming by reminding herself that she was on her own and that she had to seize every opportunity that came her way. Khun Chai's arrival in her life was an answer to the prayers that she had offered up. She would not cheat him or exploit him but if he was sincere in his ambition she would guide him through to the success that awaited them. And even if she did not feel any physical attraction to him she would be a companion to him and give him her body for his pleasure, as she had done countless times before to men who were less deserving. For she did not want to be alone any more, growing old, gracefully or otherwise. She wanted someone to be there for her and to care for her and if possible be legally committed to her. Eduardo had held out a carrot then taken it away. Now Khun Chai looked like being the ticket she was waiting for and she was not going to let him slip from her grasp.

When things started getting out of hand, she admitted to herself that it was her karmic action that was the cause of her troubles. It was just as the Buddha taught. There was no one else to blame for the consequences. It was her desire for success that set the wheel in motion, that blinded her to reality. From the beginning she should have known that her relationship with Khun Chai was going to be more complicated than she had thought. Before a month had gone by she was already noticing how sensitive and clinging he was. At first she put this down to the sadness that he still felt over the loss of his mother two years earlier. On the very first night that they slept with each other Khun Chai had tearfully shared with her his mother's long illness and slow dying and Marisa, listening to him, found herself unprepared for the feelings of tenderness that he evoked in her. She wanted to comfort him and take the sorrow away and she was sure that she had the power to do so. This was the first time that anyone had stirred up this protective urge in her. But it was natural, she told herself. All the men she had gone with previously had been older and more confident or at least they had pretended to be. Khun Chai was twenty four, young enough to be her son, and he did not hide his vulnerability from her.

But in the weeks that followed she began to realize that the maternal instinct that he awoke in her was to be used as a way of manipulating her. Quite quickly Marisa found herself the recipient of a devotion towards her that she had never experienced till then. Men had fallen in love with her in the past and been attached to her before they moved on but with Khun Chai she saw an unusual dependence that was nothing to do with their age difference, but which came from a much more complex side of him. Even without knowing anything about her he seemed to want to hand over to her control over his life, to let her make all the decisions, from minor ones such as where they were going to eat that evening, or what colour shirt to buy to those which were crucial to their project. At first Marisa was puzzled by this willingness to let her be so totally in charge but at the same time she was encouraged by his attitude. It was as though he believed in her wisdom and in her experience. Up till then, professionally, Marisa had never tasted such power over a man. She had always been the one who followed the decisions made by those who needed her image and her charisma but who rarely took any notice of her opinions. And in her private life she had only known what it was to be the object of desire, to be claimed, seduced, used and eventually abandoned. Now, with a young, naive lover who wanted to follow her around and hang onto her every word, she found herself in the commanding position. Go there, do this, come here, she could tell him and he would readily obey. Had she been younger and more easily assured, Marisa might have enjoyed this almost divine feeling of power that Khun Chai's devotion gave her. But his unexpected worship came at a time in her life when, having herself recently been through the sickness of the heart, she was suspicious of all extremes of emotion. The intensity of his feelings was too overwhelming. She felt that if she let herself be swept along she would drown in them.

Marisa knew all these things right at the beginning of their relationship, yet she still chose to go ahead because the desire for success and recognition outweighed the dangers that were looming on the journey. Contrary to the vow that she had made, she now decided that she would indulge his game of dependence while it was necessary and try to keep detached and focused on the goal she had set herself. In other words she would let him use her and in turn herself make use of him while it suited both of them. This would be their unwritten contract. But she would not let herself be drawn into any emotional entanglement from which she could not extricate herself.

This arrangement, so neatly established in her mind, might have worked out had she not underestimated the demons that haunted her partner. It was only when he revealed to her another, more precarious side to his character that she understood that the stakes involved in her plan were much more than she had reckoned. For within a couple of months of their affair Marisa came to realize that Khun Chai's dependence on her was nothing compared to his addiction to drugs and alcohol. From the beginning he had not tried to hide anything. It was Marisa herself who refused to see what was happening in front of her eyes. At first, when he got drunk in her company, she pretended to be amused. She had known drunks before who were vicious or abusive. But Khun Chai was not the violent type, so she tolerated his behaviour. To the friends who saw him in various states of inebriation, she even made excuses. But then as time went by and she saw that alcohol was not the only substance that attracted him and that he could barely function without first getting high, she realized how serious the problem was and how involved she had become in his destructive patterns. He insisted to her, like all committed junkies, that he was in control and could handle the intake. But what she saw was that he took whatever drug that was available, like a glutton who knew no limits, and being a rich young man in Bangkok society made him all the more vulnerable. In the world that they inhabited there were always those ready to indulge him and provide him with the pills and powders that he needed in his trip to the dark places which seemed to hold a fascination for him. She could not understand why he wanted to punish himself when he had everything at his fingertips. The contradiction between his desire to be creative and his determination to obliterate himself was bewildering to her. If she had been in love with him she might have probed into the causes of his sickness. But her defensive instincts told her that if she was going to follow him into his darkness she would have to go all the way. And she was not prepared to do this. Still she needed him and because of this she used every tactic she could think of to stop him from freefalling into the abyss.

But none of them worked and little by little she found herself exactly where she did not want to be with him; protecting, defending, mopping up whenever he got too wrecked. "It is my karma to be with him," she told her friends, who, on the whole, were unconvinced that she was suffering so much. The reason that she let things drag on, they agreed, was that she had never been in such a strong position in her entire career. Khun Chai had made her the managing director of his company, which was now moving into distribution. Not only did she have no reason to complain, they said, but the fact that Khun Chai was almost permanently incapacitated by drugs and alcohol, far from being a burden, gave her free reign.

Marisa had been present at nearly all these conversations and the ones that she did not hear she could guess at. And, while in their company she had played along with the gentle mocking that they dished out, inside she was furious that they should think they had the right to judge her and make her out to be such an unscrupulous schemer. It was true that she was looking after her own interest but these so-called friends had been born into privilege. They had never known the hardship that she had been through to get to where she was in the world.

She realized before the year was out that she was now hooked into taking care of him. She was caught in the dilemma of being unable to leave him for fear that he would self-destruct and at the same time resenting the fact that her dependable presence was itself the safety net that allowed him to walk the high wire.

Yet despite the constant dramas caused by Khun Chai's behaviour and against everyone's expectations, they managed to collaborate in establishing a production company and to accomplish all the things that they planned. A competent writer was hired to put together the script, a team assembled, and an optimistic young director, who had recently been made redundant, persuaded to work with them. The plot which grew out of an idea that they had sketched out together had all the ingredients expected of a modern Thai drama and touched on many of the relevant social issues that were being debated. It was about a contract killer on the run who makes the mistake of visiting his sister, a go-go dancer in a cheap, sleazy club. The budget was a mere one hundred million baht and the film was shot in eight weeks on location in Petchburi, Hua Hin and Bangkok during the rainy season (which gave its mood) without any of the logistical problems that sometimes bedevil a production. Khun Chai's family lawyer dealt with the financial side and drew up all the contracts. Marisa, using her experience and past contacts had no difficulty finding a good cast. The star was a handsome new discovery from the north-east, vaguely resembling an Asian Elvis, who had been a real life thug and a dealer in his teens and who brought a convincing energy to his role. The love interest was played by a young woman whose looks reminded Marisa of herself at the age of twenty. When the editing was finally over it was shown to a sample audience in Chiengmai who enjoyed it mainly for the raunchy mawlum songs that were written especially for the film. The invited audience at the Bangkok premiere applauded it enthusiastically. The critics were already calling 'The Sad Killer' Thailand's best film of the year, comparing it favourably to a classic made in Jamaica over thirty years before called 'The Harder They Come.' There was talk of it being sent to film festivals in Hong Kong and Japan as the official entry. All in all it looked set to be the signature debut that its producers were aiming for.

So finally Khun Chai passed the test of fire and was now accepted into the Thai film scene as a kind of wayward genius. Marisa too won the respect that she had sought. Her dream of making it to the other side of the camera had come true. The film was packaged and marketed. The work was done. Celebrations and congratulations piled up. The money was already flowing into the bank account. The praises were more than she had expected. Further projects were now possible.

⇒‡⇐

She should have been elated with all that she had achieved in that year, and content with the direction which her career had taken. But the sense of achievement she had expected was absent. It was natural perhaps that some kind of anticlimax would follow. In the days when she was a star Marisa had known the feeling when she had finished making a movie. The exhaustion and then the goodbyes and the parting from the rest of the cast and crew. The eager expectation of the outcome and then the flat fallow period that followed even if the film was a success. The intensity and the adrenaline of the working months always left behind a grey dull depression that was countered by jumping back into the social whirl. But after the completion of 'The Sad Killer' she did not experience any of this. There was no coming down from a high. It was as though the making of the film had just been another step she had taken, another meal eaten, another book read, none of which had added anything thrilling or special to her existence. It was the first time that she had felt such apathy and it disturbed her.

On a visit to Dr. June, who was now retired and living in Ayudhya, she told her old friend that what she felt at the end of that year was a strange, cold emptiness, as though she were standing knee deep in a flat expanse of water, looking out in all directions at once and indifferent to everything around her. If a new project turned up she would probably go ahead, but she did not feel particularly motivated to do anything. As for her relationship with Khun Chai she would merely let it drift on until it petered out by itself. The doctor listened to her and smiled.

"What is it you're afraid of?" she asked.

"Why, nothing," Marisa replied quickly. And they left it at that. But on the drive home she knew that the doctor, as usual, had intuited the truth; that underneath all the numbness which she professed to be feeling, she felt more anxious and insecure than she had been since she was a child.

CHAPTER 6

It was late. Arun had attended the reception of 'The Sad Killer' at the Asiatique and he had seen Marisa there in the distance at the centre of a group of people. He did not know her, but, of course he recognized who she was. Now back in his small house in a cul de sac off Soi Ngaam Duplee he stood in the middle of his studio, which covered half of the ground floor and lit up the small, carefully rolled joint. He was relieved to be back in his own place but the mixture of whiskey and wine that he had drunk earlier still made him agitated and ill tempered. He hardly touched alcohol these days precisely because it made him feel uncomfortable and he rarely went to social functions because to him they were a waste of time. He had been pacing around the studio, obsessively tidying up the bits and pieces lying all over the floor and throwing them in the waste bin. But he could not calm down or get rid of the restlessness and the annoyance he felt at having been conned by his sister Ladda into going to the party at all. Then he remembered that a week earlier a friend had left some grass in a drawer as a present.

"More public exposure is what you need," Ladda told him when she had rung him up that morning. "You've got to get out and talk to people about your work if you want to sell. Anyway it's going to be great. Marisa and Khun Chai want it to be the best party of the year. There will be important guests there who are already interested in your work. You'll make great contacts. With the exhibition coming up it will be the perfect time for them to meet you."

His instinct told him that it would be the kind of extravaganza that she was famous for organizing and which he dreaded. But he needed to get out of the studio and to stop brooding and for purely practical reasons he needed to get his paintings sold. It had been nearly a year since his last show and the money he had made was almost all gone.

As it turned out the party to celebrate the opening of 'The Sad Killer' was worse than he had imagined. There was the usual crowd from the film and fashion world, dressed in their most flamboyant costumes, as if they were attending a drag gathering, eyeing one another critically as they huddled in little cliques. Then there was the straight bunch: the business people looking formal and affluent and awkward in their suits, the inevitable clutch of VIPs, including an ex-prime minister to give his blessings to the event, and the gang of foreigners whose faces regularly smiled out from the social pages. They were all there to show off their wealth, beauty or wit and to catch up on gossip and affirm their loyalty to the Bangkok merry-go-round. It was the same circus that took place on any night of the week in the various luxury hotels and grand mansions dotted round the city.

As soon as he arrived Arun felt uncomfortable and out of place. Having decided to skip the screening which took place in a fashionable shopping mall, he knew that he was probably the only person at the reception with nothing to say about the film. He had taken the sky train, got off at the bridge and walked the rest of the way so that he was sweating by the time he stood in the queue, invitation card in his hand. He had come alone and he felt that he was entering a world that was removed from his own, one which provided him with material but which he preferred to survey from afar. It was a different matter to be right there in the thick of it and his first thought, as he set foot in the main hall, was that Ladda had exaggerated yet again. He doubted if anyone in the room was going to be in the slightest bit interested in his paintings. They had all been to the premiere of the film held in a cinema in Gaysorn and they would now be talking about it.

Under the heavy chandeliers the conversations were loud and punctuated by shrieks of laughter as one celebrity greeted the other. Impeccably dressed waiters and waitresses were weaving through the crowd holding trays of drinks and canapés. The air was thick with kisses. Cameras were clicking. A television crew was pushing its way through, harvesting images. Arun was relieved when he saw his sister but this feeling was brief, because the next minute she was taking him by the hand like when they were young and dragging him to one group then another, announcing, and sometimes shouting out over the din :

"This is my young brother. He's a painter."

It was embarrassing to be patronized in this way and he would have left there and then if he could. But there was hardly any room to move through the dense wall of people between him and the exit and besides, every time he glanced over, Ladda seemed to read his mind.

"Don't you dare think of sneaking away," she said wagging a finger in jest at him. He could tell that she had already had too many cocktails. "If only you knew what I did to get you in here. Do you know there are people who would kill to be inside this room tonight? The party's only just beginning. Loosen up a bit. Enjoy yourself. It's good to see you get out in society once in a while."

At one point when his sister had finally left him alone Arun found him standing next to a tall thin woman in a gold dress with pink streaks in her hair. He did not recognize her because she had her back to him but he guessed that she was an actress. He found himself admiring her bare shoulder whose skin was so smooth that for a moment he wanted to reach out and stroke it just to see what it would feel like. She was talking excitedly to a group of people who hung onto her every word. He was about to take a drink from the waiter when she turned round and saw him. For a moment she frowned as though wondering where they had met before.

"How's it going ? Having a good time? Did you like the movie?" she asked, with a smile dancing in her eyes.

"Yes. No," he mumbled. "I suppose so. I didn't go."

She laughed at his answer; then, with her eyes appraising him from head to toe, she said:

"You're very good looking. Do you have Indian blood? I like your pigtail. Are you in this business?"

"Not exactly," he replied with a slight shrug, a movement he made whenever he felt uncomfortable. "My sister brought me."

A look of recognition lit up her face. "I know who you are. Ladda's brother. Of course. Your sister took me to your exhibition last year at that gallery on Soi 23. I remember your photo in the brochure."

"Oh yeah."

"I nearly bought one of the paintings but I didn't have any more room in my house to hang it."

Arun quickly tried to figure out an adequate way to respond, but as he was about to speak a young man dressed a tuxedo came up and whisked her away. As she walked off she turned and waved to him with her fingers. The rest of the evening was a blur of people with whom he exchanged a few stilted words before moving off and picking another glass from the tray. An hour and a half later, just as the first announcements were being made over a crackling microphone, he managed to work his way towards the back of the ballroom and make good his escape.

The marijuana was shifting his mood. The edginess gave way to something more relaxed. He went over to the CD player, put on some Brazilian guitar music and stretched out on the sofa. The gentle, late night chords affected him. He felt less annoyed now, more forgiving. He knew that his sister had meant well when she invited him, that there was no one to blame but himself for thinking that he should go around trying to convince her celebrity friends to buy his paintings. The Asiatique was not his sort of scene. He should not have gone, simple as that. The annoyance, he realized had little to with his sister or the party, or the people there and everything to do with the canvas that was hanging opposite to where he lay. It was two and a half metres square and filled almost the whole of the wall space. That evening it looked to Arun like a dull white mirror whose empty silence reflected his impotence and dissatisfaction. It challenged him again to make a move. But he knew that he had no intention of doing any painting at that hour.

It had been over a month since he had stretched and primed and hung it in readiness and every day he had sat looking at it unable to make the first mark. Sometimes he would walk up to it or stand back and contemplate its surface but as time went by it dawned on him that he was not going to get started. Now there were only three weeks to go till the exhibition which had been planned a year earlier; a small one man show that was going to define the next stage in his career. There were going to be gallery owners, dealers and collectors from Paris and London. A lot was at stake. He had agreed to provide eight paintings. Five were finished. The gallery owner and the representative from the Alliance Française reluctantly accepted that he could not fulfil the quota in time. So as a compromise they told him that they would settle for six, but insisted that he had to deliver. And it was precisely this last one that was the problem.

As he drew on the joint, blew the long shaft of blue smoke towards the white background and watched the ephemeral patterns that it created before disappearing, Arun was struck so forcefully by the absurdity of his situation that he laughed out loud and shouted out:

"You pathetic idiot!"

CHAPTER 7

When, at the age of thirty two he left the teaching job at the Fine Arts Department at Silpakorn University in order to devote all his time to painting, Arun was so grateful to be released from the routine of clocking in and the obligations that were required as a member of the faculty that he threw himself into his new career with athletic enthusiasm. Like a man who had come out of prison he felt that he had to catch up with the years wasted in not getting down to his own creativity. His mission was clear. He wanted to be the best artist in the land and to this end he would make whatever sacrifice was needed. A relationship with a journalist that could have continued if he made the effort was allowed to evaporate. The social life which he had till then enjoyed as a way of compensating for the boredom of his job now had little importance. Clubbing and the rest of it were a thing of the past. His old friends would find him at home working feverishly day and night, finishing up to three huge canvasses a month. The problem in those first heady days was having too little time. The moment a painting was finished he was on to a new one. All the images that had been waiting to be brought to life came pouring out into the light and the colours that Arun used reflected a sense of celebration and new-found freedom. Whenever he heard that some fellow artist was going through a bad patch and feeling blocked and unable to get started he would scoff at the news and spell out his impatience at such self indulgence and affectation. Artists were privileged. They had no reason to complain. Most people had to do a long day's grind, in a job they hated, to earn a living. It was a luxury to have the time to paint and sculpt and get paid for it. As for sitting around agonizing about the philosophical issues and analyzing one's motives, Arun felt that it was all a waste of precious time.

Now, five years and three exhibitions later, he found himself among those he had once criticized with such casual severity. The friends who had dropped in during the past weeks and seen him sitting there in the middle of the studio in front of the huge primed canvas, with his arms folded tightly like some hostage tied up by invisible rope, commiserated with him to his face and offered advice and sympathy. But he suspected that they were probably laughing at him behind his back. He was aware that his previous arrogance and lack of compassion for others in the same position invited ironic mockery. But he did not care. The intervening years had hardened him to criticism and success had made him solitary. People could think what they liked. Besides, they were off the mark.

Once he might have made an effort to explain himself, but now he did not bother trying to convince them that the reason he could not get started on the painting had nothing to do with lack of inspiration, or ideas, or discipline. There was nothing so obviously tangible holding him back from putting his brush to work. He was capable of delivering another picture easily enough. It was not a block in terms of creativity. He could start mixing the paint on the palette at any moment and be finished within ten days. He had been toying with the theme for months. There was no shortage of material to draw from. Bangkok was one big treasure chest of subject matter waiting to be recycled. Even the launch party he had just attended and the people he had seen there had provided him with images to play with. The empty canvas on the wall was already covered by the shapes and figures and details and shadows that he held in his mind.

He did not tell them any of this, nor that the real reason he could not get started was so banal that it was laughable. He did not mention Gaew to them.

CHAPTER 8

It was all Gaew's fault. The witch. Or was she a saint? Arun still could not yet decide, but he blamed her for his predicament nevertheless. Lately, because of her, he had been thinking about karma again. It was something that had been drummed into him as far back as he could remember, as if it were an immutable law of nature, but he had never been sure that he had grasped it correctly nor that he agreed with it. Still, like most other people in the country, he paid lip service to the commonly held belief which stated, as far as he could tell, that you get what you deserve in the very crude and basic sense, that a good deed will lead to the blessings of wealth, health and happiness and a bad one punished in proportion to the transgression committed, good and bad being defined by the Buddhist teachings whose moral coordinates more or less corresponded with those found in other faiths. The difference was that in the Buddha Dhamma there was no judge or final authority out there administering the verdict, nor a time scale limited by this earthly existence, it seemed. You alone were responsible for your actions, whose consequences followed you from one incarnation to the next, so that you could be suffering in this life for something you did in some previous lifetime. Eventually the wheel would come round and unless you were one of the fortunate ones to get the rewards due to you (although even these were within the overall context of suffering, or Dukkha, that was the essential quality of the earthly dimension) you would have to pay up for what you did sooner or later.

In its negative aspect karma was the law of retribution that Arun saw those around him use time and again to explain away the mystery of what happened to everyone; why the poor had to suffer their lot, why perfectly decent people suddenly lost everything they had, and, conversely why some fat cat politician got away literally with murder. ("Don't worry," his mother would say, "his karma will eventually catch up with him," and this would conjure up for Arun as a young boy the image of an implacable Fury in the form of an angry dragon that pursued each person till the end of the universe).

By the time he was in his late teens and beginning to form his own world views Arun made a half hearted effort to reject this belief in karma and rely on a more rational explanation for the way the world worked. He was determined not to subscribe to such a fatalistic approach to life because, apart from being constantly confused by the notion and the various personal interpretations of the theme, he found the whole idea of the eventual punishment awaiting every erroneous action terrifying and too controlling in its implications. But he never quite succeeded in shaking it off because, like most things that have been planted in your heart when you are a child, like the idea of God and the Devil, sin and guilt, the notion of karma was an integral part of who he was and how he thought and felt about things

⟨≈‡≈⟩

Gaew's return into his life had stirred up the confusion once more. And he could only understand the effect that she had on him in terms of karma because his involvement with her seemed so fated and perversely immaculate in its timing that it felt as though she had come back to extract payment from him for having been wronged in some distant past. At least this was how he saw it. Her unexpected reappearance just when things were beginning to go well with his life and his work had all the makings of an invisible, mysterious scheme in which retribution was being acted out. The turmoil that Gaew managed to introduce with her re-entry into his life was like a punishment inflicted by an avenging sorceress. Arun, who had always taken pride in staying detached in his relationships with the women he had known, felt that Gaew was deliberately leading him step by step into a landscape in which he had no bearings. Her words and her questioning of his motives, which were all the more powerful for the sincerity behind them, felt like a forceful rush of water that swept the solid ground away from under him. The doubts that he had managed to stash away in the depths of his mind about his art came surging back to the surface, so that within a short but emotionally intense period the fragility of his convictions had been exposed and the certainty of the direction he had chosen overturned.

His rationality crumbled before her and he found that he could not even resolve the simple riddle that she threw at him; namely, why paint when there was so much to do in the world? Of course he had all the answers at his disposal because he had been forced to think about the issues since deciding to go to Silpakorn. He had justified his career to himself and to others many times in the past with increasing confidence and certainty as the years went by. But when Gaew put the question to him he found that he could no longer trot out the same replies, which now sounded like poor excuses for inaction. And so he was left dangling and unable to break through the spell that Gaew cast on him. The result was that what he was most attached to, which was his painting, started to seem totally meaningless.

They had been students at Silpakorn together and he, like most of the other young men of his year, had wanted to go out with her. There were better looking girls and her artistic talents did not impress him, but he found her bubbly, vivacious character attractive. It was in contrast to his own guarded, morose, suspicious nature and it brought light and humour to him at a time when he needed it. This was a difficult period for him. His father, Khun Wikrom, a retired family doctor, was in poor health and their relationship, once close, was now going through a bad patch, which meant that they disagreed about almost everything from literature to the fashion of wearing long hair to the political situation of the day. Arun was by no means a rebel and he did not want to aggravate his father, whose condition was fragile, but he found himself unable to contain his opposition to his father's hard line conservatism and his insistence that the self appointed government at that time had to be obeyed to the letter if Thailand was not to fall apart. Arun, like most of his generation, was still under the influence of what had happened in the October 14th, '73 movement, which had taken place when he was too young to participate, but which nevertheless was still fresh in people's minds. The students who had gone to the mountains as a result of the subsequent suppression and were now being granted amnesty were still trickling back to the city by the time that Arun was in his late teens.

They argued most of all about Arun's decision to become an artist rather than go to medical school and train to be a doctor. His father did not disguise his disappointment nor did he understand why Arun could choose such a path. To him art, which he took to mean painting and sculpture, was a hobby unless you were a craftsman in which case it was a worthy though low level skill. But he could not accept that to stretch a canvas and put shapes and colours on it or to hack out some figure which had no practical use could count as a serious career. Needless to say the examples of modern art such as abstract expressionism made him furious with indignation that people could be so easily fooled. Behind his disdain was the xenophobic attitude that Arun had encountered through his childhood; the mistrust of Western culture. Art was seen by his father as yet another import which the Thais did not require. Arun tried his best to justify his decision from all sorts of angles, even once making the mistake of pointing out to his father that the medicine he practiced had come from the West (this had led to a battle lasting days which Ladda, his sister, finally broke up). But none of his reasons impressed his father who in the end acquiesced only because he was too sick and weak to do otherwise.

Arun kept all these problems at home to himself because he did not trust anyone enough to share his intimate feelings with them. But he felt the confusion and doubt that the conflict with his father had produced. He was glad to have the distraction of Gaew's presence in the faculty. It cheered him up and distracted him. He could not help noticing her when she entered the lecture hall or the studio and he saw from the beginning that he was not alone in being affected by her. She stood out from the rest of the students, most of whom came from repressed, polite backgrounds and were still uncertain about themselves and struggling to find out who they were outside of their families. She alone seemed confident and free enough to express herself and not to fear argument or ridicule. She questioned the teachers, brought them down from their pedestals and made them explain and justify things in a way that others, including Arun himself, would never have done. The teacher's word was final. This was how they had been conditioned. There were even moments when he was embarrassed by her frankness. But he noticed that most of the teachers responded to her with enthusiasm and were pleased that there was someone in the class who stepped over the boundaries and challenged them.

The big theme in those days was the need to find a Thai style that was liberated from the farang traditions that had been assimilated but which did not, according to general opinion, express their truth, whatever that was. Arun listened but never took part in these discussions. Partly it was because he was exhausted from the fruitless debates that had taken place with his father. But also being at heart a pragmatic person, he found the talk too abstract, philosophical and irrelevant to what he was trying to do, which was just to get on with the business of painting. He felt that questions of style and content were a personal issue, not something that could be collectively agreed on and adopted like some general policy and he mistrusted the nationalistic undertone of the debate and the wholesale debunking of all things farang, which seemed to be just another extension of his father's narrow views. The bottom line was that he did not want to talk about art. He merely wanted to paint. Nevertheless, he attended those meetings held at the back of noodle shops, or in Suan Lumpini, sitting on reed mats under the trees, or in someone's bedroom, just to watch Gaew in action, arguing and laughing and as often as not hectoring the other students to see things her way.

During those university days, especially in the final year, he tried to get close to her and he felt that she too was interested in him, because, in the gatherings they attended, she would often look at him while she spoke and address her remarks in his direction, as though she was trying to impress him. They walked together through the park once or twice and exchanged ideas and one night at a faculty dance she told him that she found him attractive. But by that time a friend had already warned him that she was going out with an older man, a professor from another university who was married, and that he should watch out if he did not want to get hurt. When he heard this Arun was shocked. He could not imagine why she would want to be the mistress of an older man when she could have anyone she chose. In any case, on learning about this he drew back and gave up on her. Soon after they graduated from Silpakorn they had lost touch. He learned that she went abroad for a while and then, as the years went by and he began his stint as an art teacher, he forgot all about her.

Their reunion took place when a mutual acquaintance from Silpakorn, called Pi Pao, brought her along to the exhibition in Soi 23. The show featured three artists; a sculptress, a potter and himself. They had been chosen for the disparity of vision and approach because the gallery owner wanted to demonstrate the broad spectrum now covered by Thai artists. Arun was excited about it because it was the first time that he was showing paintings that marked a radical departure from the style which he had adopted since his days as a student. He was anxious about how those who had known his work from before would react and, although he did not admit it openly, how the critics would judge his new collection.

Up till then the semi-abstract landscapes which he painted owed heavily to Gauguin and the Fauvists as well as to Dali. He had found his inspiration in the mountains in the north and down south on the beaches of the Andaman coast and painted big bright canvasses which celebrated both the tropical light and what he saw as the underlying poetry of locations; surreal moments that soon became the trademark of his work. Within a relatively short time, he had become well known in the gallery circles and received praise and recognition for these paintings. Local collectors bought them and interior designers commissioned him to decorate hotel lobbies and restaurants. One of his images, depicting a bird with a human head flying through a sky in which the clouds were sea shells became well known as the backdrop for an advertisement for mobile phones. From having been a teacher who struggled to make ends meet Arun became one of the few artists who could make a decent living from his art and as a result he quickly became the envy of some of his fellow artists who felt that his work was a little too glib (in other words too commercial). His close friends, also, seemed not to be too impressed by his early success. They felt that he was capable of much more depth. He defended himself against these comments. But secretly he was hurt because he knew they were right. Still, he continued in the same style because the income he derived from the sale of the paintings was, at that point, a strong consideration. Money was a measure of his achievement as well as providing him with the sense of security that he had always wanted. With it he was able to buy himself a small plot of land and build a house and a studio. Most importantly he knew that he never wanted to go back to teaching.

But after five years he began to feel stale and jaded by what he was doing. And by now he realized that he was in danger of being pigeonholed and expected to churn out the same old stuff. The scenes that he could now produce with ease continued to please his buyers, but he felt limited and weighed down by his so-called poetic tropicalism (a term used by a loyal collector in an art magazine to describe his style) to the point of being cynical. He knew by this time that the only reason to go on with the same kind of paintings was because it was easy cash. But this was no longer such an important issue. He was not an extravagant man. His lifestyle was simple and he felt that he had everything he wanted on the material level. What he desperately needed was to find a new challenge, a different approach which could express the ideas that were floating around in his mind. He was tired of the landscapes, the beaches and the mountain scenery and of the whole exotic stuff in which he no longer found any depth or true poetry. He

wanted to turn to the city, most of all to include the love/hate he felt about
Bangkok, where he was born and whose ugly beauty he felt was part of his
soul. But the moment was not yet ripe. His thoughts were still too vague
and he found himself struggling with the logistics of style. Having worked
so hard to establish his own, out of the combination of influences to which
he had been exposed, it seemed such a radical step to now drop it all and try
to reinvent another. He found himself, during this fallow period, thinking
about these matters and getting nowhere.

When the opportunity came to apply for an exchange program that would
give him two months in Spain he did not hesitate. He needed a break from
the familiar surroundings and the routine that he had established for himself
and he had never been to Europe before. The cultural attaché was one of his
collectors and helped to make sure that he was chosen for the residency at
the Fine Arts in Madrid. The program was not demanding. There were no
obligations except to give a couple of talks to the faculty about his work and
about the state of the art scene in Thailand. Arun was glad to have some
time and space away from the everyday demands of Bangkok. It would be
the opportunity he needed to sit and contemplate and to get his thoughts in
perspective. He was excited about going to Madrid, visiting the museums
and galleries and seeing first hand the paintings he had admired but he was
not particularly looking for inspiration from any source outside of himself.

He arrived in Madrid in late September. The daytime weather was
still warm but the evenings were starting to cool down. Orange and ochre
and golden dead leaves were now floating down off the branches onto the
pavements. On his second day there, with a guidebook in his pocket, he
walked round the central area of the city and through the gardens and landed
up at the Prado where he headed straight for the Goyas. But the rooms where
they were hung were so crowded with tourists that he decided to leave them
and return later. Then he made his way down to a lower floor where he
found himself face to face with Hieronymus Bosch's *The Garden of Earthly
Delights*. He had not been prepared for it and the painting struck him like a
blow which sent his mind reeling. He felt as if he had stumbled on a treasure
that he had not been seeking. Its impact on him was so great that he was
no longer interested in anything else in the museum, the Goyas and the
Velazquez, because he knew that he had discovered what he was looking
for. And from then on he went as often as he could to stand in front of the

painting. Oblivious to the other tourists and spectators, Arun would stay in silent absorption, like a monk meditating, taking in every detail of the work. Then he would go and read about Bosch in the library and find out why he painted the way he did.

The two months in Madrid intoxicated him and by the time he came back to Bangkok Arun was filled with fresh inspiration His views on painting had shifted and he was sure once more about where he was heading with his art. The ideas which were seminal before he left Bangkok were now ripe for execution. He would now turn from nature to society and make the city and its sprawling mess his subject. The everyday scenes of Bangkok would become the backdrop of the modern morality play which he would describe; the crowded avenues and back streets, the sky train and the bars, the putrid canals, the market places and the massage parlours, the luxury condos, the river life and the slums. And he would people these cityscapes with the decadent and the depraved, the hungry ghosts and freaks, the broken and the undefeated who lived out Bangkok's strange drama.

So for a whole year following that visit to Madrid, Arun painted without a break, guided by this new vision and sense of purpose. Friends and fellow artists who visited his studio were surprised by his transformation and his unstoppable enthusiasm, which railroaded everything aside and pushed what he had done up till then into an irrelevant past. He could tell that some of them did not like the way he had incorporated social commentary into his work. They felt that he had gone political and too polemic in his approach. (He suspected that these were the same ones who had previously put him down for being commercial and who now would have preferred him to stay with the safe and exotic pieces that were familiar to them). But he argued with them patiently, insisting that the shift of subject matter from nature to society was a natural progression and that the depiction of urban decadence was nothing more than a reflection of what he saw in his own life, all around him. It was the state of a world where all was permitted and all manner of pleasure and gratification provided but where, ultimately, there was no peace or contentment. Bangkok, being a place where desire had no boundaries, was the perfect allegory for a universal condition.

Arun looked forward to the exhibition, but he was also more nervous than he had ever been about the reaction to his new work. It had been hard enough to explain to friends what he was trying to do but it was a different matter convincing the wider public, who were used to associating him with the colourful tropical imagery for which he was known. The new collection was anything but bright. The paintings all depicted night scenes of a city that was caught *in flagrante*, a kaleidoscopic depiction of lowlife and depravity that were inspired by the sex ghettos dotted round Bangkok. Despite the confidence that he had expressed in private, he was anxious about the response and had already prepared his explanations about his latest works. Being a critical person he did not like it when others criticized his work, especially those who pretended to know about art. But, even though he had begun to learn how to deal with this necessary part of his profession and to persuade himself not to take their comments too personally, he still felt as vulnerable and sensitive to criticism as any other artist.

In the end he need not have worried. The vernissage passed off with success and the next day, in the write-ups, his decision was vindicated. The critics appeared to have understood his change of style and direction and praised him for the risk he had taken. Arun felt both encouraged and relieved.

But he had not reckoned on Gaew's visit.

When she walked into the hall two days after the opening of the exhibition, dressed in faded jeans and a tee shirt, he hardly recognized her. It was over a dozen years since they had last **met**. Her youthful prettiness had made way for a more angular, boyish look. Her hair which once hung straight down her back, was now cropped short and all the art school frills had gone. No more earrings or flashy rings or bangles on her wrists. All decoration had been discarded. But, with the new minimalist look, she also seemed to have lost her bouncy, gregarious energy, greeting Arun with only a few brief words before wandering off to look around the exhibition. Pi Pao, who had brought her along, told him that she had given up painting as soon as she left Silpakorn and that since returning from the U.S. she had been working as an NGO, with an organization based in Chiengmai.

When she rejoined them she smiled at him and looked down at the floor and he remembered that this was how she looked whenever she was about to launch into one of her arguments. Arun knew before she spoke that Gaew would comment on his paintings unfavourably and he braced himself for her attack.

"You've become a really good painter," she began ominously. They were standing in front of a painting that was called 'Wild Nights'. It depicted a surreal Bangkok club scene in which all the figures were engaged in some kind of orgiastic interplay on a vast dance floor and giant rats and cockroaches huddled menacingly watching them.

He sensed what was to come.

"I mean it. But do you know what you are really doing?"

"Do any of us?" He knew that this sounded weak and smacked of sophistry.

"Yes, I think many do." She glared at him as she said this. He wanted the conversation to end right there. But she was just beginning. "You think that you're making a commentary that's valid. And you have every right to do so. But the world is burning. It isn't a matter of saying: 'Oh look how decadent we are.' There are real people suffering out there."

As a student he had found her direct manner amusing. But now it grated on him.

"What am I supposed to do? Leave everything and join some organization and try to save our rotten society from itself?" he was aware that his voice was getting shaky, and that his breathing was shallow. Why was he letting her make him feel so defensive?

Seeing his reaction, she laughed. "You must hate me for walking in out of nowhere and making these comments. I have no right."

Arun could find nothing to say to this and was relieved when Pi Pao suggested they have a drink in the bar next to the gallery. There they did not discuss his paintings but kept to safe ground and had a stilted conversation about their student days and laughed at the teachers who taught them. In the course of their exchange, he learned that Gaew was still single. There was too much to do, no time for marriage and that kind of stuff, she said jokingly. And he in turn let her know that he was not attached to anybody, although he wondered afterwards why he had bothered to do so. When she was leaving Gaew invited Arun to Chiengmai, but it was an offer he did not intend to take up.

Nearly a year later Gaew came to his studio. She was down in Bangkok, she told him, to attend a conference and she felt that she had behaved so badly to him at the gallery that she wanted to apologize. Arun found that, despite what had happened, he was pleased to see her. In the intervening months he had been having an internal dialogue with himself about the point she had raised and he had come to the conclusion that she was wrong. Now that she was there in the flesh it was a good opportunity to get it all off his chest.

It was late afternoon and the soft sunlight was slanting in through the tall windows that looked out on the garden. They sat for a while looking at the painting on which he was working, the fifth one in a series of eight that he was preparing for his oncoming show, soon to take place. He was going to finish it that evening. For a long time neither said a word. It was he who started.

"So you think this is all meaningless crap."

"No. The paintings are good. Much stronger than the last ones. And your vision is right too. I can feel what you're saying. But I think that you could do so much more to contribute."

"But this is my contribution," he interrupted her. "And I don't think I'd be much good at anything else. I tried teaching and that was a disaster."

She laughed and with a slight movement of her head flicked the hair from her face. Arun again found himself physically drawn to her, as he had been when they were young students together.

"I mean, I don't really understand what you want of me?" he continued more confident now. "I'm just an artist. This is my line of business. It's what I do."

"But that's precisely my point. I feel that our country, the world too, is in such a mess that the only art is to do something good for other people. But there's sacrifice involved." She could not have known that her words reminded him of the rebuke that his father, a family doctor, gave to him not long before he died.

"You sound so preachy. It's frightening." It was not what he meant to say but it slipped out. "Listen, I respect the work you're doing looking after people. But you can't expect everyone to have the same crusading spirit. My way is to make them look and think."

"But don't you see? Only a handful of people with enough money can afford your work, which they will collect, hang and probably resell one day. What difference does it make to anyone? How does it stop people from doing bad things to each other? How does it save the children who are destroyed before they have a chance to live? There is so much to be done."

She was sounding aggressive again and he wished the conversation would end right there.

"I mean you sit here in this studio and you make statements about the decadence you see around you and the meaninglessness of people's lives. But you are part of that decadence. And what you do is just as meaningless."

"Stop. Please stop," he pleaded, but smiling.

"Oh, I'm sorry. Forgive me. I am crazy. I didn't want to come here to torture you. I just wanted to renew our friendship, that's all."

They then began to talk of other things. Her work, her life up north, the women and children who came to her centre as a last resort. He wanted to make sure that there really was no one in her life and probed gently. But she reassured him that she was unattached and that made him feel hopeful. They drank beer and listened to Cuban music. She touched his cheek when she left saying that she was sorry she could not stay because she had to meet some friends that evening. He sensed that she wanted to stay. He thought of her that night after he had finished the painting. He desired her.

The next day at the same time she came back to his place and he made her tea. Then in the middle of showing her a painting he pulled her gently towards him and kissed her. At first she seemed to respond with equal passion, but suddenly she drew away.

"I'm sorry. I'm not ready for this," she said. And he did not insist.

During the rest of her stay in Bangkok she came round often to the studio to sit and chat. Arun noticed that her attitude towards him had softened but he sensed that he had to wait for her to decide when she was going to allow him to approach her physically again. The desire in him, being inhibited in this way, merely grew more intense. When she finally went back to Chiengmai he called her every evening, sometimes twice in succession which made her laugh. And then one morning, unable to bear the distance between them and impatient to be with her he went to the airport on impulse, bought a ticket and took a plane up north, checking into a small hotel on the Mae Ping. He thought that he would give Gaew a pleasant surprise. But it turned out that, when they were face to face that evening, she seemed anything but pleased that he was there.

"You should have warned me you were coming. I'm really busy," she said, obviously annoyed.

Arun was both hurt and surprised by her reaction. He was sure that she would be happy to see him again, and glad that he had made the effort to come to Chiengmai. For him the days and nights they had spent together in Bangkok had established an intimacy between them that could grow. But instead they might have been strangers. Later they walked by the river, hardly saying a word and came back to his room just as the twilight came on over the city. But she would not spend the night in the hotel with him.

"You shouldn't have come," she said simply as she was leaving.

Arun felt flushed with anger.

"What was that all about in Bangkok, then? Tell me. Just something amusing to pass your time? Have you got someone else up here? Is that it?"

"Why does it have to be someone else?" Her voice was weary. "Why can't you just accept things as they are? I have my work and I'm committed to it. It's very important to me. Try to understand."

"Are you saying that there's no time for me?"

"No. Yes. No. I mean..."

"You mean that I have to fit in when it's convenient. Well that's not good enough."

That night Arun lay on the bed smoking and watching the fan on the ceiling slowly turn. The sounds from the streets drifted up; a love song sung off key, laughter shared by a group of friends. He puzzled over the mixed messages he was getting from Gaew. He asked himself what he was doing wrong and why, just when it looked like he was getting close to her, she withdrew, as if afraid of physical intimacy. It was a mistake, he decided, to have been impetuous. He should never have come up to Chiengmai. Still, he had to see her again. There was no way that he could work while the obsession continued to hold him in its grip.

The next morning, at the crack of dawn, Gaew came by. She called up from the lobby saying that she had already ordered breakfast for them. Afterwards, at his insistence, she took him to the centre where she worked. To get there they walked through the old part of the town, along quiet streets, until they reached the southern boundaries of the city. Then, at the end of a road that seemed to be leading nowhere, they went through a small wrought iron gate which was the entrance to 'The Women's Home'. On the steps of the old wooden building and in the small, scruffy garden out front, there were groups of women of all ages, sitting around chatting. In the soft early sunlight the scene looked peaceful. They all waied Gaew respectfully and one of the young girls shouted out:

"Pi Gaew, Pi Gaew, is that your boyfriend?"

This made them all giggle. Gaew smiled and shook her head without answering.

That morning, as Gaew showed him round, Arun began to understand what she had been trying to tell him. The place was crowded with the casualties of domestic violence and those who had been abused and exploited. There were young girls from the hill tribes who had already spent time as child prostitutes. A section acted as a hospice for those who were HIV positive. Some of these had full blown AIDS and were in their final phase. It was here that Gaew worked. The first day that he was taken into the building Arun tried his best to hide his shock. He had seen the pictures in the newspapers and the TV like everyone else, but up close, standing in front of a body that was ravaged and emaciated to a point where the bones looked as though they would pierce the thin film of skin that covered them, it was another matter altogether. Eyes stared out at him with expressions that he had never seen before. One woman, who seemed like she had no more breath left in her, even managed to put her hands together to greet him, as if she were grateful for his presence.

"Most of them got it off men, only a few from dirty needles. Some of them have children in the ward upstairs who are infected too. None of them will leave here. This is their last home."

Later, when they were walking along the river under the flame trees, Arun asked her if she was going to do this work for the rest of her life.

"If not this, if not here, then something along these lines, somewhere in the world. You see, I can't live a normal life. I've lost touch with all the dreams I once had, to be an artist, to be in a fixed relationship, to have a family. All those things just don't have any point for me nowadays."

"But you might change."

"No. Something's happened to me. It's like I've found my karma in this life. I've seen that the only meaning in this existence is to be of service. I wish I could share this with you. It is why I said all those things about your painting."

"And what if I changed? What if I gave up painting and came up here to help you in your work?"

Arun was not quite sure of what he was saying, but he felt that she was slipping away from him.

"Could you do that? Could you join me? Would you be brave enough to sacrifice what you love doing most? For me? Really?"

Arun felt confused. Her eyes were smiling. He was not sure if she was laughing at him or accepting his offer. But it was too late to take back the words he had spoken. He felt that he had been trapped. That evening he packed his bags and left Chiengmai.

⊂≈⊰⊱≈⊃

The joint was nearly finished. He dragged on the last toke, dropped the butt onto the floor and let it die. Then he walked over to the corner, where the five finished canvasses were stacked. Carefully, he pulled one of them out and leaned it against the wall. He removed the cloth that was covering the painting and stepped back to look over what he had done. 'Celebration' was the title he had given it; a large canvas depicting a river that was on fire, and in which all the boats were carrying ghostly figures travelling towards a crimson horizon. It was, he decided, a good painting. It would sell and be hung up on someone's wall. He stood staring at it for a few minutes with appreciation until he suddenly remembered a look he had seen in the hospice. And Gaew's words echoed back to him. Then quickly he put the cover back over the canvas and moved away. For a moment he wished he had the courage to take all his paintings out to the garden, stack them up, set light to them and be done with it, if that's what it would take to get her to love him. But in the next instant a thought made him laugh nervously out loud. What if he had got it all wrong, that she was only playing with his feelings and that she had no intention of allowing him into her life? What if she were mad? For a while he could not control his laughter. But when he calmed down he cursed. The thought was not funny. It was frightening.

Damn Gaew and all her crusading nonsense! It was absurd, he thought, that he should be so obsessed with her like some hopelessly lovesick teenager, that he should take any notice of her single minded altruism, that he should let himself be blackmailed into thinking that he must stop painting if he wanted to be with her. He had been through it all in his mind so many times, but he could still not reason away the feelings that were churning around in him. He felt exhausted from it all and he knew that he had to break the love spell that she had woven round him or he was finished.

Arun turned the light out in the studio and stepped into the small garden. The air, after the rainstorm was clean and fresh. The scent of honeysuckle came with the gentle breeze that was getting up. The moon was reflected in the small pond. A frog plopped into the water. The smoke was hitting him full on now. He was no longer depressed. He danced slowly round the garden to a rhythm which he alone could hear and against the bushes and the trees he looked like a lithe cat that was stalking a hidden prey. Then he paused and turned his head toward the round silvery globe that hung there in the sky like a huge fruit waiting to be picked. "Why all the anxiety?" he asked himself aloud. "What do I have to lose?"

Straightening up, he shook himself vigourously and then he nodded as if to an invisible witness. In that moment he made his decision. Tomorrow he would start work and slap the paint on and do what he knew best. In a few weeks the show would be behind him and then he would think of joining Gaew in her quest to save the world and following her wherever she led him.

CHAPTER 9

The train was crowded. They were now a couple of hours out of Nongkai, heading south to the capital. Don was seated next to the window. He had been one of the first to board, and for a long time while the train stood in the station and filled up with passengers he sat there dazed and uncertain, as though drugged, still getting used to the idea that he had actually folded away his saffron robes that morning, and put on his old jeans, taken a lift to the station in a country taxi, bought himself a ticket and was now on a train returning to Bangkok. He could not connect his consciousness to what was happening and he kept having to remind himself that he was now no longer Phra Boontam living in Wat Thammacitta, with its silence, established routines and rules of conduct, but back in the deconstructed arena of everyday life. Vendors were walking along the track next to the carriage shouting, at the top of their voices. A child was being scolded. Another was crying at the top of its lungs. A group of young men was walking through the passageway singing along to the *mawlum* folk song blasting out from the machine that one of them held on his shoulder. Everything seemed so frantic and unnecessarily loud, too raw and too close. Don found it unbearably strange to be sitting there among ordinary men and women again, feeling like some alien who had just arrived from another planet. And he felt how easy it would have been to get off and head straight back to the monastery and resume his ordained existence.

But once the train got going and Nongkhai receded into the distance it was easier. As the passengers around him settled down and the din of their voices gave way to the steady pleasant chugging of the engine, Don began to relax. Then, with the keen awareness that came with the months recently spent in meditative retreat, he began to take in all that was going on around him in that carriage, noticing the details which he would have once left unnoticed, like the texture of the table in front of him and the faded, cracked paint of the carriage wall. Opposite him sat an old lady dressed in a faded batik sarong and a cream coloured long sleeved lace top. A thick gold chain hung from her neck. Her sandy coloured skin was weathered and wrinkled and her grey hair was cut short in the old fashioned country style. She sat with her hands folded her in her lap, holding in them a string of prayer beads made of rosewood. Her eyes were tightly closed as though she were meditating or praying and Don wondered if she would wait till Bangkok before opening them again. Next to him on the narrow seat was a wiry farang woman in her early forties dressed in a flimsy sleeveless yellow cotton top and purple fisherman's trousers. Her blonde hair was bunched up on top of her head and through it there was stuck an elaborate comb. At first when she had sat down he had felt embarrassed but once the train got going he had given up trying to avoid letting his shoulder touch her. Don, glancing sideways at her arms, saw that her lightly tanned skin was covered in freckles. She had silver hill tribe jewelry on her wrist and her forefinger was stained with tobacco. Opposite her sat her companion—no wedding ring—who looked much older. He had longish thinning grey hair and a short stubbly beard. The logo on his faded tee shirt said 'Free Tibet'. His fingers lightly drummed the table in rhythm with the train. By their accents Don guessed they were Australian. They had not said anything to each other during the first hour after boarding the train. But now they were engaged in an animated conversation that he could not help overhearing because they were both shouting across to each other, fighting the sound of the engine. They presumed, he was sure, that he could not understand them and this was why they were conversing so freely. The woman was talking about the days they had spent in Laos and how she much preferred it to being in Thailand, how wild and simple it still was across the border. Then she went on to say that she was worried about leaving their friend, Jim, behind in Vientiane and wondered whether he would be safe travelling on his own up to Luang Prabang.

"I hope he's cool," the woman was saying. "and he doesn't go around trying to score dope."

Don looked out of the window. Everything was fresh and fertile after the rains. The bright green of young rice. The trees that dotted the fields. The bushes bursting with colour. The hills in the distance. These passing sights filled him with a quiet joy. In the past five years he had only left the compound of the monastery to go on the morning alms round or to accompany the abbot to the nearby villages, whenever there was a blessing ceremony to perform. Some of the other monks had asked leave to go on *tudong* pilgrimage but Don never did and the abbot did not encourage him.

"You've done enough travelling in your short life. It's time for you to be still," he said at the very beginning, when Don ordained.

Now he was on the move again and out of the robes that he had worn and scrubbed till they were threadbare. Once or twice since boarding the train he had found himself, out of habit, tugging at his shoulder to make sure that the cloth was not slipping. When he got up that morning he had opened the drawer and taken out the shirt that he had worn when he had arrived at the monastery and held it up to his body. It had the feel of belonging to someone else. Later at the station in Nongkai he had bought himself a baseball hat to cover his shaved head. It felt odd to be in civilian clothes again because it reminded him that he had just emerged from that other world, where he had spent the past five years of his life. And he could hardly recognize himself any more. His body which was bulky before was now lean from the Spartan diet at the monastery. And the poisons in his system had been purged. He felt stronger and cleaner than he had ever been.

⚬⚬⚬

For Don the decision to leave the monkhood was not something dramatic, or one which he had been mulling over for any length of time like some of the other monks he had known at the monastery, whose last months were plagued by the dilemma of whether or not to leave and return to their old life. In fact, sitting there on the train he thought how easy it might have been for him to be still there in Wat Thammacitta at that very hour, next to his fellow monks in the huge open sala by the tamarind tree, eating the sticky rice that the villagers had offered. He had suffered no crisis of faith or doubt about the teaching that had been embodied in Achaan Panya. He still looked to the Dhamma as the highest path. At various low points it had helped him through the worst of his darkness. Nor was it a question of finding the daily routine too rigorous or monotonous. At the beginning when he arrived at the monastery everything was difficult. The two hundred and twenty seven rules of the *vinaya* which were strictly imposed by the Achaan was something that took Don the best part of two years to be able to follow. Being a person who had led a life that was so devoid of discipline, the challenge was painful.

But in the end he learned not only to surrender and adapt to them but to use them in the creative way that the Achaan taught, as a tool for spiritual growth. Neither was there anything in the secular world that called him back. Of course at the beginning the sense of deprivation was acute and there were things he longed for, particularly sex and there were days when the so-called patterns of *sankara* looked set to overwhelm him. But in time with the Abbot's patient guidance as well as the practices he made them do, such as watching corpses decomposing, these impulses were tamed. After the first few years, life at the monastery had become familiar and in its way even comfortable. He could have coasted along for the rest of his life like some of the monks he had come to know, forgetting how old he was and how life outside had been, judging time by the phases of the moon and the changing seasons and the *pansa* that came and went. And perhaps one day he might have become an abbot in one of the temples in the province.

The last rainy season retreat had been especially rewarding from a spiritual point of view. He had reached deep states of *samadhi* and gained new insights. For the first time the mosquitoes had not troubled him. He had at long last learned not to resist them and as a result, almost miraculously, they had stopped biting him. And during the meditation sessions he had found long stretches of peace and freedom from the ghosts of his past that had been troubling him. Everything had gone well. It was only the dream of the Naga on that morning a month ago that stirred up a disquiet in him which he could not deal with.

In the end he did not show the abbot what he had written. But several days later as he was sweeping the leaves by the front gates the abbot walked up to him.

"Phra Boontam," the Achaan began without preamble. "I saw you in my sitting yesterday night. You want to tell me something."

He had long ceased to be surprised by the abbot's intuitive powers. So that morning as they sat in the sala by the river he recounted his dream to his teacher who listened with his eyes closed. When he opened them again he did not laugh, as Phra Boontam, half expected but instead kept nodding his head.

"The spirit of the Naga is the spirit of the unexpected. It comes from the depths," he said finally, and that was all. Don did not understand what the abbot really meant by that cryptic remark but he took it at face value.

Almost a month later, just before dawn, he woke up and knew that he was about to disrobe and return to being Nai Don Tongbai. It was time to confront the things he had avoided. When he went to the abbot that morning his old teacher was not surprised by his decision.

"Yes," he said simply. "It's time. You have to go back out there into the world and do whatever it is that is waiting for you. But remember that you can always come back."

⟨═╪═⟩

The train was pulling into Khonkaen. The vendors were already lining up on the platform waiting to board and sell their wares. Others, with trays of soft drinks and sticks of fried chicken, were preparing to do business through the open windows. The smell of food and smoke wafted through the carriage. It was now early afternoon and the sun was fierce. Don was glad that he had decided to buy a seat in an air-conditioned carriage. He had been thinking of his last meeting with the abbot which had taken place in his teacher's kuti, which he visited after completing his last rites in the *vihara* in front of his fellow monks. Phra Achaan handed him the wallet that he had kept in a wooden chest in the corner. Don had entirely forgotten about it and catching himself opening it he felt embarrassed. Achaan laughed.

"I think everything's still there," he said. "But go ahead. Have a look and see."

In it there was a picture of his mother and father, his ID and two credit cards which were out of date. Then the abbot handed him a plain white envelope saying:

"The villagers want you to receive this gift. They all contributed to it."

"But they didn't even know of my decision to leave," Don replied.

"Oh they had a feeling it was coming," said the Achaan with a twinkle in his eye and Don knew, because it was how things worked around there that the Achaan had arranged for the money to be collected. In which case how did he know that Don was going to disrobe? Was it something in the dream that Don related to him?

He had been puzzling over the dream for a month. Not only the images but the consciousness that he had experienced through it were still fresh in his mind. He could not understand what it meant only; that it had left him with a sense of great disappointment and melancholy. He could not save the Buddha from being drowned. But try as he did to analyze the dream, reading his own words again and again, he could see nothing in his life to which this referred. Yet the feelings remained and he knew that some truth contained in the dream lay behind his decision to disrobe. And this was what the abbot, his teacher, had seen too.

The train had still not left the station. Don was leaning against the window watching the activity on the platform when he felt his arm being tapped. He turned to see the farang woman, who had got up earlier from her seat, holding up a bottle of soda water in front of him.

"Would you like this?" she pronounced her words very slowly so as to make sure he understood.

"Thank you," he replied and took the bottle from her, grateful for her consideration.

"Are you going to Bangkok?" her question was accompanied by an exaggerated gesture pointing down the track.

"Yes I am," he answered.

"That's good."

She sat down and he was relieved that she seemed to give up making conversation with him. It still felt odd to be in such close physical proximity with a woman. He had tried to squeeze into his part of the seat without touching her. But during the journey with each jolt of the train her bare arm had brushed against his. A day earlier and this would have been considered breaking the vow of *brahmacharya*.

"Are you a student?" Now it was the man who addressed him. Did he at thirty still look that young?

"No."

"Do you live in Bangkok, or are you from round here?"

He smiled at them. "Bangkok."

"And you speak very good English," said the woman.

Don nodded, but he did not really want to go on with the conversation. He did not want to chitchat and to explain that he had grown up in their country as well as in England. He needed to be with his own thoughts. He saw that the old lady opposite had done the right thing by keeping her eyes firmly closed. Thankfully, with a loud crunching sound, the engines started up their din once more and the train lurched forward.

It must have been nearly four in the afternoon when Don woke up. Despite the air conditioning he was clammy with sweat. The sun was now streaming in through the smoke coloured glass. On opening his eyes he saw that the old lady was staring straight at him. The farang couple were both asleep.

"Did you have a good rest, Luang Pi?" she asked with a thick accent.

Don was shocked that she was addressing him this way, as though he were still a monk, and he was about to answer her but she put her hands together respectfully.

"I'm so sorry I did not recognize you when I got on. I've been watching you and it took me a while. The clothes you're wearing fooled me, you see. But then I thought I bet that cap is hiding a shaved head and then I remembered who you were straightaway. You won't know who I am because you always had your eyes down every time I filled your begging bowl. You are Phra Boontam, aren't you?"

"I was. But no longer."

"Of course, of course."

"What are you going to Bangkok for?" Don felt compelled to ask her this out of politeness.

"Oh I have so many things to sort out. My sister's in trouble. She married a bad man. I've been telling her to leave him for years. He's a gambler and a womanizer and now he'd in debt. He owes money to the wrong people. They're going to lose their house. But what can I do? It's too much at my age, having to deal with all this now. But my sister's at her wit's end and I'm afraid of what might happen."

Her words came pouring out and now she was dabbing her tearful eyes.

"You can only do what you can. They have to sort it out themselves."

"Thank you, thank you for your advice, Luang Pi. I mean Khun. But I feel so responsible for my sister. I brought her up, you see, and..."

Don could tell that there was a lot to the story which she probably would not be able to share with a stranger. He reached across and patted her hand, realizing immediately afterwards that he had not touched a woman's skin for five years.

"It will be all right," he told her.

"Oh your words have given me comfort, Luang Pi."

With that, as though the exchange had exhausted her, the old lady once more closed her eyes.

$$\Longleftarrow\mkern-8mu\ddagger\mkern-8mu\Longrightarrow$$

The sun was now setting and the lights came on in the carriage. The flat central plain was bathed in a golden glow, in which the palm trees stood out like sentinels marking the boundaries of the fields. It was going to be a clear night. Stars were already visible. There were only a few hours left before they reached Bangkok. Don stood in the small space outside the toilets with his elbows resting on the window that he had opened and let the hot wind blow into his face. He needed the air to wake him up. He looked back down the track and watched the last carriages curve round a bend. For a moment just before getting up from his seat he had found himself thinking that he might have been too hasty in leaving the security of the monastery, that he had not properly thought through what this would mean. But now with his head clearer he dismissed this moment of doubt from his mind. There was no going back. He had taken the decision to leave without pressure from anyone and now he must stick to it.

As the train made its way toward its final destination, Don could not help feeling nervous about what lay ahead. Five years earlier he had run away, swearing never to return if he could help it. He knew that he had changed but still he prayed that he had the strength not to get sucked back into things that he could not handle before he had found his new bearings. The imminent reality of finding himself once more in the place where he had messed up his life so badly brought up a mix of contradictory emotions that were difficult to disentangle from one another. Yet he could not help but feel excited at the prospect of seeing once again the city where he was born. It was a landscape that was so familiar that he merely had to close his eyes to be able to see the crowded streets and smell the market places that he had missed in his exile. He wanted to see how much it had all changed in the years he had been away and at the same time he wanted to see how much he himself had changed and whether he was now ready to face the past.

He wondered what had happened to the old gang that he ran with, whether any of them were still doing the same reckless things or whether they were now in jail serving time or on their way to becoming respectable bankers and businessmen. He guessed that they would be surprised by his decision to disrobe.

Going to Chiengmai would have been the easiest thing to do. But the one person he did not want to confront was his mother. whom he now pictured in the living room of her mansion in the hills. As it was early evening, she would be watching the television, waiting for the news to come on, with the poodles on the sofa beside her waiting to be fed chocolates. His sudden and unexpected arrival would have provoked a drama or worse. She had always hated surprises and given what had happened between them he suspected that she would probably have preferred him to stay ordained as a monk and as far away from her as possible. An aunt had written to him only a month earlier saying that his mother was still going around saying that she no longer had a son. She had added that his mother's heart condition had recently got worse and that she was now taking heavy medication. She told him that he should pray for her forgiveness and make peace with her before she died.

Don thought about the complicated relationship they had and he wished that it was not so difficult between them. He could not help feeling partly responsible for her heart condition. Things had never been smooth at home. She had smothered him with love when he was a child and then later, when things were going badly between her and his father, she looked to him as an ally to give her the moral support she needed, which put him in a painful position. But in the end it was something he found impossible to do. The truth was that Don could see how difficult and emotionally demanding his mother was and he could understand why his father went looking elsewhere for companionship. He could not side with her in her condemnation of her husband's behaviour. As a result she felt betrayed and never forgave him.

Later when the terrible event happened that revealed to her the side of his life that he had managed to keep secret up till then she took it as a sign that her son had incarnated all the evil traits of the father and had been sent to her as a form of punishment, which she had to bear with courage and equanimity.

During his first month in the monastery, his mother had visited him on two successive weekends, taking with her foodstuff and extra blankets and even money for him to spend. When he had gently asked her, at the end of her second visit, to come less often so that he could have a chance of adapting to his new environment and not to bring him anything, since he had no need, she became upset, then angry. She cried as she told him how she had lost her only son and then declared that if he did not want to see her then she would never come to the monastery again. And she never did. It was typical. She had cut her husband off from her life with the same sort of display of cold implacability, which belied the deep hurt of having been wronged.

He knew, as he stood watching the fields roll by, that, because of all the things that had come between them, he could not go back to that mansion where so many troubled memories lay and walk through the door like some long lost son. Maybe in a couple of days or weeks, when he had adapted to ordinary life again. But in the meantime he would go to Bangkok, and check into a small hotel and get adjusted to being back in the city. Then he would call and tell her that he had left the monkhood.

At last they were on the outskirts of the city. The train had stopped at a level crossing and was now pulling out again. Streetlights and rickshaws. Crowded lanes. Motorbikes. Large billboards. Pavements spilling over with noodle stalls. Swarms of people going in all directions. Policemen directing traffic. The sharp shrill of whistles being blown. Taxis waiting in line under a bridge. Buses roaring along the road spewing out black smoke. Sights that he had not seen for five years. But there was something distinctly familiar about the throbbing chaos and suddenly, for a brief second, it felt as though he had never left Bangkok.

There was a lot of activity in the carriage as people anticipated the arrival at Hua Lampong station. Already several of the passengers were getting their cases and bundles off the luggage racks. The old lady opposite was holding up a small mirror to herself and putting on her lipstick. The farang couple had a map of Bangkok on the table and were discussing how they were going to get from the station to their hotel at Kao San Road, the backpackers' district. Don suggested that they take a taxi, but they were now looking for a bus route. The ticket collector, his work done, was making his way through the carriage, smiling at everyone and stopping to answer questions. He was talking to a family, telling them that he was pleased to be going home to his wife and two children. Just at that moment the train's long sad siren pierced the air. They were coming into Hua Lampong. The train now slowed down to walking speed. There were crowds all along the platform. The cleaners too, with their mops and their buckets, were ready to board. Porters leaned on their trolleys. It was the end of a long day's travel but Don had a feeling that his journey was just beginning.

CHAPTER 10

Bangkok. Not so much a city as a dysfunctional sprawl dumped on a mangrove swamp. It should never have strayed so far from the Chao Phraya River and the banks of the canals that lead off from it. The wooden houses on stilts with their lopsided balconies and the thin boats tied to the steps, the old temples and the walled palaces look fine there next to the brown green water. The rest is a monster spreading its brittle fingers out in every direction; the result of relentless and often reckless construction, in the name of necessity, progress and development, and much of it done on the cheap. And yet despite the efforts to cover the spongy fertile seedbed with cement and concrete, glass and steel and turn it into some version of an urban setting, the watery element seeps through. There is the sense of oozing damp everywhere. Newly painted walls are soon stained with patches of fungal growth. The vegetation pushes up through any cracks that appear on the sidewalks. Unruly bushes of bright flowers burst out in the wastelands that dot the metropolis. The fetid smell of decay rises from the canals that are now black and unused. It is hard to imagine that they were once busy thoroughfares and alive with wild life. But still there are parts of the swampland that will not submit to the modern onslaught.

During the monsoon months a python may sometimes appear from nowhere and slither over a rain drenched lawn or across a car park looking for a lost mate or an old nest. Iguanas lurk in the water hyacinth, refusing to die. When the lanes are flooded, which can happen within an hour of a heavy storm, armies of cockroaches run out of the sewers and the rats scuttle along the gutters to find shelter under bridges. In the slum district of Klongtoey, near the docks, the children surf down the main street on planks stolen from the shipyard. Every year the city sinks a little more into the mud.

For Don, Bangkok was the Naga's city. What happened to make him think this took place exactly a week before his fifteenth birthday, when he was on holiday in Thailand from his boarding school in Melbourne. It was during a stage in his father's diplomatic career when he was stationed in his home country as deputy head of the political section at the Ministry. Previously, he had been posted to Australia and before that to England. Because of his father's peripatetic career Don had been abroad since he was six and his connection to his own culture was not a comfortable one. Because he had not grown up there, he had no friends and the boys of his own age group to whom he had been introduced did not share his main interest, which, at the time, was biology. He would have preferred to be around his school pals, who were planning to do a trip into the bush with one of the parents. But his mother had insisted that he should brush up his Thai and become familiar with his own culture. To this end she hired a private tutor to come round every morning to give him lessons in his native tongue.

They had rented an old rambling Thai style complex in a soi off Klongtan from another diplomat who was abroad. Their family home was really in Chiengmai, up north. His father had chosen the traditional dwelling in the capital instead of a condo type apartment because, he told them, he wanted to have a feel of what old Bangkok must have been like. His mother complained endlessly about this eccentric choice. Being accustomed to the comforts of immaculately tidy, well kept apartments in London and Canberra, the open plan teak buildings, however elegant and exotic, were difficult to get used to. She was endlessly complaining about the fact that, when it rained, they had to rush across the terrace to try to avoid getting drenched, and that the street cats regularly had running fights on the rooftops and that the place felt spooky. But most of all she hated the days when the canal that ran by the house exuded the rotten stench of stagnation. Then she would go around lighting joss sticks and sticking them into the flower pots to disguise the smell.

"It may be a beautiful house, but we can never entertain here," she told Don when he arrived back from Australia that summer; "Sometimes I think your father chose for us to live here in order to punish me."

Don agreed with all her complaints, but in his heart he appreciated his father's decision. For, despite all the inconveniences, the place had a romantic charm to it. He did not mind that there was no swimming pool and no convenience store on the ground floor. He liked being close to the earth and feeling the cool teak planks under his bare feet and being able to step out straight down onto a lawn without having first to take a lift. It made a change from all the carpeted formality in which he had grown up. And the best feature was the klong by the house whose stink could be so pungent that it took your breath away and yet whose very endurance suggested, as his father rightly held, a sort of link to a city that had all but vanished.

Don did not like Bangkok in those days. He had not yet discovered its subtle and weird poetry. To him, at that age, it seemed like a mess that offered very little joy. The well-ordered Australian towns were standards against which he judged the place where he was born and against these imprints Bangkok felt tawdry and definitely miss-able. He enjoyed the tourist sights which his parents took him to see during his first week with the detachment of a teenager but the rest of it did not impress him as being anything exciting or exotic. The shopping malls, the traffic jams, the pollution, the general chaos and heat seemed oppressive and unnecessary. The few glimpses through the car window of the suffering of the poor and the broken disturbed him for it drove home how privileged he was and how distant his world stood from the rest of the life of the city. This sense of alienation was compounded by the feelings of awkwardness in the social settings in which he found himself. Among the acquaintances of his own generation—and there was no lack of them—Don felt ill at ease. With the ones who had grown up in Thailand he found that he could not follow their jokes and their play on words or the way that they all seemed to be so well versed in how they were expected to behave. He noticed the wide gap between who they were when they were with each other in a group and how dutiful and polite they appeared in front of the adults. He did not judge them for this but he felt unable to perform with the same conviction. In the evening he sometimes accompanied his parents, rarely out of choice, to some social function that was taking place. But he usually felt embarrassed at these occasions and tired of keeping up the fixed smile and answering the same questions and receiving the same advice from well meaning family friends and relatives.

Consequently, during that long rainy holiday, Don preferred to spend most of his time at home, reading and listening to his Walkman after his morning Thai lessons with the tutor were over. Often, when his mother left the house to go shopping or to lunch with her friends, he would sit with the servants in the kitchen or in the water sala and listen to their gossip. The gardener, a Karen tribesman who had been with the owners' household since he was a boy, would tell Don stories of when the house was always full of guests and lively with intrigue. The grandfather, a famous politician, liked to entertain. In those days the klong was clean. The cook bought fruit and vegetables from the market gardeners who passed in their boats, on their way to selling their produce at the floating market up the river. An old monk would come by on his alms round, paddling a tiny wooden canoe, and they were always afraid he would capsize. Local children would strip off on the hot afternoons and dive in off the bridge and during the *Loy Kratong* ceremonies they would steal the coins from the little banana leaf boats that floated down the klong. Sometimes they would have to shoo the water buffaloes from the back garden while the guests were having cocktails on the terrace and often iguanas would climb up from the water and get chased off by the dogs.

Don was fascinated by these tales. Through the gardener's descriptions of the past he could sometimes imagine what life in that house must have been like. But mostly, listening to them, he felt touched by a certain irrational nostalgia, as though he had lost something precious which he never had. When he looked down into the klong, all he could see was black water in which the detritus of the city floated by, and it made him wonder, even in those young years, how the city had been allowed to sink into such a level of decay.

The four servants of the house were his only friends that holiday. He came to hear about their problems and their dreams and ambitions in a way which gave him a sense of being put in touch with a world which was much more fascinating than the predictable stage of the hotel restaurants, dinner parties and shopping malls to which he was periodically dragged along by his mother. He on his part tried to tell them about his own experiences at school and about the places he had lived in abroad since he was a child. But he always noticed a glazed look come over them whenever he spoke of these foreign lands. It was not that they were disinterested. But it was too far from their reality.

Towards the end of the holidays Don fell ill without warning. It happened that his parents were away one weekend attending a funeral in Chiengmai. They had taken the plane on Friday evening and were not due back till Monday. He had begged to be allowed to stay in Bangkok. The thought of travelling all the way to the north to go to the cremation of an elderly friend of the family whom he had never met did not appeal to him. For a change his mother did not insist. Two of the servants were away too, so there was only the cook and the gardener in the house with him. That Saturday morning he woke up with his head feeling as though it was being struck with a hammer from the inside. The cook, of course, contacted his parents, who said that they would cut short their stay and be home by the next evening. Don talked briefly to his mother, who seemed a little annoyed by the news because it meant that she would not have time to see a property that she was thinking of buying. She told the cook that she thought it was the flu virus that was around and that Don should be given a double dose of aspirin and be kept in bed.

By the afternoon his temperature was 41. The cook called Chiengmai once more and this time Don's father came on the line and said that if his son was not better by the next morning then they would try to change their flight yet again and be there to take Don to hospital. But it was impossible for them to leave any sooner. He did not listen to the cook when she told him that she did not think it was flu. He rarely listened to her about anything except what they were going to eat that day. So she did not tell him that she was certain that Don's symptoms were those of *Kai Lued Aug*, Dengue fever. Both she and the gardener had seen it before in their villages. All the signs were obvious. Both had seen people die from it.

The gardener had a friend who lived in the group of wooden shacks that stood where the soi ended and the patch of wasteland began. This man had once been a monk and had a reputation as a *maw ya*, a healer who used herbs and massage, potions and incantations in his craft. In recent years, as the locals began to depend more and more on Western medicine, his skills were less appreciated. In fact the term *maw ya* for some people including Don's parents was now synonymous with being a quack. But there were still a few who went to him for treatment, especially the older ones in the neighbourhood who insisted that his cure for diarrhoea and arthritis was better than anything you could get from the hospital or the chemists.

It was the cook who suggested getting him in to see what he could do for Don, because the aspirins were clearly not working and she was beginning to get nervous about what might happen before the parents arrived back from the north. So the old healer was fetched from his shack and on arrival he was taken straight to Don's bedside. Without so much as touching the boy, he immediately recognized the symptoms and confirmed what the cook and the gardener had thought.

"There's no time to lose," he said to them. "This is a serious case. The boy is hurting badly."

He went away and returned an hour later with a brown paper bag filled with dried roots, which looked gnarled and shrivelled, and grey coloured leaves that felt like they would crumble into dust if squeezed too hard. He told the cook to boil up the contents of the bag and to let it steep for an hour before administering it to Don, who by this time was almost delirious with the pain and the fever.

"It's very strong medicine. If he takes it today he'll be all right soon. Then he'll need to rest for a month. The poison was bad," said the healer, before leaving.

After drinking the concoction that night Don felt an immediate relief. The headache subsided and he was even able to get out of bed for them to change the sweat-soaked sheets. Exhausted from his ordeal, he looked forward to getting a good night's rest. Just before he turned the lights out his parents called again and he was able to reassure them that he was much better. He did not mention that the healer had been round, nor that he had been given the herbs to drink, because he did not have the strength to deal with the inevitable reaction that it would have provoked.

Some time during the night Don woke up feeling clear headed, fresh and full of energy. It was as if not only the sickness of the dengue but all the tensions and stress in his body had dropped away. There was an absence of pain in a way that he had never experienced before. Apart from the lightness of his body and a sense of physical ease all the doubts and fears and insecurities that he had suffered seemed to have melted away. Instead of the usual heaviness that had recently been weighing down on him he felt as if there was a light radiating from his heart.

That afternoon he could barely sit up but now Don sprang out of bed and strode out onto the terrace, then skipped down the steps onto the lawn. He had a strong urge to be outside and to touch the earth and when his feet felt the dew his whole being seemed to tingle. There was no moon that night and the servants' quarters were all shut up and dark. The only light came from a streetlamp down the soi which had been damaged in a recent storm, so that it was now flickering like a strobe. With each flash Don saw the moisture glisten on the well cut grass and the trees along the tall garden wall come alive.

The only sound was a bird call that echoed from the tree tops. An answer came from somewhere far away. Don stood for a while listening to this exchange and then slowly he walked across the lawn to the sala by the *klong*.

There he leaned over the wooden parapet and stared down into the water. He noticed that the smell coming from the *klong* was new. Usually, at its worst, it was the sour, putrid stench of an open sewer. Other times it merely gave off an odour which he detected through the streets of the city, something that suggested gentle ongoing decomposition. He had got used to it during the months in Bangkok. But this was completely different. For a start it was pleasant, like the scent of lemon grass mixed with mint, something that was clean and fragrant and vital. And it seemed to grow stronger and more intoxicating by the minute.

Suddenly Don noticed that there was a light under the surface of the water, just below where he was standing. Surprised, he blinked, then looked away up the klong and noted that the houses were all dark. Then he turned and looked back across the lawn towards the house. The streetlamp seemed to have gone off entirely. All the shapes were now silhouetted against the night sky. Most vivid of all of them was the jagged top of the palm tree. He could make out a bird sitting in one of the branches. Then finally he turned back to the water below him. And the light was still there.

Something told him to avert his eyes or close them quickly but before he could do so he felt his gaze locked open and it seemed for a moment that the light came from two enormous eyes that were staring up at him from below the surface of the klong. He remembered afterwards that he felt no fear even when he realized that he was caught by this sight and could not move either his head or his body away. And then he began to hear a message that came to him in a language he did not know: it was not in Thai, English or French. Nor could he be sure that the voice he thought he was hearing came from outside him. But the message was clear.

It told him that the spirit of the city, of its river and waterways, was the Naga and that the dark deep beneath the skyscrapers and the shopping complexes and the asphalt avenues was its home. Once, the inhabitants understood how important he was, how life giving and fertile and sensual, and at the same time how unpredictably destructive. Long before they had heard of the Buddha's teaching, he was worshipped and respected as the manifestation of the power of water. Later, when the Dhamma, with its rationality and its rules and laws, had taken root there was still acknowledgment that the Naga was the primordial force that could lift the Buddha himself above the flood, protect him from the raging storm and at the same time wash away the foundations of his teaching and suck even the firmest men and women into the tide of desire. But that was long ago. Human memory is short and now hardly anyone remembers, even though they continue to perform rituals and ceremonies to show their respect and their gratitude, and their fear. But the real connection is no longer there and the waters on which the city stands are neglected. The rivers and canals are left polluted so that the very veins of the city are clogged and its lifeblood, with nowhere to run, turns black and heavy and clots up. The Naga had been relegated to myth. He had no place in the quest for solidity and certitude that had come to dominate the minds of people who have chosen to make Bangkok their home. The obsession with ownership, the fascination with cars and gadgets and wealth, left little room for the fluidity of poetry. But even so he was still there, in the mysterious and murky undercurrents which pulse out the subtle rhythms of what takes place from day to night in the city. Since he now dwelt in stagnant pools, the vapours that he generates are no longer fertile or life enhancing. Instead they come from his shadow and they awaken the shadowy side of the city's inhabitants. The Naga still had the power to suck those who dwell above him into his dream, without resistance. Only the dreams, which once gave vision and inspiration, are now disquieting. The sense of drowning is never too far away. And he himself dreams of rising to the surface and feeling the light on his back just once more before he is gone forever.

Don never shared his experience with anyone. He did not know how to put any of it into words without sounding crazy or a liar. In time the memory of that evening faded into the shadows. But the conviction remained that Bangkok was the Naga's lair.

PART 2

CHAPTER 11

It was now November, and officially the cold period had begun. A sense of oppression hung like a soggy blanket over the city. The rains should have stopped or at least died down but there was none of the certainty that once marked the seasons. In fact there was little sign of any cool weather arriving. Every day the sky was hazy with pollution and the city was like a steam bath. The mornings were not so bad but by the afternoon the air was thick with acrid exhaust fume while the pavements shimmered with a heat that sent the street dogs slinking into the shadows. During these intense weeks only the beggars stayed at their posts, on the footbridges crossing the busy thoroughfares or on the corner of an intersection, plying their trade with that detached air of resignation that makes them almost invisible. And then, in a corner of the sky, storm clouds would quickly gather and bring the rain crashing down, so that within a short time many of the smaller, badly drained roads and sois would be under water. The *Loy Kratong* festival that marked the month's full moon was coming at the end of the month and public festivities were being planned on a grand scale, but most people believed that the rain would spoil the fun.

That November, three weeks before the festival, a funeral ceremony was held at Wat Taadthong which was the most significant media event of the season, because it marked the climax to a scandal that had been keeping the city's inhabitants enthralled for months. It had already been a vintage year for scandals. The ones that had thrilled those who were hungry for their shot of sleaze had been suitably colourful; a well-known society doctor who, in a bout of jealousy, cut up his wife into little pieces, then drove to Paknaam and fed them to the fish, after first enjoying a meal at a popular seafood restaurant on the pier; the arrest of the head of a drug trafficking empire, who turned out to be a woman whose day job was running a stall selling Isan-style grilled chicken and papaya salad in Laadprao; the murder of an abbot by one of his bodyguards and the subsequent revelation that the monk had over a million baht in his bank account; the politician's son who had undergone a sex change but, dissatisfied with the result, ran amok through the hospital, wielding a surgical blade and injuring members of the staff as well as a number of foreign patients. There were others, including the inevitable tales of graft and corruption, and crooked land deals which were hardly of interest to a cynical and hardened audience.

But the saga of Pi O topped them all. The sex was hardcore, the corruption and the intrigue more dramatic than a television soap, with the whole affair threatening to become a political headache and perhaps a serious loss of face for the government. Along the way there had been startling revelations and grade A gossip provided by Pi O himself, in the interviews that he gave describing the sexual activities of various high ranking officials. And then to cap it in a way which even a crime writer might have thought was too cliché, Pi O was shot in the head five times in the car park of one of the nightclubs he owned. In a city where death can be fast and cheap, where a punk from out of town can be hired to shoot down the person of choice for less than a hundred dollars and underworld killings take place every day of the week, one man's assassination might not have been significant. But given all the other factors in the case, everyone knew that this was not an ordinary murder, but had all the trademarks of an official directive, which made it immediately a different and potentially hot issue. Already there was a call from the opposition, keen as ever to capitalize on whatever crumbs came their way, for a public enquiry.

The fact that Pi O was known by this friendly acronym by all the inhabitants of the city, even those who had never met him, showed just how familiar he had become to the public. The tabloids had dubbed him many years earlier as the Sex Czar of the Capital, by virtue of the fact that, up till his death at the age of 55, he had ruled over an empire of up-market massage parlours and establishments where sex was the main commodity on the menu. In life he had been both admired and vilified. According to those who took the narrow line and claimed to be able to tell the difference between good and evil, he was a totally shameful, immoral pariah who gave the country a bad name and whose violent end had been his own karma coming full circle. But there were a greater number of Bangkok's inhabitants who, even while they accepted that Pi O's chosen direction had not been exemplary, would not have agreed with this wholesale condemnation. To them he was a home grown libertarian and the nemesis to the corrupt officials who were shown up by his refusal to be blamed for the things that were normal practice. These supporters argued that Pi O had exposed the hypocrisy of our society. There was even a group calling itself 'The Friends of Pi O' made up mainly of the pimps, hostesses and masseuses who worked in his establishments, appearing on national television to proclaim what a good, honest man and a fair employer Pi O had been and how he was the victim of the police for having exposed the system of bribery that took place. Given the staunchly held opinions, the contrasting reactions and the strong sentiments whipped up by an enthusiastic press and the fact that the story had been on the front page for almost a month—which amounted to a record—the affair had generated an atmosphere of mounting tension. For a while it mattered which side you were on because it supposedly reflected your own set of values. From a casual glance it seemed that the city had been polarized. But, like many such matters in Bangkok, the issues were never as clearly defined as they seemed. The two camps were filled with prejudices and contradictions. Among those who saw him as a champion of the people, there were some who, with the same conviction that they defended Pi O's defiant stance, felt that Bangkok needed more law and order and they applauded the hit squads who were roaming the city killing the drug dealers and cleaning up the streets. And it was no secret that, among the ones who considered that Pi O was an example of the rampant sensuality and decadence of the city that had to be wiped out once and for all, there were a good few who frequented his establishments whenever they had the opportunity to do so. Given all of this, the funeral, in its way, was a rare moment in the history of Bangkok when, in one man's passing, a mirror was held up in which the citizens of the capital saw themselves dimly reflected.

One thing, though, was certain. In the middle of the confusion generated by the views and opinions, the claims and counter-claims, made by Pi O himself and on his behalf immediately after his death, it was obvious that the truth, whatever that might have been, was quickly becoming drowned in a sea of information. It all depended on how you wanted to view the scandal. As for the man himself, he would remain forever an enigma.

CHAPTER 12

Up until he hit the front pages with the regularity that was the envy of politicians during the last six months of his life, Pi O had managed to keep a low profile by the skilful use of his wealth and influence. Only those who worked closely with him actually knew what he looked like. He was camera shy and preferred to stay in the background. It was said that because of this he could visit the clubs that he operated without even his own employees being aware of his presence in the premises. On the rare occasions in the past when his name was linked to a land deal or some business venture in the city the papers had referred to him as the shy tycoon, because of his reluctance to be photographed or to give interviews, which made his eventual public appearances all the more intriguing. Little, in fact, was known about him until the fateful morning when quite unexpectedly, whole page advertisements appeared in all the newspapers, including the English language ones, accusing the government of trying to use its influence illegally to prevent him opening a casino on a prime site just off Sukhumvit Road. A picture of Pi O covered a quarter of the page. It showed him in a stiff pose wearing a theatrically serious expression and holding up an accusing forefinger. Around the photograph was the text arguing his case, point by point. Basically the message was that he felt that he was being treated unjustly. It was never clear why he chose to go public about an issue that he might have solved by using the well trodden pathways and paying the standard asking price to settle such disputes. Even those close to him were puzzled by his decision to bring the matter out into the open. Not only was his action, which was made without consulting any of his associates, a move that went against both style and character, but, given the circumstances, it looked like he was gunning for a headlong collision out of which he would almost certainly be the loser.

In any case, on that April morning Bangkok woke up to a conflict that left them begging for more. At the outset the government countered mildly by saying that there were irregularities in his proposal. Soon it turned into a session of mutual accusation. Before long the gloves were off. Each time

Pi O spoke out he had more to reveal about the nature of business deals in the city and particularly those regarding the entertainment industry; which sections of the police force were involved, which politicians had benefited, how the risks were covered. Pi O did not hesitate to name names, nor to be forthcoming about the whole set-up in which he had been involved, to the point where the public were left wondering whether he was on a suicide mission. And yet, during all those months, despite the public appearances on chat shows and the interviews in the press, little was revealed about Pi O besides the most basic facts which were already common knowledge. Nobody seemed to get close to figuring out who exactly he really was, how he had arrived at his enormous wealth, what his origins were. This was partly due to the fact that everyone was too caught up in the intensity of what was going on to care much about the past.

It was only after his assassination, which seemed so inevitable from the beginning that no one even bothered placing bets on it, that the newspapers, during a frantic week, published interviews with colleagues who had worked with him in the past and those who had recently known him. There was his driver Nai Lek, who survived the shooting, and one of his mistresses, whose name was Nong Goong and others who had been business associates or one of the army of pimps and runners in his employment. Out of the stream of reminiscences, gossip, hearsay and eyewitness accounts that were accumulated the picture that emerged was more complex than those who wanted to condemn him could have wished. And yet, at the same time it was curiously banal. Phrases like "hard working", "generous", "dedicated to his job", even "religious" cropped up often in these testimonials. He seemed to have the same dreams and ambitions of being wealthy and successful in his chosen profession as anyone else. If you put aside the fact that, for over twenty years, he had controlled the upper end of the flesh trade in Bangkok (and it was rumoured that he had extended his business into Australia and the West Coast of the U. S. A.) the descriptions that were applied to Pi O might have been the same ones used for any bureaucrat or government official in the city.

His real name was Wasan Songsaeng and he was born in Lopburi, the second son of a woman called Duangjan. The father, a professional thief, disappeared from the scene when he was two and he moved to the capital with his mother and older brother. After that there is a gap. Pi O did not speak about his past to anybody. We meet him next as a young police officer. And even this stage in his life might have remained a blank were it not for the colleagues who trained with him in the police academy and who later worked with him in the force. But there is no official record of his early career because somewhere along the line Pi O managed to get his file removed from the official archives. And no one from that period could remember clearly learning anything about his personal life. But they all agreed that more than any of them he seemed to be totally committed to the job and tireless in his ambition to climb the ranks. During his spell with the drugs suppression unit he made a name for himself as an enthusiastic officer and a ruthless suppressor of criminals, who did not hesitate to shoot on sight during the raids he took part in. And he was also noticed for his organizational skills as well as his facility with figures. A fellow officer from that period told of how they left it to Wasan to share out the monthly extras that their department collected, knowing that he would be honest and correct in his calculations. With his qualities he might have gone on to be promoted all the way to the top, which would have meant the usual perks and advantages. But Mr. Wasan was more ambitious. He was sure that he could branch out on his own and that there were more lucrative ways of making use of the contacts he had made. So when he was thirty years old and about to be promoted he quit the force. (He continued to use his official title as police captain for the rest of his life).

Wasan went into business as a security specialist, running nightclubs and bars in the Silom area. Then, as his reputation was established, he started to help to organize big festivals in Muang Tong Thani. Steadily he consolidated his power in this field and gradually began to form links with a major syndicate in the so-called entertainment industry. This euphemism covers a large area; straightforward brothels, massage parlours, bars, nightclubs, private key member establishments, short time motels, all the places where sex is the commodity. Within a few years he had either bought out his associates or seen to it that they were no longer interested in directing operations. By now he was thirty-five years old.

But soon after gaining control, Pi O, as he had come to be known, decided to get rid of the popular establishments off Patpong and in the Ratchada district. This was the beginning of the nineteen nineties and the city was still in its boomtown phase, with tourists pouring in and the locals with more spending power than they had ever dreamed of. Pi O saw his chance and put his business up for the highest bidder. The sales were perfectly timed. But it was not only profit that motivated Pi O to sell off his assets. This was part of a much bigger plan. His policy from the beginning was to move as quickly as he could to the top end of the market and leave the cheap dives to others. He saw no point in owning and managing places that attracted the regular customers, who were looking for instant gratification after an evening in the bar. In Pi O's eyes the regular massage parlour business and the girlie bars were no challenge. They were inefficient and sordid (this was the word that he used, according to one former lieutenant). The girls were as tired and bored as the customers.

There was a niche in the industry. He wanted to set a standard, cut out the seediness and create high class palaces of recreation where rich Western tourists as well as wealthy Asians, particularly those who came from the countries where professional sex was not so available, would be provided with what they required, and at a price. He had a vision of a five star market where the goods on sale would be of the highest quality, catering to all tastes. Sexual pleasure would be the central product, but instead of a cheap setting the exchange would take place in luxurious and well equipped surroundings: spas offering traditional treatments, fine restaurants showcasing Thai cuisine, fitness centres. These would all be part of the package.

During those years in the no-holds-barred economic climate nobody seemed disturbed by Pi O's vision of a latter day Babylonia. Banks eagerly lent him what he needed to acquire property through the city and to construct what he would later call his palaces of love. The 'Club Bahia' off Rama IX, the 'Bangkok A Go Go' on Sathorn, The 'Elite' in Pratunam were soon filled with members who came from all over the world to enjoy what "Amazing Thailand" had to offer. To the few who bothered to make their objections vocal, he would always reply that he was a realist. Sex was here to stay and the Thai sex industry was famous long before he came onto the scene. All he wanted to do was to transform it from a low level industry to one in which the highest standards were applied. He argued that in doing so he was providing jobs and bringing in valuable foreign exchange, and he would emphasize that he looked after his employees and paid them well. His boys and girls were given regular check ups, given paid leave and received 50% of what they earned.

Despite the candour with which he spoke about his business Pi O always managed to avoid disclosing the secrets of his success. Land deals, massive loans, construction, the basic ground of his empire seemed to present none of the problems that bogged down other would-be developers. As for his human organization, which was rumoured to number over a thousand, he seemed throughout the years to have none of the troubles that other employers had to deal with. Those who were suspicious of Pi O or envious of his success suggested that his business methods included all the tactics that he had learned from his days in the vice squad; that he had a group of well paid and highly efficient thugs do his dirty work behind the scenes and that he used whatever tactic that was needed to get his way. Blackmail, it was said, was his favourite method of persuasion to ensure agreement. Pi O supposedly kept files on everyone he had dealings with. These accusations were, of course never proven. Many people would have liked to point to him and blame him for the corruption, but no one could ever find solid evidence of any misdeed. And even if they had, in a land where corruption is anything but uncommon, it was not something which would have lowered his status in the eyes of his compatriots. On the contrary, Pi O had achieved the kind of kudos that the very successful have, fuelling the dreams of those less fortunate that they too would one day reach such heights from the same humble beginnings.

At any rate, by the time of his death he had acquired the reputation of being one of the godfathers of the city on whom politicians depended and in fact he could, if he had chosen, become a politician himself. But Pi O, up till his untimely exit, steered clear of the political arena.

The question of why such a cautious operator as Pi O, who had managed so meticulously to avoid the public eye for so long, should suddenly decide to mount a head-on confrontation with the government remained a mystery for nearly twenty years after his death and even then the explanation was not universally accepted. It was an historian, researching that period in Bangkok's history and the long defunct sex industry, who dug up an old government file that stated that Pi O, one of the last of the city's godfathers, left everything in his will to his niece. An appendage to the report affirmed that in the end she did not, in fact, inherit anything, since the state confiscated all the surviving assets. The researcher diligently followed up the clues and discovered the niece, by now a widow in her late sixties. After much persuasion, she told him that her uncle had discovered that he was dying (she would not specify the ailment, though the historian guessed that it was probably AIDS related) and felt that he wanted to expose the corruption and hypocrisy surrounding him, because he himself had reached a point when he was disgusted by what he did. This was her version of what happened and the historian reproduced it faithfully in his book, which provoked a fair measure of public controversy. There were many who could still remember the incident vividly and among these there were some who disagreed vehemently with the niece's explanation, saying that she was merely making excuses for her uncle. They claimed that his motive for going public was because he was arrogant enough to think that nothing could ever stand in his way and that he wanted to exact revenge on the people who had thwarted him in his ambitions. Then again people came forward and wrote letters to the newspapers, after the book's publication, expressing their satisfaction at having been vindicated in their admiration of Pi O at the time, arguing that, had Pi O been the degenerate and immoral man that he was made out to be, then he would surely have made public all the dirt that he had acquired about the rich and powerful who had benefited from his acquaintance. The fact that he had, according to his niece, stipulated that all his papers should be burnt after his death showed that he was a compassionate man. So the debates went back and forth and it was clear that, long after he was gone, Pi O still had the power to create divisions in the city.

CHAPTER 13

Due to the unusual nature of the death, it was decided by the one relative who came forward that, instead of the customary week-long chanting which would have been fitting for such a well known person, the chanting and the cremation were to take place in the same ceremony. That day a bank of heavy clouds, looking like a distant mountain range, had been forming steadily in the sky to the south-west of Bangkok since dawn. By 4 p.m. their colour was beginning to change to a greyish shade, which meant that there was a strong possibility that it would rain. Some took this as an unlucky omen but the general opinion was merely that it would be bad news for the people who, either by choice or a sense of duty or mere morbid curiosity, were intending to attend the ceremony at Wat Taadthong which was to take place at five o'clock as announced in all the newspapers that morning. There was intense speculation throughout the city, among those who had not the least connection to the whole episode except as witnesses to an unfolding drama, as to whether it would be a well-attended affair, in which case the traffic would be even worse than usual, or whether those who knew the dead man would shy away out of a sense of discretion and self preservation.

That afternoon Marisa, Don and Arun made their way through the heat and the crowded streets to the temple. Each had decided to attend the ceremony after much internal debate and hesitation. Up till that November day they had not met, although their paths had crossed over in the subliminal way that inhabitants of a big city brush by each other in the street or a shopping mall or a hotel lobby; random encounters which leave traces only in dreams. Naturally Marisa, being a film star, was known to both men from the pictures that they had seen of her in the newspapers, magazines and on the billboards, advertising soap and shampoo. They had seen her in the films she had been in and they had watched her on one of the TV chat shows, where she was a regular guest. But precisely because of the exposure and the fact that she had become an impersonal icon who belonged to the media world, neither would have recognized her if they saw her in the flesh, without the makeup and the hairdo, and out of the usual unreal context. Nor would they have expected her to be attending the funeral in the first place.

The two men had been closer to making social contact. When he was in his first year at Silpakorn University, Arun had once noticed Don from a distance. It was in a jazz club and Don was getting drunk and loud in a corner with a group of girls. Then later, as he was leaving, Arun saw that a fight had started involving Don and one of the girl's boyfriend. But he would have found it hard to recognize the same person, with the short crop of hair and the quiet manners, who was to sit only five metres away from him at the temple.

As for Don, he would not have remembered the incident in the jazz club because those years went by in a long haze. Nor would he have recalled sitting at a table next to Marisa in a smart Italian restaurant when she was accompanied by a tanned, handsome farang with a well trimmed moustache and a fashionable stubble. Don was with a party of male friends. All of them had been smoking marijuana and drinking bourbon and by the time they got to the place they were stoned and behaving badly, spilling wine and throwing bread around like spoilt rich kids, which was what they were. The other customers tried to ignore them at first, then complained to the manager, who asked them to leave, which they did obediently without making any protest. On the way out Don had turned to wave at Marisa.

It was at Pi O's ceremony that they began to exist for each other, and for each of them it felt as though their meeting was not a matter of chance or coincidence but engineered by some display of synchronicity that was beyond comprehension. They could easily have gone to the temple and then drifted off in their separate ways. After all, it was not exactly the kind of occasion for making new friendships or initiating conversation with a stranger. This was going to be a very open, public scene, with the whole of the press corps laying siege. There was going to be no opportunity for formal introductions or, given the particular circumstances, even polite conversation. Those who already knew each other would stick together and the rest would be the object of interest and scrutiny. Already each of them had made up their minds to do their duty as fast as possible and then to leave as quickly and discreetly as social etiquette allowed. But an extraordinary event happened towards the end of the ceremony that pulled their lives together and wove the three strands into a plait with such impeccable and unexpected force that even Arun, the sceptic among them who insisted that he did not believe in fate or God or anything that was not scientifically explicable, admitted much later on that he felt that it was all meant to happen.

CHAPTER 14

The reason why they were going to the cremation was because all three had known the dead man at different stages of his life and in ways which each had tried with considerable success to keep from being revealed. But even though they would have preferred to keep their relationship to Pi O to themselves and out of view from the world for the rest of their lives, if that was at all possible in a society that thrived on gossip, there was a sense of duty and propriety that had been so deeply rooted in them that in the end it cut through all the dilemmas and overrode all other considerations. A person coming from a society in which death and the rituals surrounding it do not play such an important role in the life of the community would find it hard to understand how a Thai is conditioned to feel if he or she does not make the effort to attend the ceremony and physically pay the last respects to the dead and to make peace with the karma that had come before. Without doing so when there is no good excuse, the doors leading back into the past cannot be properly closed.

Arun's connection was the most obvious, by virtue of the fact that he was Pi O's nephew. His father had been Pi O's elder half brother. There were seven years between them and, because of this, Pi O always looked up to him as a father figure, since the real father had left the family almost as soon as the baby was born. They came from a poor background. Their mother, Duangjan, who came from Cambodian stock, was a strong dark skinned woman. Her first husband died young and she had no interest in marrying again till she met Pi O's father, a charmer and womanizer besides being a thief, who already had two other families. She never expected him to stay but she was surprised by the rapidity of his disappearance. Left alone with a boy and a baby she scraped a living helping in a shop and doing whatever seasonal work there was in the fruit orchards in that district. When Pi O was barely a year old a distant cousin called to say that there was a post available as a cook in the house of an old widower, who had been told that she was a single mother with two children and did not mind; she could not believe her luck.

Khun Pairod, the man who employed her, was a retired civil servant from an old Bangkok family who had been widowed years earlier and who was childless. He had a private income to add to his small pension and, while not being a rich man, he was well off and comfortable. As a young man he had been deeply influenced by the democratic movement and during the Second World War he had joined the clandestine free Thai. When it ended he shared the hope that Thailand would become a modern state in which the people would decide their future. By this time his politics leaned towards the left. But, after Pridi's exile and the suppression of many of his old friends, Khun Pairod seemed to have given up, either out of fear or disillusionment. During the succession of military governments he kept his thoughts and opinions to himself, got on with his work in the Ministry and lived the everyday life of someone in his position.

He told Arun's father all this because he wanted to explain to the young man, who after a few years in the household was treated like a son, why he had felt so good to have been in a position to help the single mother and her two sons who appeared at his gate one rainy evening. For he had decided that true democracy would never be allowed to take root in Thailand, and that the only politics worth pursuing was a personal one, based on the loving kindness that the Buddha had taught. It happened that his old cook was too old to work and wanted to end her days in her village in the northeast. A friend of hers working with another family had recommended Arun's grandmother.

Khun Pairod died when Arun was too young to remember much about him, except that he had stiff white hair that stood up and that his fingers were so gnarled and misshaped from arthritis that he had to hold his glass of water with both hands. And he recalled how the old man had once smiled at him as he put a boiled sweet into the palm of his hand. But through his father he learned what a kind and generous person this Khun Pairod had been to them and how it was precisely this kindness that was his undoing in the end.

From the beginning he treated the family as though it were his own. Three years after they arrived in Khun Pairod's house, which was in a soi off Sathorn Road, Arun's grandmother died from a third and lethal dose of dengue fever. From then on the old man began to look after the children left behind as his own. By then Arun's father Wikrom was twelve and showed academic promise, so Khun Pairod made sure that he received the best education and by the time he was nineteen he was enrolled in Chulalongkorn medical school.

But while he was fond of Wikrom, the feelings of love and paternal tenderness were reserved for the younger brother, whom Khun Pairod adopted into his heart as the grandson he never had. But the young Wasan did not respond to the old man with equal affection. Instead his behaviour in the household seemed to be fuelled by an anger that would often explode into small acts of savage violence towards anybody or any animal that happened to be close by at the time. He seemed to realize from the beginning the power that he had at his disposal. Khun Pairod never told him off but forgave him every time, telling the rest of them that the loss of his mother was the cause. And as a consequence, over the years, as if he knew intuitively how to use the means he had, the boy would taunt and insult his benefactor to his face and make demands that he expected to be met as if he were the master of the house. When he was fourteen he asked for a motorbike which he crashed within a month and left in a heap on the roadside. He insisted on joining an exclusive gun club and persuaded Khun Pairod to buy him a set of handguns with which he would practice in the back garden. Arun's father could only stand by helplessly witnessing this spectacle and wondering why Khun Pairod put up with it. Eventually, when Wasan joined the police academy, he seemed to quieten down.

By this time Wikrom had already left the house and moved into a small apartment with his new bride, a trainee nurse called Noi. His excuse was that he wanted to be closer to the hospital where he was interning. But the truth was that, despite wanting to be around Khun Pairod and look after him and repay him his generosity, he could not bear to see his younger brother acting like the lord of the manor whenever he was home.

Ladda was born a year after Arun's parents were married and already there was danger in the air. The birth of the child plunged Khun Noi into a depression. It was not the first time that she had suffered such a bout. She had already been diagnosed as having bipolar imbalance. Khun Wikrom knew of this before he married her, and he had witnessed her manic highs as well as her dark periods. Being a doctor he also knew what it would take to look after her, but he loved her and was prepared to devote his life for her. It was a hard struggle but at the beginning of their marriage there were signs that his love and affection could break through the strange destructive patterns which were embedded in her psyche. Three years later when Arun was born there was every chance that the sickness was behind her. There were no more attacks and for the next four or five years all was calm in the house. Wikrom was by now a specialist in lung diseases and working hard in the clinic at Chulalongkorn Hospital.

During these years they saw little of Wasan, who was in the police force. Whenever Wikrom and his family visited Khun Pairod, Arun's father would try to make sure that his brother was not home. On these occasions the long lunches would be relaxed and homely. Grandpa, which is what he insisted the children call him, would reminisce and tell them about Bangkok in the past and the days during the second World War when bombs dropped near the house, and the life of the city that none of them would ever see again. But sometimes, with no warning, Wasan would turn up and then Arun could feel the tension in the air between his father and his uncle. He would look to his big sister to see how he should behave but he would get no help and he would sit at the table with a fixed grin praying that there was not going to be an awkward scene.

In fact, whenever Wasan was there he would make a point of joking and playing with Arun, but rarely did he sit down to speak to his brother. It seemed that neither of them could get past their old mutual antipathy. Arun remembered how he was always slightly frightened of his uncle. The gun in the leather holster that Wasan took off and placed on the chair by the door, before joining them at the dining table, always looked like an object of death and once, when his uncle took him out into the garden and tried to show him how to fire it, he ran away crying. He always felt intuitively that his father was right in keeping his brother at arm's length.

On one of these visits to Khun Pairod's house something happened which split the two brothers even further apart. It was when Arun was six years old. His mother had been behaving strangely for a few days. She could not sleep and walked round the house singing loudly, laughing and dancing and picking him up, then running round the small yard at the back of their house, almost falling over. Arun remembered how powerful and infectious her joy was. But it also frightened him. One night when he was getting a glass of water from the bathroom he overheard a conversation between them.

"It's no good. I can't be a mother to them, and I love them so much," she was saying as she sobbed. "And I love you. But I am just making you all suffer."

He tiptoed back to his room before he could hear his father's reply.

That weekend they went to have lunch with grandpa. Wasan happened to be there that day.

During the meal Wasan was telling a story about a recent raid in which he had taken part. He was addressing his words to Khun Pairod who sat at the head of the table, too old now to take much in but still nodding his head in encouragement as his adopted son spoke. Then all of a sudden Khun Noi pointed a finger at her brother-in-law and said firmly:

"I've had enough! You're a cruel man. I can see that you have no respect for life. You're a bad person who should not have anything to do with the law."

There was a moment of silence. Then Wasan laughed and answered her:

"And you are a mad woman. We've all heard about it."

That was when Arun's father chucked a glass of water across the table into his brother's face. Both Arun and his sister, Ladda were shocked. It was the first and the last time they saw their father angry and express himself so openly.

"I never want to see you again," he shouted at his brother and then, to protestations from Khun Pairod, he gathered the family from the table and the half eaten meal and they all left.

Three weeks after the incident Arun's mother took the children to school, then drove to a small town West of Ayudhya called Sena. It was on the river. (They never understood why she chose that particular spot). She persuaded a local woman to rent out her small wooden boat, saying that it had been a long time since she had paddled on that stretch of the river. The woman told her to be careful of the current but Khun Noi reassured her that she could handle the boat. Then in the bright hot morning she climbed down the steps and set off from the pier.

Her body was found that evening, tangled up in the thick mesh of water hyacinths that bordered the river a kilometre or so from the town. The verdict was death by accident.

Wikrom did not allow his brother to attend the funeral. Khun Pairod had to be brought in a wheelchair. Arun and his sister stood in dutiful silence as the guests came down the steps and offered their condolences. Arun held back his tears. But at that moment, when he was barely eight years old, his childhood came to an end.

Three years later Khun Pairod died peacefully in his own bed. It had always been presumed that the house would be sold and that the money would be shared by the two brothers. But when it came time to settle the inheritance it was discovered that Wasan had managed to convince Khun Pairod, many years earlier, to change his will and to leave the property solely to him. For Arun's father this was the last straw. He cursed his brother in front of his children and told them never to mention his name again in their house, and that from now on Wasan did not exist for him.

Arun always believed that the stress of all that had happened took its toll on his father's health. One day, two years after Khun Pairod's death, he came home to be told that his father was seriously ill. He had begun to have pains in his abdomen and the test revealed that he had stomach cancer. He was only forty two. Arun was by that time filled with all the confusion and uncertainty that a young male of that age goes through. The death of his mother and now his father's sickness were dark winds that shaped his character. The sadness made him morose and introverted and he was consumed by a sense of powerlessness. In his mind his uncle was largely to blame for his father's state and, although he contradicted his father's word on most matters as he went through his teenage years, he kept true to his father's injunction not to have anything to do with his uncle again.

CHAPTER 15

Arun had not bothered to follow the scandal which confirmed everything that his father had ever told him about his uncle and when he saw the announcement in the papers giving out the details of the assassination he felt no sadness. If anything he was now released from an association which he had always been embarrassed about and kept secret from those who knew him. He had already decided not to go to the ceremony. But at dawn on the same day Ladda called and told him, to his sleepy surprise, that she was organizing the funeral, since their uncle had been single with no other family and that she was expecting him to be there.

"He may have not been a very good person. We all know that. But you have to treat the dead with respect and you have to forgive what they did," was what she said, and for a moment Arun felt like saying something insulting or sarcastic, but he checked himself. It was too early for an argument. But he remembered how, after the family conflict came to a head with the issue of the inheritance, his sister had been the first person to curse Ah O and swear that she would spit in his face if she ever saw him again. That had been over fifteen years ago. Arun wondered what had happened to persuade her to make her feel so charitable towards him.

"Please. I'm not going. OK?"

"Oh, but you must. You owe him. We both do."

"How come?"

"I never told you this before because Ah O did not want you to know. He saw how much you loved Pa and how loyal you were to him. But how do you think we survived when Pa got ill and had to give up working? Do you think he had a big stash saved in the bank? Well you're wrong. Pa never saved, and he didn't think of taking out insurance. We were in a real mess. I didn't tell you at the time because I didn't want to worry you. It was uncle who paid for practically everything, from the medical bills to your education."

Arun was stunned by what he heard. After his father's illness Ladda took care of the money and he had always presumed it came from his father's savings. The news that his uncle had paid for them made him feel that he had somehow betrayed his father. But at the same time he could not deny the debt that was owed; the hospital fees, the operations, the medicine, all of which were of the highest quality and must have cost the earth, and then his four years in university. The realization that his uncle had offered all this without asking for any gratitude confused him. This was why he decided to attend the ceremony at Wat Taadtong that afternoon.

CHAPTER 16

At four o'clock Arun left his car in the parking lot near the gallery and hailed a taxi. It was Friday and all the roads were sure to be clogged up at that hour. He was in no mood to deal with the Bangkok gridlock. He wished he was lying on a beach in the south looking out at the sea, with none of the demands that were being made on him, by Gaew or his sister or anyone else. The day had started badly. The dawn conversation with Ladda left him in a strange, agitated mood. His image of his uncle had been turned upside down and his decision not to attend the funeral reversed within a matter of a few minutes. Then, after breakfast, he remembered that a week earlier he had arranged an important interview with a Japanese art critic at around the same time as the funeral, which he would now have to cancel or postpone. When he called the woman at her hotel, she told him, frostily, that it was impossible as she was about to leave Bangkok that same evening.

At the gallery that morning he was busy finalizing the arrangements for the transport of the paintings that had been sold and for packing and storing the rest in the warehouse at the back of his studio. It was the last day of the exhibition, which had gone moderately well, considering that the economic situation was not one conducive to people splashing out on art. The end of an exhibition always left him with a kind of sadness. It was a farewell, perhaps forever, to a part of himself. It was the end of an episode. He was in the middle of helping to load one of the paintings onto a truck that was going to take it up to a collector in Chiengmai when Gaew called. She told him that she had come down to Bangkok to interview some Canadian volunteers for her centre. They had not talked since the day he called her to say he had decided that his path was to be a painter, not a social worker, and that he could not give up his work for her or anyone else. She told him that she understood. They did not make any plans to see each other again. Now she wanted to come over and visit him. She sounded bright and cheerful. But he did not respond. He felt that he had managed to break through her spell and he was not sure whether he wanted a repeat of the same intense exchange so soon. His lack of enthusiasm made her angry enough to put the phone down on him and then to ring back almost immediately. It seemed that now he was pulling back she was keen to be with him. They ended up having three long conversations which led nowhere except to convince him that it had been a mistake to get involved with her at all. Then, as he sat down to recover from the exchange, Ladda called just to make certain that he was not going to change his mind and renege on his promise to attend the cremation.

By now his head was throbbing from the conversations and he decided to turn off the mobile phone for the rest of the afternoon. Sitting in the taxi looking out at the crowded pavement that was spilling over with pedestrians and stallholders, he was trying his hardest not to listen to the driver's monologue, which was in full swing. The man, who was from the anti Pi O camp, thought that the whole affair painted a bad picture of the country. He was ashamed at how the farangs would be laughing about it. The government was right to promote more law and order. But personally they did not have a chance of winning the battle. According to him the military had to come back and take charge. Then they should shoot anybody who was caught selling drugs and tear down all the slums. Arun was determined not to be drawn into the absurd discussion which he knew the driver was expecting and continued to stare out of the window, only grunting now and again out of politeness. He could see the clouds forming on the horizon. The different shades of grey pierced here and there by the sunlight interested him for a while and then he remembered that it was going to rain. He suddenly wished that the storm would come before he reached his destination, so that he would have an excuse to tell the driver to turn round and take him home. But he knew that he was not going to be in luck and as they turned in through the front gates of the temple he resigned himself to going through the motions that his social obligation dictated.

Ladda was standing near the entrance to the main section of the temple where the cremation ceremony was going to be held. She was dressed in a long black dress and looked very much the part of the bereaved relative. She was waiting and speaking to the guests who were arriving steadily. Arun saw her as soon as he stepped out of the taxi and marvelled at how at home she seemed in these public situations, doing the correct thing with effortless nonchalance. She could have been at a gala dinner or another film premiere. As he approached her she looked at him up and down and made a face. As a gesture of protest he had chosen not to put on the suit and tie that she had told him to wear but a plain black shirt. It now struck him that this was a mistake.

"Well at least you turned up," she whispered, as he greeted her with a friendly pat on the arm.

"Does anyone here know that we're his relatives?"

"They didn't before today. But I've been telling them. What's there to be ashamed of? He was there for us, wasn't he? Are you going to help me with the guests?"

Arun quickly shook his head. He did not want to get into a conversation with her about this. Besides, people were coming up behind him. So he quickly moved off and made his way to the seats that were lined on either side of the passageway that led to the crematorium. He chose one next to a woman who was reading a book of chants and prayers and who paid no attention to what was going on around her. Arun wanted a cigarette badly, but knew that he would have to wait till the chanting was over. He was still hoping that there was some way out and looking over the temple roofs took note again of the clouds that were now growing and slowly moving across the sky. In his mind, as he waited for the ceremony to begin, he was already considering whether to use the impending storm to leave early, knowing that this would have been bad form now that he had taken the trouble to come, or join the inevitable rush to get under the shelter of the nearest sala when the first drops came down.

He could feel Ladda's fierce gaze on the back of his neck. That he had given in to her by coming did not surprise him. Even if she had not told him about what Ah O had done he would not have been able to say no to her, simply because she would have found a nasty way of making him feel terrible if he had. She was born in the year of the Tiger, their mother had once told him when they were little, and she had the power to frighten ghosts and robbers. But as usual he did not obey his sister entirely. It had always been like that between them. He kept just enough back to make himself feel that she did not have absolute control over him.

He turned to check and true enough she was glaring at him. But fortunately she was tied up with the guests, who were now streaming in. She had somehow managed to get three young boys from the temple to hand out the small bouquets of flowers made from fragrant wood that were later to be thrown into the furnace. Arun could not help but admire her skill at organizing people. He himself had always found it so difficult to relate to people, particularly in a crowded social setting. He felt bad for not helping her to greet the guests but he knew that she could handle all of them single-handedly well enough.

Sitting there in the sweltering heat of the late afternoon, looking at the white coffin surrounded by flowers, the wreaths on either side and the photo of his uncle in his police uniform and the strangers who were now filling all the available seats that were left, Arun thought about what Ladda had said. Forgiveness. It was difficult to know what she meant by it. Certainly he could never forget what Ah O did to his father, the pain and the bitterness that he caused. As a young man he had blamed his uncle for his mother's final breakdown and the collapse of his father's health. But the truth was that he had not given Ah O a thought for years. It was as if he had ceased to exist. Up till that day the bitterness seemed to have disappeared, melted away. But now, as he thought once more about the past, he saw that the feelings were all still there. He could not see how or why he should forgive someone who had callously swindled his own brother and then gone on to make his millions without so much as saying he was sorry. His attendance at the temple was a matter of etiquette. But he knew that in his heart there was no forgiveness.

CHAPTER 17

Marisa was sitting four rows in front of Arun but on the other side of the passageway. She had been among the first to arrive and now she felt an ache in her lower back from maintaining the same seated posture for too long. She wanted badly to stretch her legs and have a cigarette but she did not want to draw attention to herself. She would have to endure the pain until it was time to approach the dais. That afternoon she wore thick dark glasses and hardly any makeup, hoping that no one would recognize who she was. But she knew from the few double takes aimed towards her that her presence at the cremation was not going to go unnoticed. She had placed herself at the end of the row so as not to be hemmed in on both sides by people she did not know. The snatches of conversation and greetings that she picked up gave no hint of what background they came from or what their connection to Pi O might have been. She was glad that they did not want to talk to her. Since it was a cremation it was not considered rude not to greet the person sitting next to you. There was no need for introductions or polite chit chat, as there might have been in the evening chanting ceremony leading up to the final day. Although it all seemed a little odd and hurried, Marisa was grateful that they had decided to dispense with the preliminaries and cremate him immediately. She kept her gaze fixed towards the front most of the time but once, when she turned round briefly, she noticed a man probably the same age as Khun Chai make his way past the other guests as though he was in a hurry to take his seat. He did not wear a suit and tie like the other men but had on a black shirt that did not look ironed. His long hair was tied in a ponytail at the back, and he looked vaguely familiar, but she could not remember where she might have seen him before. She wondered if it had been at the party the previous evening, another long boring affair where Khun Chai had once again overstepped the mark.

Marisa sat there enclosed in her silence, her fingers clasping the black silk fan which she had not used despite the heat. Her outer calm belied the whirlpool of thoughts and emotions that had been taking place inside her ever since arriving at the temple. Earlier that afternoon as she was about to leave her apartment Khun Chai had propped himself up on the bed and insisted on going out with her, although she had not told him where she was going. He was still groggy from the alcohol consumed over lunch and the only reason that he wanted to be with her was because he did not want to let her out of his sight. Recently his insecurity bordered on paranoia. It was as though he sensed that she was no longer committed to him. Every conversation with another man was taken as a sign of her rejection of him. The rows which resulted left her exhausted. When she told him that she was going to attend the ceremony he looked alarmed.

"But this is the first time I've heard about it," he whined. "Why? You didn't even tell me you knew him. How well did you know him?"

As she stared at the coffin containing the body of the man to whom she had come to pay her last respects, she thought that if Khun Chai, or for that matter any of those present who recognized her had any idea of the truth, they would probably crucify her for having cheated and betrayed them.

She had been following his case for months, wondering what had possessed him to act so recklessly. It seemed so out of character with the elusive and secretive person she had known. Khun Chai's question was more poignant than he could have guessed and as she sat there enveloped in her thoughts Marisa answered it in her mind. Yes. She knew the dead man. And this particular funeral, far from being just another social event that she had to attend, was like an unexpected answer to one of her prayers, a prayer that she had been offering up ever since she began her career as an actress. In fact as soon as she heard that Pi O had died she had felt so elated that she wanted to shout for joy and tell Khun Chai that she was now free. Neither of which she did because it would have meant explaining the past and revealing to him an episode of her life that she would have sooner forgotten.

She was almost certain that nobody at the Wat that afternoon was aware of her connection with Pi O. It had been his idea to wipe out all trace of her past. He had done this in the same masterful way that he had wiped out his own. But of course, as she well knew, the past could never be totally eradicated. There were always clues for anyone who cared to follow them up. She did not worry about this as she once did, but still, sitting there and noticing the inquisitive looks that were directed towards her, she felt vulnerable once more.

The story that the public had been fed was that she was had been discovered while she was a school girl from Saraburi who helped out in her mother's corner store. Her father had been killed in a car accident. She and her mother had to work hard to make ends meet. One day a publicity agent from Bangkok was driving through and stopped to buy a bottle of water. As he opened the ice box he looked up, saw her and was impressed by her fresh beauty and her sweet manner. He got a film company interested and later arranged for her to do a casting for a film that was about to be made and her career took off from there. It was the fairy tale that her fans loved to hear. And even if some cynics hesitated to swallow the myth wholesale, by the time Marisa was in her mid twenties it had become part of her iconic quality, proving to young women throughout the land that if the stars were with them anything could happen. And nobody cared about the past.

The truth was not so rosy and innocent. Marisa was sixteen when she met Pi O, who was thirteen years older and in the drugs suppression division of the police force. Through his work he had made connections with the underworld and the entertainment industry and he now had ambitions to use them in order to branch out and break into the film world. She had never known her father, who was a European. Her mother originally came from Saraburi and had been a bar girl in the sixties and now helped to run a small cafe in a shopping mall. Marisa went to a temple school and was working on the side as a waitress, in an agency that catered for high profile functions such as a gala opening or a motor show. All the girls in the agency had been hired for their looks and their willingness to supplement their income by accepting invitations from the VIPs. But unlike the others she had up until then never gone out with any of the guests. Not that she had any reservations about it. She had already lost her virginity to a boy in the back of a pickup truck. But her mother told her to be choosy and not to make the same mistakes she had made, to wait for the right person to come along, who would help her get ahead in the world.

It was at a fashion show to launch a new designer clothing brand that Marisa, or Nong Daeng as she was then called, met Pi O. Marisa's job was to usher the guests to their seats and hand them their complimentary gift package. She remembered that it was a glamourous event, full of well-known celebrities. She recalled seeing Pi O for the first time. The sharp moustache, the slicked back hair. He was out of uniform that evening and wearing crocodile skin cowboy boots, a plain white shirt, tapered jeans, all of which made him look like a villain in a Thai movie. After the formal part was over she had noticed him standing close by, watching her all evening and then, when the guests were all milling around sipping wine and the directors of the company were climbing onto the stage to make their speeches, he walked straight over to her and said simply:

"You have a future."

Then he led her to the back of the hall where there was less noise and began to seduce her with his smooth talk and his flattery, telling her that the models who had been parading down the catwalk were not a patch on her. He was sure that, with her good looks and her unique charm, she could one day be a big star and that he would help her by being her agent if she wanted. She found his directness disarming and his promises of fame and glory irresistible. Instinctively she felt that Pi O was the man her mother had in mind and when, a few days later, she took him home her intuition was confirmed. Her mother scrutinized her would-be benefactor throughout the meal and after he left she told her daughter that there was no doubt in her mind that Pi O was the one to launch her career, that this was the break and that she should grab the opportunity while her star was on the ascendant. Marisa's mother was not a trusting person. Life had taught her to be wary and to sense danger before it happened. But it had also taught her to be on the lookout for a genuine opening. She knew that Pi O was not a loser trying to make a quick buck out of her daughter but a serious opportunist who could deliver. He had good *ngo heng*, all the signs of a winner. There were dollar signs in his eyes. She had once, long ago, heard the same promises and dreamt of hitting the big time. She was glad that her daughter would now get a shot at it. (In fact, Marisa's mother did not live long enough to see just how far her girl went, because less than five years after that encounter with Pi O she was killed in a car crash on the way to Hua Hin).

A few evenings later Pi O spelt out for them the plan he had for Marisa, that he would now take charge of her life, like an older brother or an uncle. But she had to be prepared to sever the links with the past and be reinvented from scratch if she was to be successful. It was his idea to establish a new background for her and to kick off her story with her being discovered by a talent scout in a noodle shop in Saraburi and brought to the attention of a film studio. That was to be the foundation of the fairy tale that other young girls would want to share. He would build her up like a dream come true, the model for a whole generation. But to do this her looks and her style all had to be transformed so that even the girls she had been to school with would not recognize her. He would take care of everything. But they had to trust him completely.

Looking back Marisa marvelled at their readiness to comply with this stranger who had eased his way into their lives. Her mother did not object even when he told her that he wanted Marisa—this was the name that he chose for her—to move out as soon as she could to a condo off Rama IV. She had to get away from the old neighbourhood and learn how to live by herself and to learn independence. Pi O had the power of persuasion and a gift of speech that neither of them had ever encountered before.

If there were ever any doubts that lingered in their minds they disappeared overnight. True to his word Pi O wasted no time in setting up private acting lessons for his protégée. He bought her fine clothes to wear. He paid for her to have her eyelids Westernized. He found her a personal trainer at a fitness centre who taught her Kung Fu and jazz dance and a struggling musician who gave her singing lessons. Twice a week he fetched her mother to visit and gave both of them generous allowances to spend. And through all of it he behaved like a gentleman. In fact so much so that it seemed odd to both Marisa and her mother that not once did he ask Marisa for any sexual favours. Given what he was doing for her it was natural that Pi O should have the right to enjoy her body. In fact, Marisa was infatuated with Pi O at the time. She was bowled over by his attention and impressed by the connections he had and the confident way in which he dealt with people. Yet when it came to intimacy he seemed strangely reticent. In the end it was she who initiated their first touch.

But becoming his mistress did not change his attitude towards her. Apart from the brief moments of physical contact it was business as usual. He never stayed with her in the condo but visited her at odd hours of the day or night, whenever he was free. Sometimes he would disappear for days on end and when he did turn up they would not always make love and when they did there was a marked absence of passion. Marisa got the impression that Pi O went through the motions as quickly and mechanically as possible. He seemed disinterested in sex, as though, like a seasoned pimp, he was already numb from too much carnal experience. Power and wealth seemed to be more exciting to him. Sometimes he shared with her his dream of one day controlling the entertainment industry. At those moments she saw the excitement in his eyes. She did not know what he did when he was not with her but she understood that she was not meant to ask.

Over the months the lessons continued and he took a keen interest in her progress. He told her that he was negotiating a contract for her which was soon going to come off. Then one evening he sat her down and explained that in the film business there had to be certain things she had to be prepared to do if she wanted to get ahead. It was a real test of her character, he said, and if she could do them then she had a real chance of hitting the big time. He did not have to spell out for her what this meant. She reassured him, obliquely, that she did not have any qualms about doing what was necessary in the game plan. She trusted him.

Not long after this conversation he drove her out one afternoon to Bang Saray, a fishing village just beyond Pattaya. They cruised through tall metal gates, past a group of uniformed guards until the sea was in sight. Then they entered a big pink Roman style mansion with a gigantic swimming pool at the side and a well tended garden that ran down to the beach. Inside it was all silk and marble and very formal looking. Marisa had never seen anything like it in her life, but she controlled her excitement and resisted the temptation to run her hands over the plush furniture. Pi O introduced her to a tall, deeply tanned German with shoulder length white hair wearing an extravagantly patterned shirt, tan linen trousers and embroidered velvet slippers. In the car Marisa had been given all the background information that she needed. Her client was a businessman and his latest project was a spa resort on Goh Chang, which was going to be a joint venture with the government. This made him a VIP, an honoured guest of the country. The man liked Thailand, she was told, and his hobby was golf. His wife had recently left him for a young gigolo. He was lonely and needed company. These were the basics which Marisa had memorized by the time they arrived at the mansion. On the journey she had been nervous and worried about letting Pi O down.

But the moment that they shook hands she knew that it was going to be all right. The German, whose name was Mr. Johann complimented her straightaway by telling that she resembled a beautiful and famous Chinese movie star from his youth. That night, after Pi O had left, Marisa and Mr. Johann sat on the terrace with a soft breeze blowing across the beach, carrying with it a faint scent of frangipani. They were gazing at the stars twinkling in a clear sky and the lights of the fishing boats bobbing on the horizon. Two servants stood at a discreet distance, ready to serve them their meal. It could have been a dream scene from a romantic movie. But they had little to say to each other. The man seemed shy; they were using English as their common language, and Marisa was not yet confident enough with it, despite the lessons she had been given. This was her very first assignment and she felt awkward. She did not know exactly what was expected of her. But there was no going back. So that evening she smiled across the table at the sad, leathery looking businessman and drank her champagne and later, when the Viagra had done its work to stir up his manhood, offered herself to him like a young virgin.

During the three days that she spent in the mansion at Bang Saray Mr. Johann treated her courteously. He was on a short holiday, he told her, and he was happy to be lazy. This meant getting up late, then having a swim before breakfast, a boat ride to an island to do some diving, a game of golf in the afternoon, dinner in one of the hotels in Pattaya and then back home to bed. Marisa understood for the first time how easy it was for the rich to spend money. And in that first test she also learned how little it took to satisfy a man and boost his vanity and how grateful he was for some tenderness. By the time Pi O came to fetch her, Marisa was a wiser person.

That year there were four other clients, all of them wealthy or famous or powerful. One was a politician from an African country on official visit, who wanted to have her smuggled into his suite in a five star hotel very late one night, after his staff had gone to bed, and who was so pleased with her services that he gave her a thick gold necklace. And then, a few months later, there was a famous Hollywood film star (who she was one day to meet again, when she was a celebrity and he was on the way down). This man's public image was that of a stallion. But it turned out that he was more into drugs than into sex. He merely wanted to have a stunning looking female on his arm whenever he stepped out into the limelight, just to show the public that he was the greatest stud on the planet. When it came to the bedroom he was content to snore the night away.

Marisa performed her duties without flinching. From the beginning she had suspected that there were going to be demands and she was not naive. She knew that there were sacrifices to be made in the business. Her trust in her 'agent' never wavered. She was sure that he would never sell her cheap.

But she could not help the impatience that was creeping up on her at the end of that first year of apprenticeship.

Then on New Year's Eve, when she was preparing to take her mother out for a meal in a restaurant by the river, she received a phone call from Pi O telling her to drop everything and get herself dressed up as beautifully as she could because he had just landed her the job that could be the breakthrough they were waiting for. There was a well known Hong Kong film producer in town, who was putting up the capital for a local production which was due to begin within weeks. It was a ghost story, a rehash of the well known Nang Naak Phrakanong tale, but set in the future, about a young woman who drowns and returns to haunt the city. The man wanted female company that evening; only the best. Marisa had to be ready within an hour.

Pi O's instinct was confirmed. He guessed that the man, who was known in the film world simply as Mr. Kwok, would see Marisa's qualities. He had already told Mr. Kwok that Marisa was the most promising starlet in Thailand, which was a lie that made the producer laugh, since he was thoroughly acquainted with the business in Thailand and knew who was who.

"A starlet who's never been in a movie. I look forward to seeing her," he said and they both laughed.

Nevertheless when he did meet her Mr. Kwok was so pleased with her young looks, her slim body and her skills that he insisted that she move into the suite with him for the two months that he was going to be in Bangkok. He not only wanted her for regular energetic sex but also had ambitious ideas about moulding this teenager into a star. He found her a part in the film. Not the main one because the casting had already been settled but one in which she got noticed by the press when the film was finally released. And so, with her career kick-started, Marisa began a new phase of her life. She was a fast and willing learner. When the film was finished Mr. Kwok had to return to Hong Kong to face charges of being an accomplice in the murder of a Kung Fu star. He was acquitted and sent word to her that he would soon be back in Bangkok. But soon afterwards he died in mysterious circumstances. It was said that he had crossed the Triad on whom he had depended for his successes once too often and had to pay the ultimate price.

Mr. Kwok was Marisa's last client. After that Pi O saw to it that she had a bigger part in an historical epic that took over a year to make and which turned out to be a flop, although Marisa won more valuable recognition through it. Then curiously he disappeared from her life. She remembered the afternoon when they met in an Italian restaurant on Langsuan and he told her that she was now on her own, that she did not need him any more. He explained to her that he was about to break into the big time himself and that from then on he had to devote all his energy and attention to the job at hand. He handed her a card of an actor's agent who he said was a good man who was unaware of their relationship, so that she could start from scratch. She felt confused and insecure as she listened to him. It was as if, just when she needed his guidance more than ever, he was abandoning her. Towards the end of their meal he received a call on his mobile and told her that he had some urgent business. Then he paid the bill, got up, bent over to kiss her cheek then left the restaurant. And that was the last time she ever saw him in the flesh. He called her several times to make sure that she was doing all right, but she did not feel that he wanted her to get in touch with him again. It was as though he was afraid of his feelings for her.

Yet afterwards, through all the years, whenever she thought of him, it was his power over her that she could feel, not least because he was the only person in the world who knew her secret, being the one who had invented her myth and who had traded her body to the highest bidders. His shadow had always hovered over, threatening to tell the world that she was not the sweet young schoolgirl from upcountry who had been discovered by an agent but someone who had been through the complete initiation into the entertainment business. Whenever she thought of it she would shudder with quiet panic, thinking how easy it would be for him to take advantage of his knowledge and blackmail her, and even now after his death she could not fully understand why he had never done so.

The memories were rising and falling and the speculation of what might have been continued to play out in her mind as she held her hands together in prayer while the monks chanted. To anyone watching she was the picture of tranquil piety. They could not have guessed that, mixed in with the gratitude and relief that she felt, there was also a sense of foreboding, that something was unfinished, that his passing on did not mean that the past died with him. He had already made a public promise that if he were to die from unnatural causes things would be revealed about everyone he had ever had dealings with. He told the journalists who had reported his every utterance till the very end that he had kept files and records and that these were important enough to ruin reputations and possibly bring down the government. Was it possible, she thought, that he might have saved some scrap of information about her past relationship with him, and if so how would she be able to get hold of it and destroy it?

CHAPTER 18

When he arrived at the temple Don stood in the queue behind a long line of guests waiting to get seated. There was already a big crowd and it did not look as if there were enough chairs to go round. The assistants were rushing about trying to find extra ones and room to place them. Don had already decided that he would stand at the back, walk up to the dais when the moment came and leave as soon as he could, but he was ushered towards a single empty chair. To his left sat a man who looked round briefly as Don sat down but who showed no sign of wanting to introduce himself or of making conversation. The couple on the other side did not even seem to acknowledge his presence. They were talking to each other as if no-one else was there and Don could not help overhearing what they were saying. The man seemed to be upset by the inadequate seating arrangements.

"There's far too many people," he said emphatically. "Let's just go home."

"No, no," said the woman annoyed at him. "We've come all this way through the traffic. We can't leave now."

"Why not? We hardly knew him."

The remark reminded Don of his own ambivalence at being there in the Wat. He had seen the news of Pi O's assassination in the papers and spent the whole morning trying to decide whether or not he should go to the ceremony. He had no connections to the family and he had only met the dead man once in the back of a car. On that occasion, when they parted Pi O had said to him:

"This meeting never took place. Remember that. You do not know me. Always deny that our paths have ever crossed."

In the end he decided to go to the temple not because he wanted to go against Pi O's wishes, but because he felt strongly the need to make some sort of gesture of thanks to the person to whom he owed his freedom.

Five years earlier, on June 16th (a date he would never forget) at five thirty in the morning, in a soi off Pratunam, Don had driven over a small boy and killed him. The newspapers reported it as an accident. The boy had run out of the lane, chasing a football and had not seen the car coming. The driver was not going too fast. The only reason that it was newsworthy was that Don was the son of the late Khun Sombat Tongbai, a well known and much respected diplomat, who as a result of the political pressure put on him had committed suicide four years earlier. Apart from that there was no other interest. It was a tragedy that was all too common in the city and the news did not last more than a couple of days.

But as is often the case the story that was put out was not the truth. What really happened was that Don went to a club that night with his friends and took speed, washing it down with whiskey. Then later they had all gone on to a house near Rangsit where they took some more pills and partied. Someone then suggested racing up to Ayudhya but by that time Don was feeling too wired up to join them. He needed to get home, but the party was still going strong. At one point he found himself in a room with a big yellow balloon in the middle. A group of people were huddled around a table in the corner and passing around a pipe. The smell of the smoke drifted over. It was sweet and metallic, nothing he recognized. A farang woman beckoned him to join them. Her face was long and thin. She was wearing strings of heavy beads round her neck. Her hair was the colour of young rice. Her long gown was made of red velvet. These details haunted him for a long time afterwards. She smiled at him and said:

"You'll enjoy this. It's just like floating in a warm sea." Then she laughed.

He could not remember much of the rest. Time seemed to pass by very slowly. Everything took place at a great distance from him. It was still dark when he got into his sports car. He felt a strong need to get back to his own bed and sleep. He drove faster than usual and swerved all over the road. Fortunately there were no other cars about. The music was blaring out from the speakers, his mind was elsewhere and he kept having to remind himself of where he was going. The streetlights flashed by. And then at some point during the course of his journey, without knowing how he got there, he found himself lost in a soi in the Pratunam district. He felt nervous, as if he was caught in a tunnel and raced down it looking for an exit. Then, as he was screeching round a corner, craning his neck, looking for a sign, he felt the car make contact. There was a bump, and a body bounced off the bonnet. Then he heard a woman screaming. He braked hard, jumped out and saw the boy lying there in the road. There was blood on the white shirt of his school uniform. The mother was bending over and patting his head as though she was trying to revive him. Don slapped himself hard to make sure that he was not hallucinating. The dark buildings looked down at him accusingly. One of them had a picture of a dragon or a serpent whose eyes flashed their anger at him. All at once he was shouting out:

"I'll drive you to hospital. He'll be all right."

The mother wordlessly scooped up her child who must have been only five or six and climbed into the back seat. Then Don realized that he was still lost and asked her for directions. There was a private hospital not too far away, she told him. The boy was bleeding all over the seat and groaning. They went to the emergency ward. Mother and child were immediately whisked away. Don, still in a drugged daze, sat and panicked and prayed while he waited for the news. After half an hour a nurse came out and told him that the child was still in a critical condition and they were not sure if they could save him. Don used his mobile phone to call his mother.

"Mae, I might have killed someone. A little boy. I ran him over," he told her quite simply.

There was silence on the other end before she asked him how it happened. Then she told him to stay exactly where he was and not to talk to anyone.

"Remember. If there are any questions it was an accident," she said coldly.

"But it wasn't."

"Yes it was."

As he sat waiting, Don went through all the things that were now going to happen to him as a result of what he had done. The effect of the drug gave him a heightened sense of paranoia. He felt that the nurses and the orderlies who walked past him were staring at him accusingly and already condemning him for his deed. They would tell the whole world what had happened. He would go to hell and be punished. He wished he could turn the clock back. He was trembling with fear. He needed to get out of there.

It seemed that a lifetime passed, but then suddenly the door at the end of the hall opened and two young men walked in and headed straight towards him. By their haircuts he could tell that they were some kind of officials.

"Come with us. Right now," said one of them, without any introductions. Don did not see any choice but to obey.

"Am I being arrested?" he asked as they reached the lift, but there was no reply from either of them.

The parking lot was empty except for a blue Mercedes in the corner.

Don was gently pushed into the back seat, where a man was waiting. He was wearing dark glasses even though there was hardly any light. The thought crossed Don's mind that it was like a scene from a gangster movie. The door closed behind him leaving the two of them alone. The man told him who he was.

"Your mother called me. Now tell me exactly what happened."

Don knew that his voice was slurring but he tried his best to stay focused on his account. The man seemed to know exactly what state he was in. And when he was finished the man sat back and for a minute looked ahead out of the smoky coloured window with a pensive expression, before giving Don his instructions. When he had finished he said very quietly, but in a way that left Don with no doubt as to the disdain behind the words,

"I'll sort this out. It's what I owe to your mother. Now our karma is settled. But I want you to leave Bangkok. Go away and don't come back. Make a wreck of your life somewhere else. There's no room for you here."

Don answered the questions at the police station exactly as Pi O had told him to, and later, in the interview with the press, he stuck to his story. The mother of the dead child corroborated his version of what took place that morning and said that she would not press charges. Pi O had seen to every detail. He had stepped in to save him from the inevitable fate of going to jail. That same afternoon Don was back home and the next morning he left for Nongkhai and ordained as a monk in Wat Thammacitta.

As soon as he settled down to the routine at the monastery Don knew that far from having been saved he was now faced with the full consequences of his reckless act. The reality of having taken an innocent life now began to eat away at his soul. There were no diversions and nowhere to run. He soon discovered that the freedom from conviction and imprisonment that he had managed to retain with Pi O's intervention was itself far more enclosing and constraining than a cell with four walls. And in those first months not a minute passed by in his waking hours when the horror of what he had done did not weigh on him like a faceless shadow in a bad dream. The mix of guilt and remorse that constantly cut into his consciousness made him understand that there was no escape from what he had done.

In time the intensity of this turbulent initial period gave way to calmer waters. The abbot helped Don to take the steps towards forgiving himself and the practice of *metta karuna* that he prescribed helped to bring about some rays of light through the clouds.

"Let the act that you've committed be your teaching. Do good for the rest of your time on earth," the old man told him.

But these words did not help. Following the rules and regulations and keeping pure and celibate did not cleanse him of the dirt that clung to him like a second skin. And even later when he went around the villages giving advice to the young addicts and their families, it still did not feel that any contribution he made to others' wellbeing would in any way free him from the shame and guilt that he carried. So during the years at the monastery the incident remained like a dark stain in his heart that would not be washed away, no matter what practices he did and what rituals he performed. From time to time he was filled with such feelings of self loathing that he could not see the point of carrying on with living. The five years spent in the monastery did not heal him from this but left him with a melancholy that only those who have committed acts of violence can know. The karma that he had created remained unresolved and Don knew that he would probably carry the darkness with him till the rest of his days. But in other respects the monkhood and the simple, demanding discipline of the monastic life did have an affect him in a way that could not have been predicted by anyone who had known him in his wilder years. He was no longer the privileged young man who was so bored and directionless that he needed to test the limits and toy with danger just to feel alive, who once thought that there was no point to rules and morality in a world that was totally corrupt and in decay, whose god was unrestricted hedonism.

⸎

Don's thoughts and memories were interrupted by the arrival of the monks who filed past those seated on their way into the main sala. Don watched them being respectfully greeted by a woman wearing glasses as they entered. Then after saluting the Buddha image the monks took their positions on their cushions and one of the attendants approached them, got down onto his knees and began the customary request for the blessings, which was duly answered by the head monk. The ritual had begun.

As Don listened to the familiar words and rhythms that were starting up and transported, crackling, by microphone to outside the sala where most people were sitting, he found himself, out of habit, joining in with the chanting. But his thoughts were not on the meaning of the ancient Pali words. Instead he was wondering about the strange gathering around him; an unlikely mix of strangers, many of whom, like himself, probably had some debt of their own to pay the dead man. He considered why each of them was there and why he himself had felt it so important to attend the ceremony. It was his first outing, so to speak, after his return to Bangkok. He had not yet re-established his bearings and he felt nervous about being there in that very public setting, and yet he knew that there was no way of avoiding it. There had to be some kind of symbolic gesture of repayment for the debt that he felt he owed to Pi O. It was not just that the dead man, like some guardian angel, had been there to save him, but in their brief exchange, when Don accepted Pi O's help, his fears and his limitations had been unwittingly exposed. After that he could no longer pretend to be the person he once showed to the world, the cynic who shrugged at the consequences of his actions. The thin veneer of arrogance and bravado had fallen off. There was no more need for those brittle barriers that he had constructed to keep others at a distance. The false character he had assumed had been dismantled for good. There was no way of returning to the life he had led. And for all of this he was grateful.

The monks were pausing before beginning the last chant. After that the coffin would be wheeled round the funeral dais three times anti-clockwise, with anyone from the gathering who wanted to do so walking behind. Then those present would throw their artificial flowers and candles into the fire and everything would be over. Another body reduced to ashes and the ashes scattered in a river or in the sea. Don had been to hundreds of these ceremonies and each time it left him with a sense of the fragility of life.

Don settled back in his chair. Finally he was glad he had made the decision to attend. It was not just that he had done his social duty or that he had made his peace with the dead man. But being there and sharing in the mundane ritual of death underlined the fact that he had well and truly left the monkhood and was now in the realm of ordinary people, who did not have the benefit of rules and vinaya to protect them from themselves and their own passions. As he sat in the stifling heat of the afternoon Don felt the strange sensation of having come full circle and returned as an ordinary man to the city that he thought he had left for good. But there was also the feeling that he was now a stranger to it, like a farang newly arrived in Bangkok, unencumbered by personal history, with space to be what he chose to be. And as he followed the chant through to its final blessing the abbot's words floated back to him:

"Do good for the rest of your time on earth."

He saw that more than anything he wanted to atone for what he had done and although he had absolutely no idea what this would entail he knew that attending the ceremony was the first necessary act, and that by taking this first step he was now ready to do something that would require all of his courage and determination.

PART 3

CHAPTER 19

There was confusion. The monks had left the sala and, all except the one who was to lead the procession round the precinct, were now heading to the dais to prepare for the final chant while the fires were being lit. The guests who had decided to join in with the walk were already beginning to get up from their seats. Others remained firmly seated. Many looked as though they were about to leave and go home. Among these was Marisa who was sitting two rows away from the entrance to the sala. She had seen several acquaintances in the other section across the passageway and waved to them. But she was in a hurry to get out of there. The atmosphere was stifling and she did not want to talk with anyone. She had not realized that they were going to walk with the coffin, which would have meant a good twenty minutes more. She told herself that she was worried about Khun Chai and that she needed to be home as soon as possible. But she could not see how, short of pushing people out of the way, she could get near enough to the exit.

Don had decided soon after arriving that since he was there he would stay for the whole ceremony. People were trying to squeeze by him and he found that it was easier to stand up than remain in his chair. But the moment that he did so the person to his left, who was heavily built, began trying to make his way past. This resulted in him being gently pushed into the passageway in the middle. Here he found himself next to a man with a long ponytail who was trying awkwardly to light a cigarette. They were both shuffling on their feet and turned towards the sala.

Suddenly a sound cut through the air which was so surprising that all the frenetic activity came to an abrupt halt. It was not a scream or anything that sounded human; more like the savage grunt of a ferocious animal that seemed to hang in the heaviness of the afternoon, like a shot that had just been fired. In unison everyone was immediately straining to see what was going on. From where Don and Arun stood there was a clear view.

The young woman who had uttered the cry was standing a few metres in front of the coffin with one arm pointing accusingly at it. She was slightly built and her skin was dark. She was not wearing black like everyone else, but a green silk dress that was crumpled and stained and hanging loosely on her thin frame. Her hair was piled on top of her head and tied together by a green ribbon. Her face wore a wild, determined expression and this together with the bright red lipstick and thick mascara all added to the impression of a demented creature in their midst. The attendants and the young monk who were about to take the coffin seemed stunned by her presence and stood to one side watching her, as did everyone else. In fact several people gasped as if they had seen an apparition. Others looked away as if, by refusing to acknowledge her, they would not have to deal with it. For her part she did not seem to notice anyone around her. Her eyes had a blank look as if she was in a trance as she took a few steps forward. No one stopped her. With great force she kicked over the vases of flowers and threw the wreaths aside and then she spat at the coffin and for a moment looked as if she was going to cry out once more. But the sound that gagged from her throat was more like a deep bark.

By now the attendants had her by the arms and a struggle ensued. An angry voice from inside the sala, which Arun recognized as his sister's, shouted out:

"Get her out of here. Who let her in?"

"This is insult," shouted someone else. And then there were voices from every direction.

"Show some respect for the dead."

"Shame on her!"

"Disgusting."

"I've never seen anything like this in my life. This is a cursed day."

Marisa was standing still as they led the woman out. They were pushing her and manhandling her roughly. It looked as though one of the men was about to hit her. They were passing right by her. At that moment Marisa stepped up, put her arm out and held the young woman tightly to shield her and began to move with her into the passageway and towards the exit. The crowd parted and those standing nearby stood back deliberately to make way, as though they wanted to avoid physical contact. At the same time one of the young men, with a dark blue suit and the regulation short back and sides, tried to bar the way, calling out:

"Let us handle this. We'll take care of it."

Marisa's eyes met his and she tightened her hold on the girl. Now another man came towards them with a menacing gesture, as though he was prepared to hit both of them. At this point both Don and Arun, who had been watching the whole scene passively like everyone else, stepped up on either side of the two women and provided an escort for Marisa and her ward.

"It's all right," said Don in a commanding voice. "We know her."

They carefully made their way through the silent crowd and out into the car park.

The photographers were rushing round trying to get a closer vantage point holding their cameras high in the air, hoping to get a good shot. Flashes were going off but there were people in between blocking the way. The television crew who had been filming earlier over near the cremation dais were too far away to manoeuvre.

When the four of them reached Marisa's car the young official was still behind them. Marisa turned and seeing the man shouted out:

"Do you know who I am? Tell me your name. I'll see to it that you go back to looking after your water buffaloes."

"We don't care who you are. Get that bitch out of here before we beat the shit out of her. Who does she think she is coming here to insult such a good man?"

His words were drowned by the crack of thunder that split the sky. Then there was a roar, accompanied by several flashes, before the first fat drops of rain started to fall. By the time they had opened the car door and all piled in there was a downpour.

The young woman sat in the back next to Don. She still wore the same angry expression and continued to stare straight ahead as though none of them existed.

It was only they drove out of the temple car park into the congested streets that a collective sigh of relief broke out. Then they sat back in silence. It was Arun who first spoke.

"What did we just do?"

CHAPTER 20

They could hardly see out. The windscreen wipers even at their fastest speed did not have time to brush the water away. The car inched forward through the traffic. It was Don's idea that they should take the young woman to a hospital. He told the others that he was certain she was in need of medical attention and they nodded their consent. On the way there they hardly spoke except to exchange basic information. Like accomplices plunged into a scenario that none of them had chosen, they quickly shared the necessary social coordinates in order to get them out of the way. Above the din made by the rain beating down on the car roof they established that Arun was Ladda's brother and Pi O's nephew, that Don was the son of the late politician Khun Sombhat and that Marisa was who both the men thought she was. After that they sat in silence listening to the pounding of the rain.

Marisa, who had chosen to drive herself that day, was not at that moment thinking about her action in protecting the young woman, nor of its consequences. She was too intent on getting them to their destination in one piece. She went slowly and carefully along the avenue and focused all her attention on avoiding the motorbikes that were sliding all over the wet surface. Now and then she wondered, vaguely, what Khun Chai was doing and why he had not called her on the mobile, since it had become his habit to do so every few hours to check up on her movements. She worried that he was still ill from the drinking.

Arun looked out at the wet pavements and went over what had just happened to him. He still felt the rush of adrenaline and was both excited and amused by the absurdity of being stuck in a car with two strangers and possibly one psychopath, not knowing where any of it was going to lead. He disliked surprises but found that he was enjoying this adventure. There was no logical explanation as to why he had stepped in and joined Don and Marisa in protecting the young woman. It might easily not have happened at all. He had not been conscious of making any decision. It was as if some invisible force had pushed forward his hand to take the young woman's arm and help guide her through the crowd.

He knew that the act had jolted him out of the blurry dreamlike state in which he had been trapped for months. Up till that afternoon almost every aspect of his life had become predictable. His relationship with Gaew was turning out to be a burdensome, unsatisfying affair which seemed more trouble than it was worth. There was not even the compensation of sex to make it enjoyable. The exhibition, for which he had worked so hard, had come and gone and left him with a feeling not of satisfaction or success but of emptiness. He could already see himself carrying on along much the same direction and soon becoming a recognized and respected figure; one of those characters who are interviewed by the newspapers from time to time and asked for their opinion about the latest artist to hit the scene. The unexpected incident at the temple had propelled him back into a vivid sense of the present.

He watched Marisa from the corner of his eye. It was odd to be next to the woman who had once been the object of his teenage fantasies as if he had just been written into a scene from one of her movies. In the flesh she was smaller than he had imagined, her skin was darker and there were lines round her eyes. But she still had the kind of rare beauty that made her stand out from the crowd. She was leaning onto the driving wheel and peering through the windscreen with an intense expression on her face. He wondered what she was thinking and whether, unlike himself, she had known what she was doing when she put her protective arm round the girl.

He looked round briefly and smiled at Don. It was then that he thought that he remembered having seen him once in a bar, with long hair and without glasses, behaving like a lout, someone a world apart from the quiet serious person sitting in the back seat. He wanted to ask Don if his memory was correct but he did not think it was the right time to bring this up. He turned back to the front and now peered into the mirror. The young woman was sitting directly behind him and he did not want to make it obvious that he was trying to take a look at her. But the back of his seat hid her from view. Nevertheless, he had already retained her image clearly in his mind, especially the scar that ran down her left cheek, which added to her wild image. He was pleased when she had spat on the coffin. He would have done it too if he had the nerve to break such a sacred taboo and he guessed that there were others attending the funeral who might have wanted to do the same thing.

He kept wondering who she was, where she came from and what Pi O had done to her. Her dirty green dress, the clumsy makeup and the wild demented look in her eyes reminded him of one of the figures in a Goya painting. She was definitely an interesting apparition.

Don was staring out of the window watching the cascade of water tumble down and the frantic activity on the sidewalk; he was feeling sorry for the stall holders trying to fasten the plastic sheeting over their merchandise and the pedestrians running for cover under leaky awnings or huddled up in groups in the entrance of a corner store. He could see the sewage that was pushed up from below, pouring out of the drains along the avenue. And some of the lanes they passed were now rapidly disappearing under the rising water level. He was impressed by the power of water to change the city in such a short time.

The young woman was leaning against him, resting her head on his right shoulder. Her coffee coloured skin was firm and warm. He could feel her through his shirt. He felt a strong urge to put his arm around her and to speak words of comfort. But he knew that it would have been presumptuous and out of place, so he remained as silent and as still as possible. When Arun turned round to smile at him it made him feel uncomfortable and self conscious, embarrassed by the physical contact with the young woman.

Her outburst at the ceremony made him recall an incident at the temple when a monk, who was younger than himself and who had never been anything but kind and gentle, one day became violent and uncontrollable. He insulted them all, calling them parasites on the poor and layabouts. Then he tried to physically assault the abbot, at which point he was restrained and taken to the nearest hospital, which was in Nongkai, where he was sedated and tied down to a bed. A week later he came back to the monastery, his old self again and apologized to everyone. He begged the abbot to let him stay on and the abbot agreed, but with the caution that if he behaved as he had done again he would have to leave forever. Within a month of returning, this monk went down to the river one evening and drowned himself. They knew that it was not an accident because, when they dragged his body out, they saw that he had carefully tied bricks to his legs before jumping into the water. The incident had saddened them all. The abbot called an assembly and told them that the monk was sick, that there was little anyone could do, and that sometimes there was no explanation for our human behaviour.

Later, at the private clinic, Marisa, Arun and Don watched their ward being taken away for a check-up by a middle aged female doctor. The young woman had not spoken a word in the car, nor did she answer any of the questions that were put to her earlier by the receptionist. She did not appear to have the strength to respond or resist. The doctor looked at her curiously when they were introduced. But her attention was immediately diverted. As soon as she recognized Marisa she seemed to stop being interested in her patient. She was so pleased to meet her idol in the flesh, having been a life-long fan, that she seemed to be only vaguely aware of the task at hand and only half listened to their explanation of what had taken place at the temple. She showed no apparent surprise that the person they had brought in was a total stranger to all of them.

When they had gone through the door to the surgery Arun turned to the other two and asked, nervously:

"Are we aware of what we've taken on here? We know nothing about her. She's clearly out of her mind; she's done something outrageous and we've taken it on ourselves to protect her. What do we think we're doing?"

As soon as he had spoken, Marisa knew that she had no choice but to stay. She had thought of making some excuse, telling them that she had something important to do and that she had to leave right away, but now she saw that it was impossible. For a moment she felt annoyed that she had gotten involved. She could not understand what made her step in and help the poor girl. It was not usual for her to do anything without a lot of premeditation, and when she did it was almost always a mistake. This time it looked like a matter of having to spend the next few hours, possibly days, sorting things out.

"I'm sorry if I've dragged you into this. I feel responsible..." she began.

"It's going to be a mess," said Arun, shaking his head from side to side. "We don't know who she is or what her past relationship with Pi O was. Maybe his men will come looking for her, and for us. And then there's the press. They got your picture, I think."

Somehow Marisa found Arun's worried and gloomy way of looking at the situation amusing.

"My word. You've thought of all the angles," she told him.

"I'm like that. I get anxious about everything. It's my nature," said Arun, smiling back at her.

At this point Don joined in.

"She just needs care and proper medication. She's very fragile. She's been through some crisis," he said.

"Well that's for sure," said an exasperated Arun.

While waiting for the result of the examination, they discussed what had happened. None of them explained why they were there at the ceremony in the first place. Finally the lady doctor and a nurse returned with a young woman whose face had been cleaned up and who was now wearing the uniform of an in-patient. The doctor told them that there was nothing wrong with the young woman. Her organs were all healthy, her blood pressure normal, her lithium count showed no sign of imbalance, there was no alcohol or any other substance detected. The only thing she was suffering from was severe exhaustion and she seemed to be going through a psychological trauma, for there was no other reason for her not to talk.

"Our psychiatrist should have a look at her. But I'm afraid he is not here till tomorrow," she said. Then she suggested that they keep her in for a few days. But when the young woman heard this she let out a long groan and shook her head from side to side like a child expressing a definite and stubborn refusal to comply. But before the discussion went any further the nurse's mobile phone rang and when she answered it her expression immediately showed alarm.

"There are reporters and photographers downstairs. Everywhere. They are asking who the young woman is and which ward she has been taken to."

"How did they manage to follow us here?" asked Marisa in frustration.

"You're in the media. You should know," replied Arun sharply.

Don put up his hand to silence them.

"We can't leave her here. They'll finish her. We must get her away."

The doctor nodded quickly.

"There's a back exit we use. But you must go now."

CHAPTER 21

They were in Arun's studio waiting for the evening news to come on. The young woman, who they had decided by common consent to call Nong Da rather than leave her nameless, was asleep on the sofa. She had not protested when Don gave her the sleeping tablets that the doctor had prescribed. They had been talking about Pi O and the whole affair but still none of them had mentioned their personal connection with him. It seemed to have been tacitly agreed that this was a subject that they would discreetly avoid. After all, they had only just met and even though the day's event had pushed them close together in a way which only an intense shared experience can, they were still wary of one another.

Marisa, whose earlier annoyance had dropped away and who had now fully accepted that she had a responsibility towards the girl she had saved from a beating or worse, sat cradling the glass of wine that Arun had offered her in both her hands. She felt strangely comfortable with these two men, who were younger than her and who she found attractive and different from the people she usually met in her circle. Arun's paintings that were leaning against the wall seemed to her disturbingly beautiful. He was talking about them and telling them how he had once been in Spain, and had been influenced by the paintings of Hieronymus Bosch and how he felt that they made him want to adapt this vision to modern-day Bangkok.

"Look at this one," he said leading them over to a large canvas that stood alone in the corner. He pointed to the central group of characters who were standing half naked under the chandeliers and looking away from one another.

"Do you recognize this scene, Khun Marisa? I took it from the reception that I went to for the premiere of your film, 'The Sad Killer'. But of course I changed it a little." He laughed.

"I didn't even know you were there," Marisa mumbled. She felt vulnerable, as though she had been judged. "Did you think it was that awful?" she asked him.

"Well normally I never go to those parties if I can help it. But I must admit that it was interesting."

"That sounds condescending."

"I know. But I can't help it," he said and this time they both laughed.

This conversation was interrupted by the jingle of Marisa's mobile, which she extracted from her handbag and took out into the garden to answer. When she came back she told them that it was a call from her boyfriend, who said that the press were besieging her apartment block, asking everyone where she had disappeared and who the young woman was. She did not tell them that Khun Chai was worried and made her promise him that she was not seeing someone else.

Pi O's funeral was the main story on the news that evening, which was to be expected. The reportage began with a general background leading up to his assassination, which was still being investigated, because so far the police had no clues as to who might have carried it out. Then it cut to the funeral itself; the usual pictures of black-suited guests arriving through the temple gates. The commentary mentioned that the attendance was larger than had been expected and seemed to demonstrate the popularity of the deceased, since those who attended the ceremony came from all walks of life and many were clearly upset by Pi O's death.

Then the reporter, practically unable to control her emotions, was shown standing in front of the gates, sheltering from the rain as the guests filed hurriedly passed her on their way out of the ceremony.

"There's been a terrible incident," she shouted as though another murder had been committed. "A young woman came in at the end of the chanting and did something very violent and insulting to our culture. According to those standing nearby she kicked the flowers aside and then spat on the coffin. Unfortunately we did not record the moment it happened because our cameramen were far from the scene. And then the crowd prevented us from getting close. But some press photographers managed to get some pictures of what happened immediately afterwards and we'll be showing these in just one moment. But the most surprising news is that the young woman who behaved in such an ugly way was then led out of the temple by none other than our own star, Khun Marisa. Can you imagine? We do not know at this moment where they have gone. It appears that two men, possibly companions of Khun Marisa, were also involved. But we do not know who they are. And it is certain that after leaving the grounds of the temple they went to a private clinic, the Thevada Health Centre, where the young woman was examined by Doctor Chanida Boonsook. Anyway here are the pictures that were taken..."

The photographs that came on the screen showed Marisa grimacing, with one arm around Nong Da's shoulder and the other pushing her way through the crowd. Arun's face could not be seen since he was behind them. But Don, standing taller than those nearby, with his glasses and short crop was also clearly distinguishable.

Later there was a panel who were asked their opinions regarding what had happened at the Wat that afternoon. It consisted of an actor and TV presenter who had known Marisa for many years, a monk and Ladda, Arun's sister. The actor did most of the talking and seemed to be enjoying himself. He was shocked and appalled by the incident like everyone else, he said. It was the first time that he heard of anyone daring to do such an ugly act. Even if Pi O had harmed the young woman, a funeral was a time of reconciliation and forgiveness, not of revenge. He hoped that the woman would be sorry for what she had done. As for Marisa, he did not even know that she was acquainted with Pi O, and he was curious about their relationship, especially since she had portrayed herself to be so clean. Wasn't it strange? He was surprised that she should now have decided to disappear and to be so mysterious. When he finally ran out of things to say and it was Ladda's turn to talk, she merely expressed her sorrow that her uncle had been treated so unfairly during the last days of his life and in death had been so insulted. She hoped that the police would find the young woman and put her in a lunatic asylum. She added that she was very angry with Marisa for what she had done.

The monk sat in silence throughout the discussion, with his eyes half closed and a blank expression on his face, giving the impression that he did not want to be there at all. When the interviewer turned to him he remained silent for a while, as though he did not want to offer any opinion whatsoever. When pressed to offer some comment on the matter, he finally said: "It's a matter of karma following karma."

They turned the television off and sat quietly, digesting what they had just seen. Then Arun spoke.

"My sister obviously did not see what I did. Otherwise she would have called me again by now." There had been a message on the answering phone asking where he had disappeared to after the ceremony and ordering him to get in touch.

"Well, lucky you," said Marisa sarcastically. "So you'll avoid getting an earful. But what about you, Khun Don? How's this going to affect you? They got a good shot of you. Will it be embarrassing? Will there be a lot of explaining to do?"

Don smiled and shrugged. "I don't know. But it's happened and we all have to face the consequences."

"Yes. That sounds very noble. Worthy of an ex monk," said Arun. "But why did we run out like thieves instead of facing them all right there? And why are we here hiding away? Have we committed a crime for protecting our little Nong Da, whom none of us have laid eyes on before today? I know that she did something for which people like my sister will think she should be sent to hell. Maybe they would have beaten her up. I saw those hoods. But then, as you say, she has to take the consequences for her action. But we didn't let her, did we? I mean what's stopping us from just going public this evening? Is it really just our concern for Nong Da or is it because we're all nervous about what will have to come out once we reveal ourselves? You get my drift, don't you?"

Don nodded. "You're right. I am afraid of what will follow."

Arun said: "Karma follows karma. That's what the monk said. And that's what we've heard since we were born. I never really understood what it meant. If it's something to do with deserving what you get then why are all the crooks and corrupt politicians in our country carrying on so well? Where's their punishment? In another lifetime? I've never been convinced by that line. The question is, why were any of us there at the funeral in the first place? I know that if it wasn't for my sister pressurizing me I wouldn't have gone. I hated the man. He hurt and cheated my father, and probably caused his death. I was glad Nong Da spat on his coffin. If I had the guts I might have done the same. What puzzles me is why both of you went to her rescue. What did he do to you? Why were you there in the first place?"

He looked from one to the other. Marisa turned away. Don was the first to reply. He told them the story of his past; how, coming down from a drug binge, he had killed a child; of how Pi O saved him from being arrested and most likely jailed and how he had been haunted for the past five years by his action. He told them that, other than his former abbot, they were the only people with whom he had shared his past.

The other two sat digesting what they heard for a while without saying a word. It was hard for either of them to associate the mild mannered man who was sitting in front of them with the callous person he had just described.

"So it's natural that you don't want any of this to come out. I understand," said Marisa after a while.

"No you're wrong. I don't mind the truth any more. And if I have to go to jail for it then I am prepared. But there is something I need to do first."

"Surely you don't resent Pi O for what he did?" asked Arun. "If it had been me I would have been grateful."

"But you don't know what it feels like to have killed someone. I am not saying that I don't owe him my freedom from prison. But in the end I'm not sure that his interference helped me."

"You mean you still have to pay."

"I took a life. It was a mindless, senseless act. I've been paying ever since. But I am not at peace."

"And what about Nong Da? Why did you help her?"

"I don't know. It just happened. I wasn't thinking. I had no choice. I just acted."

When it was Marisa's turn she hesitated, looking from one to the other several times for reassurance that they would listen and understand. Then she drew a deep breath and, in what felt like one long sigh, she told them of her own past and how she had been used by Pi O, how afraid she had been that he would expose her one day, her relief when he died and how she wished she had stopped herself from protecting Nong Da and left things to take their course.

"I don't know what drove me to do such a reckless thing, when I was nearly home and dry."

"Perhaps it was so that once everything is out in the open you will have nothing more to fear," said Arun finally.

CHAPTER 22

They sat late into the night going over much the same ground and as the hours passed by they found themselves giving out more and more details about their past and their relationship to Pi O. None of them were tired even after such a long and eventful day. They talked like teenagers who had recently discovered a new and binding kindred spirit. It was as though for the first time in their lives they did not have to play any more social games or keep up the polite facades. They could drop their masks and reveal their true face. And in the course of this first long, intense conversation in which their fears and anxieties were exposed, a deep and improbable friendship was formed. And without having to affirm it they each knew that there was now a bond between them founded on trust and honesty that none had imagined possible and to each of them this opened up a dimension that had been missing in their lives.

In the course of their discussion they agreed that their priority was to carry on protecting the young woman, Nong Da. It was Arun's suggestion that she should not remain in Bangkok. He told them about the centre in Chiengmai and said that he would contact Gaew, who by chance was in Bangkok, and ask her to fetch Nong Da and take care of her in the centre. In the meantime she would stay at Arun's studio and he and Don would take turns keeping watch over her. Meanwhile Marisa would face the press. She would tell it like it was, and if at some point this meant that they were going to delve into her past, then she was prepared to tell them. They talked of the damage this might do to her career and reputation and the mockery and general malice that was going to follow. But she told them that if they were there for her she was ready.

As for Don, he told them that the one thing he wanted to do first was to go to the family of the little boy he had killed and to apologize to them for what he had done. After that, he did not mind what happened to him.

Marisa got back to her condo near the river at around three in the morning. She passed the uniformed guard at the entrance. He stood up to salute her and as he did so stared intently at her. She knew that he would be the first one to spread the news of her return. She parked the car and used the private lift up to her apartment. Opening the door she saw Khun Chai slumped in the armchair in front of the television, which was turned off. There was a half finished drink on the floor near him. He woke up with a jump, like a cartoon character, knocking the glass over.

"I've been waiting up for you," he said in a slurry, sleepy voice.

"So I see. Well you can go to bed now."

"Where have you been? Did you see the journalists in the lobby? The porter says that they won't leave and intend to camp here for the night. Did you talk to them?"

"No. I used the back lift."

"They came up here earlier and asked for news of you. But I was rude to them. Where were you?"

"I was with some friends. We were protecting a young woman."

"Yes. I saw it all on the news. Several times. Who is she?"

"I don't know."

"And who were the two men they spoke of? Were they really your friends?"

"Yes."

"Where did you meet them? How long have you known them? Why haven't you introduced them to me?"

"Stop it. Don't start getting jealous. I only met them today. I mean yesterday, at the funeral. But they have become my friends. And I will introduce them to you if you like. Now I need to get some rest. It's going to be a very long day tomorrow."

CHAPTER 23

It happened much as they expected. The following day Marisa gave her interview to the papers and went on national television to explain what had happened at the funeral. It was clear that what really interested the reporters was her connection to Pi O. She told them that he had helped her in the early part of her career, but she would not go into detail. She did not have to. They had already drawn their own conclusions as to what this implied.

Marisa had prepared herself in the way that she had studied for her film roles and, when the time came to face the questions and the cameras, she more or less carried it off without getting too bruised by the ordeal. She gave them straightforward answers and insisted that the reason she protected the young woman, who was a stranger to her and whose whereabouts were now unknown to her, was because she was afraid for her safety. Yes, she had taken her to a clinic to be examined and afterwards some friends of the woman had taken her away. No, she did not know who the tall man with the short hair and glasses was. She had never met him before. Yes, he did accompany them to the clinic, but they did not exchange any information.

"Wasn't that strange?" asked a male interviewer.

"No. It was an emergency. There was no time to socialize. And afterwards we went our separate ways," was her answer.

"And what about the other young man? There were witnesses who saw another man get into the car with you."

"Same thing," she said shrugging her shoulder.

The answer did not satisfy him but there was no way that she could be made to provide any more information on the matter. But the lack of total openness was accompanied by a sincerity relating to other matters which went some way to disarming some of the interviewers, although others unkindly called it her star performance.

Afterwards the tabloids of course had a field day and for a week after her going public they began put out stories about her on their front pages. They dug up old movie stills of her clad in a skimpy bikini and juxtaposed them with photos of the young ladies who worked in some of Pi O's clubs. People in the film industry who had known her and worked with her were all asked for their opinion.

There was little factual information besides what she herself gave out about her past, since she had so meticulously swept clean all the paths that led back to those times. Nevertheless, in the effort to discredit the myth of her having been discovered as an innocent, virginal schoolgirl, a journalist for City Today managed to track down a receptionist at the 'Club Cubana' who claimed that she could remember the young Nong Daeng, who later became the film star called Marisa.

"How could I forget her? She was the most beautiful girl in the whole place. A real gem. She was Khun O's favourite. I once overheard him praising her skills to a customer. A very rich man. I knew she would be famous one day."

Marisa did not bother to respond to this slander or to any of the other half truths that they wrote about her. She was only surprised that they never managed to dig up anybody from her past who might have given them a more reliable picture. In the end, when the editors decided that their readers had been fed enough of Marisa, the story fizzled out and the focus went back to the political repercussions of Pi O's assassination.

Marisa did not suffer unduly from the outcome of these articles. Everybody in the country had now been told that she had not been discovered behind the counter of her mother's little flower shop. This was something that most of her fans had suspected from the very beginning. As for the story put out that she had once been a high class teenage prostitute who got lucky and hit the jackpot, it came too late in her career to do much damage. Besides, Marisa had already decided that she could live with anything that the press chose to throw at her. Others had skeletons in their cupboard which were probably more sensational. The public embarrassment was a price she was willing to pay for not having to pretend any more about her origins. Her image was tarnished. She would no longer be the prim and proper figure that had been projected. Perhaps some of her fans would be disappointed but on the other hand it was time for a change. As for the critics, she would merely have to grit her teeth and prove to them how capable she really was. She had long developed a protective layer to shield her from the critics who had panned her acting skills over the years.

The public exposure also left her exhausted, with a longing to be far away from the limelight and allowed to be left in peace. But she knew that there was still work to do promoting 'The Sad Killer' and that leaving now would be admitting that she had been defeated. This was the last thing that she wanted. The sense of survival, of beating the odds, was the one motivation that had always kept her going. She was not going to let go of it now.

CHAPTER 24

Don, who normally did not read the tabloids, kept up with the news all through the ordeal and called Marisa several times to give encouragement. He felt bad that she was handling it all alone. But they had decided that it was best. Otherwise the press might have gone on to insinuate about the relationship between himself, or Arun, and Marisa, which would have added more confusion.

Three days after the funeral he made his way back to the soi where five years earlier he had run the small boy over. While he was at the monastery he had often thought that one day, when he was ready, he would return to Bangkok and see Pi O and ask him the name of the family and where they lived. But now Pi O was gone and the only way that he could find out was to retrace his steps. He took the sky train and walked to the hospital where he had taken the boy and his mother. At the emergency ward he persuaded a nurse to find the files that were kept from that time. She was reluctant to search through the cupboard but his gentle manner won her over.

"Why are you so interested?" she asked as she flipped through the folder. "Are you a relative? No? But you still want to know. And it was five years you say. I don't understand. So many die here every day. People think they'll live forever but death comes easily in this city."

Finally she found the page, but there was no record. Pi O's men had been thorough.

Don left the hospital and made his way along Pratunam, which was packed with tourists who were taking their time to stop at the stalls, merely to browse or bargain for a fake watch, a souvenir tee shirt, or a designer handbag made in Korea. In between there were the food stalls and the trestle tables piled high with pirated CDs. He wondered if the boy's mother might even have been one of these stall holders. The place he was looking for was in one of the back streets. But even though the main buildings were still the same, the familiar landmarks had shifted, so that he was not sure where the turning was that he had once taken. All he could remember was that it was a short cut and that on the corner where the incident took place there was a shop selling medicine. This detail had stuck in his mind.

Finally, after walking through narrow side streets and getting lost a couple of times, Don arrived at the corner where he had swerved and hit the boy. He recognized it more by instinct than recollection. But he was not sure it was the exact spot until he looked up and saw the sign: 'The Phaya Naak Pharmacy: Traditional Herbal Remedies'.

Below the letters was a painting of the Naga, much like the image on the match boxes, with big red eyes. They were the same ones that glowed down at him that dawn.

He stood there for a long time, going back to the feelings he had felt, recalling the person he had been, praying also for some kind of redemption for what he had done. He knew that the only way this was possible was to beg forgiveness to the mother and father of the child he had killed. He had no name to go by, but if she lived in that area he would find her, even if it meant knocking on each door.

He decided to begin with the herb shop. There was a woman, he noticed, who had already been watching him. She was thin, and middle aged and she looked at him suspiciously as he entered the premises.

"I'm trying to find someone," Don began. But before he could go on she turned her back on him and, ignoring him, busied herself tidying the shelves that were laden with jars and coloured bottles filled with oils and tinctures.

"I'm sorry, but I really need your help," he said, raising his voice.

This time she faced him and said slowly and clearly, as though she had been saying the same words all her life.

"I don't know anything."

"Please. I only want to ask about a woman whose little boy was run over just in front of this shop five years ago."

She looked horrified and put her hand to her mouth.

"Please," Don insisted. "I'm so sorry to come in like this and interrupt you but I need to find out where the mother lives."

"Don't bother her!" a stern voice shouted from behind the curtains at the back of the shop. She's only just come to work here. And she's not well."

An old woman dressed in a traditional sarong and using a walking stick hobbled from out of the shadows. As she did so the younger one shifted past her as though she was relieved by her presence. When she had disappeared the old woman said:

"That's my niece. She hasn't been well for a long time. It's a psychological problem. The herbs I've been giving her over the years have helped a bit. But it's been hard for her and for the family. I've taken her in now as a favour to my brother. She has nowhere to go, you see."

Don nodded.

The old woman sat down on a chair that was at the end of the counter and stared at Don without saying any more. Then at last she spoke again.

"I heard what you said to my niece."

"Yes. I need to find the mother of the child who was killed."

Again the woman deliberately took her time.

"You're the one, aren't you?"

Don nodded.

"Well you're lucky you came here before you went asking anywhere else. They'll kill you if they knew that you've come back. Do you know what you did?"

Don nodded again. "That's why I'm here."

"That child. Ai Nok. We all knew him because he used to walk round here in the neighbourhood getting sweets off people. He was such a cuddly little boy. His mother sometimes left him while she went to the market. He was quite at home with any one of us. He didn't mind. He was an easy child. You killed him. And you got away with it. That's how the rich do things in this city."

Don took in her gaze which was neither angry nor accusing but filled with pity.

"What's your name?"

"Don."

"And how old are you?"

"I'm thirty."

"So you've come back. After all this time. What do you want? Your money saved you but it can't bring the child back."

"I want to see the mother and talk to her. Even if she shoots me dead."

The woman looked at him hard.

"And what good would that do? Let go of the past. You can't do anything about it. Or can't you let go?"

Don shook his head slowly. "You're right. This is all for my benefit. But I still think it is the right thing to do."

"Well you're out of luck. Mae Hom left this area three years ago. The shop where she was working was going through a bad time and she herself was involved with some taxi driver. A drunk. And a bad man. They went off somewhere. I don't know where exactly. Samut Prakhan maybe."

Don waied her and thanked her. But as he turned to go she said,

"I told you not to go asking about her. They'll beat you to death. I mean it. Help me over to the phone. I'll find out some more details for you, if I can."

After two calls to locals who had known Mae Hom, the child's mother, the old woman told Don that the last thing that anyone heard of her was that she was selling vegetables in Prakhanong market.

"There. Now I've helped you enough. I don't know why I shouldn't just call the police or the neighbours but I have a feeling that it's something I've had to do. And now my duty is finished. Ok. You can go. I won't say good luck because you don't deserve it for what you did. But seeing you now in the flesh I won't judge you. Go on. Get out of here and don't show your face any more in this neighbourhood."

It was not difficult to find people in the market who had known Mae Hom, although they acted strangely when he mentioned her name. None of them had seen her for a year or so. One woman told Don that she and her taxi driver boyfriend had rented a room nearby in a street behind the market. Another told of how drunk they would get every evening and the fights they had from time to time, which nearly always resulted in Mae Hom coming to the market with a black eye and bruises on her arms.

The address that he was given turned out to be a repair shop for motor bikes. There were two teenagers, both in oil-stained tee shirts and ragged jeans, standing around examining a bike which looked like it had been in a serious crash. The old man whose place it was asked Don what he wanted and then told him that Mae Hom and the boyfriend had lived above the workshop.

"They left ages ago," he was quick to add. "And good riddance. They were a nuisance. I got complaints from the neighbour. Did they owe you money? Is that why you're looking for them?"

When Don asked if he knew where they had gone he answered with a cynical laugh.

"Dead probably, the way they were headed."

One of the teenagers turned and said:

"They got sick. They went to hospital and then afterwards they didn't have anywhere to go so they went to a centre somewhere in Klongtoey."

"What did they have?" asked Don, although he had already guessed.

"You know," replied the young man with a casual shrug. "The usual disease."

Don had a bowl of noodles in the market before hiring a biker to take him to Klongtoey, which was only a short weave through the traffic from Prakhanong. The man told him that he had heard of the centre, but he did not know precisely where it was. When they reached the railway track that acted as a natural boundary to the district, the biker stopped and let Don off. He pointed vaguely into the street that was ahead and said,

"I'm not going any further. This isn't my patch. You'll find the place. They all know it around here."

Don was slightly annoyed that the man had not taken him to his destination. It was early afternoon and the sun was beating down. He was tired and hot and dizzy from having to deal with the noise and the fumes, and emotionally he felt tense. The task that he had set himself suddenly seemed too daunting. Don hesitated and for a moment stood looking down the track. There were fragile wooden dwellings with their tin roofs that had been constructed on either side of it. Children were playing. An ice cream vendor was going from door to door ringing his bell. He knew that he had to go through with what he had begun.

The centre was called 'The Karuna Hospice' and it was a ten minute walk from where the biker had left him. Everyone in the neighbourhood knew where it was. Don, who was born in Bangkok, had never been in that part of the city. The name Klongtoey, when he was young, conjured up all sorts of bad associations. He could remember his parents talking about it as though it was the most sordid and uninviting place in the world, even though it was only down the road from where they lived. It was supposed to be full of thugs and addicts. It was a violent area. But walking through it that afternoon there was nothing threatening. In fact there was a friendliness and sense of community that was in contrast to the atmosphere in a shopping mall or the vast supermarkets that were now all over the city. Here there was still connection among people. There was the street life that in other parts of the city was fast disappearing. There were also all the marks of poverty; the open sewer, the smell of garbage, the damaged young men and women with vacant eyes hanging around the doorways, the food stalls that looked unsavoury. Perhaps his younger self—the protected, spoilt kid from the high class background of servants and drivers and big hotels and private gyms— would have felt shocked, or at least ill at ease with what he saw. But the years in the monastery and living among the poor in the north-east had changed him.

The hospice was a large two story wooden building that looked as though it could have once been a school or an old government office. From the outside it looked shabby, in need of repair and a fresh coat of paint. The marble steps leading up to the open lobby at the entrance were worn down and stained and the sign above them was hardly legible. The place was run, Don learned later, by a voluntary organization that had been in Klongtoey for over twenty years, working to set up women's groups and a legal aid centre. But gradually the problem of AIDS became such a pressing issue that the founding committee decided to devote most of their efforts in that direction. And, as soon as the news spread that they would look after people with the disease, they were full. People came in not just from Klongtoey but all the other districts of Bangkok, like Laadprao, Bangsue and even as far away as Petchburi. There was a vetting system but no one paid much attention to it. Sometimes a sick person would be brought in a taxi and dumped on the front steps. Or a whole family would come with their son or daughter and camp out in the lobby until there was a spare bed. There were three female nurses and a male nurse who were in charge of the day-to-day care and who lived on the premises, thirty staff recruited from the neighbourhood who were paid irregularly and very little, and a doctor who volunteered his services once a month. Apart from these there was a team of volunteers that included several farang men and women. Despite the lack of proper facilities and adequate funding, and without active support from the government, Karuna had managed to keep going over the years as if by a miracle.

Don was received by a receptionist who sat at a table in the ground floor office and who asked immediately if he was a relative. She did not show any reaction when he said no, but called to a girl who was sitting on a bench outside and told her to show him to the ward where Mae Hom was staying. The girl, who looked no more than twelve or thirteen, was bright and smiling and introduced herself as Nong Fon. She had just bought herself an ice cream at the corner store. He guessed that she was someone's daughter and there to visit a parent. She took him up to the first floor, which was the women's section. They made their way along a balcony which stretched the length of the building. There were three dormitories with a dozen beds in each. As they passed the first one Nong Fon turned and said.

"That's where I stay."

Mae Hom's room was the last one. All the beds were occupied. The bodies that Don saw on each one were no more than skeletons covered by a thin layer of skin. On that first visit it was all he registered. During the following week he would look closer and notice the marks and scars and growths that distinguished each one. But that afternoon it seemed as though he had come across a dying species. And as he walked passed them to the corner where Mae Hom lay their eyes followed him and he could not make out what they were expressing. One woman, as he passed, pulled herself up on one elbow and coughed, retched into the spit bowl by her bed and then reached out an empty hand. The girl, Nong Fon, quickly handed her the glass of water that was on the small bedside table.

"Easy there, Pi Toi," she said.

Don would not have recognized Mae Hom if the girl had not pointed to her and said,

"Here she is."

He would not have recalled her from that morning even if she had been well. All he could remember was a woman crying for her dead child. Now that same woman was there in front of him lying on the bed with her eyes huge in their sockets staring up at the ceiling and the fan blowing the wisps of hair that were left on her head. He stood silently gazing down at her with a mixture of pity and disbelief. There were sores on her lips and the skin on her face was blotchy. Her ribs showed through the thin cotton top that she was wearing. A Pamper, which looked too big, covered her genitals. And then the legs which were like two fragile sticks.

"Mae Hom! Mae Hom! You've got a visitor. Here he is. A man and quite handsome too." She laughed, but there was no response from Mae Hom, who continued to stare up as though she had not heard.

"She used to be so talkative," said Nong Fon. "But she's gone downhill lately. And fast too."

Don was shocked that the girl was speaking so openly, in such a matter-of-fact way, in front of her.

"She can't eat any more. That's the trouble. Can't hold anything down. And she coughs a lot. It tires her."

At this point Mae Hom turned towards them.

"Yes. Tired," she whispered as she fixed her eyes on Don.

"Well. I'll leave you to it now," said the girl and skipped off.

When she had gone Don drew up a chair from the corner and sat by the bed. All the words that he had prepared to say to her seemed empty now that he was in her presence. Without knowing why he reached out and held her hand.

⚬┼⚬

For the next five days, until she died, he was there at her bedside. It was on the second visit that he told her who he was. Her response was a slight nod. It was only before he left that evening that she beckoned him to draw closer with a gesture of her index finger. And then when his ear was near her mouth she said,

"I've never forgotten your face."

She did not have the strength to sit up, let alone to speak. Most of the time she was asleep. When she was conscious he would hold a glass for her while she sipped the water from a straw. Or he would wipe her body down and put a wet flannel on her temple when the fever was high.

It was from one of the nurses that he learned that she had been admitted a year earlier, along with her boyfriend who had died soon after arriving at the hospice. It was he who had infected her. He asked her if Mae Hom had any family and the nurse replied that she once told them that she had a son who was run over and killed. But when Don pressed her as to how this had affected Mae Hom the woman merely shrugged.

"She didn't go on about it. Everyone here's got some terrible story, you know."

On the sixth morning Don went in as usual to find her bed empty. The girl opposite told him that she had died in the night.

"No fuss. They didn't even have to give her oxygen. I hope I go like that," she said.

Mae Hom's funeral that same afternoon could not have been more different from Pi O's. It was held in a small Wat on the river near the docks, a temple where the poor were cremated. The hospice had a special agreement with the abbot there who asked for only the basic cost to cover the electricity used in the oven. There were no wreaths and the undecorated coffin was made of the cheapest wood.

Don had called Marisa and Arun and they, together with the nurse from the hospice, were the only people who joined him in attending the short ceremony. Before the coffin was put into the oven it was opened and the red plastic bag holding the corpse was undone, so that Don could place in it some coins, a flower and a letter that he had written, before sprinkling the body with scented water. As he looked at Mae Hom's head, which, despite its skeletal state, now wore a peaceful expression, he prayed for her forgiveness for the last time before closing up the bag. Then the four of them sat in front of the monks as they chanted and the coffin slid into the burning furnace. It was then that he could no longer hold back the tears.

CHAPTER 25

In the weeks that followed Nong Da's departure to Chiengmai (she was driven up in Gaew's pickup truck) the three of them saw each other every day. The consequences of the event at the cremation had pulled them tightly together. It was as though they had found a special friendship that each had been looking for and were discovering its strength together. Marisa introduced Khun Chai to the two men one evening in a bar on the rooftop of a skyscraper. Khun Chai had insisted that he wanted to meet them and Marisa thought that this would be a good way to dispel his jealousy. But by the time they met up Khun Chai was high and incoherent and the encounter was a disaster.

Afterwards Arun said:

"What are you doing with that guy? Mothering him?" Then realizing his rudeness he made to apologize. But Marisa laughed.

"You're very shrewd. That's exactly what I'm doing."

Marisa had planned the Loy Kratong party months before. She and Khun Chai wanted to use the occasion to thank the cast and crew of 'The Sad Killer'. She had considered taking them all to a resort on Goh Samet island but Khun Chai insisted that he did not want to leave Bangkok. When, a few days before the full moon Arun asked her whether she was still going to go ahead with it after what had happened, she told him curtly:

"Those who no longer want to be associated with me won't be there. It's as simple as that."

Despite the brave words she was nervous about the event and a part of her wished that there was some way of getting out of it. But she knew that if she were to cancel it that would again have shown her weakness and she would never again command their respect. She was grateful that both Don and Arun agreed to come along to give her moral support, knowing that behind the politeness and smiles they would all be gossiping about her that evening.

Marisa and Khun Chai had discussed the party at length. They had originally planned to hold it in a palace belonging to Khun Chai's aunt. It was a mansion built in the late nineteenth century by an Italian architect and its gardens sloped down to the river where there was a wide landing pier built for royal visits. It was the perfect setting, with plenty of room for the guests to float their *kratongs*.

But at the last minute the aunt called up and told Khun Chai that she was going to use it herself to hold a dinner for the French ambassador. Marisa suspected that this had everything to do with the revelations about her but she dared not confront Khun Chai about this. Instead, with customary efficiency, she hired a boat and a rock band and arranged the catering with the food and beverage manager of a five star hotel.

In the end she was glad that they had chosen the river trip. That evening, with the moon rising and a cool breeze brushing the surface of the water, they all climbed on board. The only person out of those she had invited who did not turn up was Ladda, who sent a note via her brother which read:

"Khun Marisa, I have been a fan of yours since I was a young girl. But what you did in protecting that evil woman who desecrated my uncle's coffin was unforgivable. I never want to see you again and I pray that our paths will not cross because I do not know if I shall be able to contain my anger towards you if we come face to face. As for my brother, I have also told him that from now on I am cutting off all ties with him. He might as well be dead."

When Marisa had finished reading it she handed it to Arun, saying:

"I'm sorry. This is so awful."

But Arun shook his head and smiled.

"No. This is just her style. She came round a few days ago and gave me a really bad time. One of her friends told her what happened that day and she went ballistic. But she'll calm down soon. You'll see."

The boat, which was one of those normally used by a tour company for their 'Romantic dinner on the river and temple sightseeing' package was called 'The Jewel of the Chao Phaya'. It was moored at the pier under Taksin Bridge. The eighty or so guests who turned up and went aboard were in the mood for a party. Khun Chai, who had been visiting his mother that afternoon, was the last to arrive and Marisa could tell from his gushing manner that he had stopped at one of his haunts on the way there. Nevertheless she felt pleased that nobody, other than Ladda, had let her down.

Everything went well. The wine flowed and the conversation sparkled. The guests were relaxed and enjoying themselves. There was no mention of the recent events until one of the makeup artists, a pretty man in his thirties stood up and shouted out:

"I want to propose a toast to Khun Marisa. I wish more people had the guts to come clean about her past the way she did."

There was clapping and cheering all round, which did not stop the gossip about her from being immediately resumed once the moment had passed.

The river was especially beautiful that evening and the festive atmosphere seemed to lift everyone's spirits. In the boats that passed them other revellers waved and shouted out greetings. On the banks, as the twilight gave way to the inky darkness the fairy lights that were hung in the riverside restaurants and hotels and temple gardens all came on. And then over one of the temple roofs and between two tall buildings they could see the full moon rising. It had a rainbow halo round it that evening.

They decided to stop at a temple up river after the buffet dinner and float their *kratongs* from there. By the time they arrived there was already a large crowd who had come by boat or who had driven out from Bangkok. It looked chaotic but there was room for everybody to eventually take their *kratongs* to the water's edge and say a prayer before floating them off. Street kids from a nearby orphanage were diving in to take these *kratongs* as soon as they drifted some way from the pier and steal the wishing coins from inside. One of the caretakers from the temple was shouting and threatening them with punishment but they laughed back at him. Elsewhere on the landing a group of well-dressed socialites, who had walked there from a dinner in a nearby restaurant, were waiting their turn holding champagne glasses. By the time that Marisa and her party had finished the moon was directly overhead.

The band struck up soon after they had all re-boarded and the boat had hoisted anchor. Most of the guests were high by now and nobody needed to be invited to dance. The lounge area was packed with writhing bodies. There was a sense of abandon in their movements. It was as though they were seizing the opportunity to let the wildness that they normally held in check out into the night.

Khun Chai did not enjoy dancing. It made him feel awkward and self conscious. He preferred to stay in the small office at the back, normally kept for storage, and watch the spectacle. With him was the makeup artist who had proposed the toast and a starlet who had been given a minor role in 'The Sad Killer'. They were sniffing cocaine and drinking whiskey and howling with laughter as they commented on the dancers and their furious antics.

On the deck at the back, Arun was bent down close to the floor sheltering from the breeze and lighting up a joint. When at last he straightened up a long stream of smoke emerged from his mouth, followed by a short dry cough.

"Do either of you want some of this?" he said stretching out his hand. But Marisa shook her head without answering and Don replied,

"No thanks. I'm an addict type. It's better not to start up again."

Arun shrugged indifferently and continued to suck on the joint. Then, after exhaling, he said:

"It's my medicine. It gets me through living in this city."

"Is it that bad?" asked Marisa playfully.

Arun laughed. "I know. There's nothing for us to complain of. Look at this scene. It is beautiful. We have everything. Not like most of the country. But that's the point. I'm not happy. I'm not even at ease."

"Maybe you should try meditation," said Marisa. "Like Don."

"Oh no. Don't listen to her. You often get much worse when you sit still and face yourself," said Don with a smile.

"But then you get better, don't you?"

"Sometimes. But it doesn't last. We come back to the same anxieties. That's the nature of Dukkha. It's just that we don't get so caught up."

Arun laughed louder than before.

"I think you should be a lay teacher of the Dhamma. I mean it. We need people like you. I can never understand what the monks are going on about. You make it sound simple."

"No. I'm a bad person."

"That's all the more reason. I don't trust the good ones."

"Seriously though," said Marisa. "What is it that stops you from being happy?"

"I can't answer you. That's the point. But you're the same as me. I can sense it. Don is different."

They sat for a long time that evening, sometimes talking, sometimes silent, enjoying each other's company and watching the moon hang in the sky.

The boat had gone up river well beyond Pakret. It was farther than the original schedule but Khun Chai insisted that they were having such a good time that the trip should be extended just a little longer and the captain, who had joined in the festivities, complied. On this stretch there were few dwellings on the river bank. The trees and the fields spread out on either side of the river were flooded by the silvery blue glow of the moonlight. Most of the guests had now come to cool off on deck and get some fresh air. It felt calm and peaceful. Only the sound of the engine and the occasional bird call that was answered by another. Soon the boat turned round and they were on their way back to the city.

Hardly anyone noticed at first. It was Khun Chai, coming up the steps who exclaimed,

"I may be a little wobbly but it feels like we're coming into a wave."

This drew a laugh. But within seconds they could all feel it. The boat was beginning to roll as if an undercurrent just below the surface was agitating the water. And then it felt as if they were on a stormy sea and people were holding on to the rails and to each other and some were shouting out nervously. At the same time they seemed to have entered a bank of fog which felt wet and clinging.

Marisa was clutching Arun's arm tightly. They were both sitting on the floor of the deck. She wanted to say something but the movement of the boat made it impossible. Don was standing next to them holding on to the flag mast and staring out into space as the boat continued to roll. He felt as though he had taken some drug which was making him see eyes and faces coming towards him out of the fog, and for a moment he remembered the night when, as a young teenager, he had an encounter with the water spirit, and he remembered too the dream he had in the monastery.

Then just as suddenly as it had begun the waves stopped. The river was calm again and the fog had lifted. One of the guests shouted out:

"What did you put in the cocktails?"

"When do we get back to the pier?" asked another.

Gradually they all made their way back down below deck. Marisa sought out the captain and asked him what had happened.

"I don't know," he replied. "But I've seen it before in other parts of the river. The people who live on the banks say it's the Naga. The fog and the swell of the river are signs that he is on the move. They take it as a bad omen."

There was a sense of relief all round when they approached the lights of the city.

PART 4

CHAPTER 26

It was now six months later. The cold season—what there was of it—had come and gone. April had brought the hottest two week spell that had ever been recorded in the country and the drought that cracked open the land looked set to hurt the crops badly. This meant that the peasants in the far provinces on the Laos and Cambodian border would suffer and the number of those coming to the capital looking for work would once more swell the ranks of the poor who were already jostling for work. A year earlier the economy looked stable. But those who made the financial decisions on the global arena decided that China, despite its political contradictions, its natural disasters which seemed to be a yearly occurrence, and the epidemics that followed, was after all now ripe for picking. And so in a short space of time the investment managers, guided by the great god of profit, diverted their funds in that direction, with the result that Thai factories were closing down overnight and the manufacturing sector in particular looked set to collapse. All of this was little short of disastrous for the recently elected prime minister, who had made a strong, and probably foolhardy, promise of eradicating poverty entirely within his term of office.

The reason that his party had won at all was not because the voters believed in these grand words, delivered with the confidence of a demagogue, nor that they were impressed by his record as a politician. In the distant past, when he was still an officer in the army he had been a member of a group that had failed in a coup attempt. And once, while minister of public works in a later government, he had appeared before a judicial enquiry into the mishandling of funds in his ministry. But what swung opinion in his favour was the public's disenchantment with the previous government. And much of this was due to the revelations that the Pi O scandal had thrown up and the subsequent mishandling of the murder enquiry, which ended up with ministers in the cabinet accusing one another of corruption. Finally, a major conflict arose between the army and the police force, which threatened to turn nasty had not the government, following a rare vote of no confidence, resigned and new elections declared.

As if reflecting the political chaos and the worries about the economy and all the confusion in the air, Marisa's life, over the same period, seemed to be unsteady and insecure. Although she managed to weather the repercussions of the incident at Pi O's cremation and her subsequent confessions and come through relatively unscathed, Khun Chai's family used the information that she had made public to pressurize him into cutting off both business and emotional ties with her. Since his income was a matter decided by the family trust and controlled largely by the lawyers, under instruction from the aunt who had always mistrusted Marisa's motives—the same one who refused them use of the palace at the last minute—the pressure was not merely a question of dishing out moral judgment but completely practical. It was explained to him, not too subtly, that if he did not stop seeing Marisa he would not be given further access to the considerable sums that he demanded to keep his production company afloat.

When Khun Chai related all of this to her, over a dinner in a recently opened Japanese restaurant on the twenty seventh floor of Bangkok Towers, Marisa knew from the way that he fiddled with his food and the fact that he was completely sober that evening that he had already capitulated to them. He told her that he did not know what to do, which she read as "I'm sorry but my own well being comes first and I am going to have to sacrifice you for it." She did not give him a hard time or start to say unpleasant things about his family which she felt like doing. Instead she controlled her anger and agreed with him. His aunt was right, she said, in being concerned for the family's reputation and she understood how her conduct and the things that they now knew about her must have shocked them. Nevertheless there was the slight problem of how to settle the business arrangements they had made in a correct way. She spoke gently with him and they ended the meal on a friendly note, talking about the success of 'The Sad Killer', which now looked as if it would their one and only joint venture.

At home that night Marisa went through many emotions. Khun Chai's words had come as a complete surprise and caught her off balance. From what they had been discussing recently, and the plans they had made to begin production of a new film in less than a month, it seemed unfair that he should now spring this on her. But from the way he talked and his whole demeanour she could tell that he himself was innocent in the matter and that he had reverted to the fearful little boy that she knew him to be. She blamed his aunt for her meanness and snobbery and for the power she had over him. And she blamed him for being so weak and selfish as to give in to them so easily. And, of course, she blamed herself for being a fool again in thinking that she was secure and protected.

It was not like with Eduardo. where she felt betrayed and used. For, if anything, it had been her this time who had been the manipulator. And yet there was a feeling of regret that things between her and Khun Chai were going to end in this way. For even though she was never in love with Khun Chai, she had developed a fondness for him which had become a habit that after three years was going to be hard to break.

But she was determined not to let the situation pull her down. Her anger would be her energy. She was not going to be their victim. In her mind she was already making plans to salvage not only her pride but also the financial debt that she felt she was owed. She cursed herself for having let Khun Chai's family lawyer have any part in drawing up the agreement establishing the company. She would have to wait till the morning before seeking the advice of her own lawyer and studying the fine print of the contract once more. If it was going to be dragged through the courts then she was ready for battle.

The more she thought about it the more hopeful she felt about her chances of winning at least a decent settlement, despite the circumstances and the influence that Khun Chai's family had. She, who had nothing to lose any more, had a trump card and this was Khun Chai's drug addiction, which was well known all over Bangkok but which would be welcome fodder for the press and devastating to the family's image. It felt unpleasant to be thinking this way about a man whose bed she had shared only twenty four hours earlier. But she had learned that to survive there had to be a willingness to cut away all sentimentality. This was what Pi O kept telling her in those early years. Still, despite her positive attitude there was a lot of doubt and insecurity in her mind as to the outcome of breaking up professionally with Khun Chai and it was because of this that she allowed herself to be persuaded by her maid, Mae Nee, to consult a seer.

CHAPTER 27

The exact number of fortune tellers who ply their trade in Bangkok has never been established, but even the casual visitor will be immediately aware that there is an army of them spread throughout the city. They sit, these men and women, in hotel lobbies, on noisy pavements, in a corner of a temple courtyard, in a small glass booth on a landing pier, under a shady tree in Suan Lumpini, at a counter in a shopping mall, anywhere that they can lay out a table or a small stall that advertises their activity, as though they have been there since time began, and they never have to wait too long before a client walks up for a consultation. Their job of telling the future is done by a number of methods. They use the charts of Thai astrology, or read a face according to the Chinese tradition. They throw sticks, or interpret from a pack of cards, or refer to the palm of the hand as the psychic map. Several are known to rely on their laptop computers to yield the patterns that contained the information they require. Or they may simply devise their own method and hope for the best; that is to say, that their intuition and guesswork will be near to the mark, which need not be the truth but should be what the client wants and needs to hear. Everybody except the most hardened skeptics uses them. They have a role that is well beyond that of soothsayer. In fact, nobody cares much whether the advice dispensed is right or wrong. The point of their popularity is that they are not there merely to make predictions. Their main task is to listen and to mirror back the clients' hopes and fears and expectations, to reassure and sometimes to warn them. The modern fortune teller's role is somewhere between a priest and a therapist and as such indispensable to a population that feels insecure in the shifting coordinates of the cityscape. The consultation is the context in which men and women can tell their story and unburden the conflicts and doubts of their souls.

This is not to deny that, either through natural talent or through the skilful reading of the signs, be it the movement of the stars, the lines on a hand, the numbers that come through the cards, a fortune teller sometimes manages to transcend the linear illusion of time and, in what seems an impossible way,

accurately and vividly foretell what is to come. And of course everyone who
has ever consulted one will swear that his or her seer got it right.

Mae Nee, Marisa's maid, was a religious person. She went to the temple
every holy day to pray to the Buddharupa and to give offerings of candles,
flowers and incense. She tried to live by the Eight Precepts, ate vegetarian
food once a week and during the rainy season. Like most of the public she did
not see the contradiction between consulting fortune tellers and her Buddhist
beliefs. The woman who she liked to consult would come once a month to the
temple where Mae Nee went to worship, which was in Thonburi, just across
the river from Marisa's condo. This woman, whose name was Yai Lek, came
from Ayudhya and had relatives in the area. She was not really a full time
professional seer, but she was grateful for the extra cash that was offered her for
a consultation. Whenever she was in Bangkok Mae Nee would make a point
of arranging to meet her in the courtyard of the temple where they would
sit under the large banyan tree. Mae Nee, whose life, unlike her employer's,
hardly ever strayed from the predictable routine that she had known for all
of the fifteen years that she had been in Bangkok and worked for Marisa, did
not, at first glance, have anything which could have necessitated the advice of
a fortune teller. But she enjoyed the meetings, which over the years became a
high point to each month. Having nothing pressing to ask from the fortune
teller, Mae Nee had for a long time consulted her on Marisa's behalf. This was,
of course, with Marisa's full knowledge and approval. In fact, Marisa would
sometimes provide Mae Nee with the questions to put to the old woman. For
example she had asked for advice about Khun Chai and was told that this
was going to be the love of her life. But later this misreading was offset by her
accurate assurance that 'The Sad Killer' was going to be successful.

For a long time Mae Nee had seen how badly things were going between
Marisa and Khun Chai. She had begun by being fond of Khun Chai but now
she could not tolerate his drunkenness and the drug taking and the way that
he treated her mistress. It made her angry to see her being humiliated by his
family, when she had done all she could to help him.

That month, on the morning that the woman was going to be at the
temple, Mae Nee went along ready with the questions clear in her mind,

and she was almost certain how Yai Lek would answer her. But that day something odd happened. The woman was sitting on the stone bench under the banyan tree, as usual. Mae Nee approached her and waied respectfully, but before she could say anything the woman told her that she was not going to give a consultation.

"It would be disrespectful of me to do so while the real one is here, in the city," she said cryptically. Mae Nee looked puzzled.

"Compared to him I know nothing," the woman went on. "I just use my intuition. But the Phaya Naak, he's the one. I've seen him. He's the real one who has the power. I've been to his meetings in Ayudhya. They've brought him down here to Bangkok because some rich widow wants to consult him. He's here in the city right now and I can feel his presence. Do you understand?"

Mae Nee had never heard Yai Lek, who she had come to respect, speak in this way before and it made her both nervous and curious. She made the woman tell her about this mysterious seer and found out that he was not like the others. He did not read the stars or the cards but was a medium who went into a deep trance.

"Whatever you have to ask, go to him. Go to the Phaya Naak. He will tell you. But you have to have *satha* (faith) if you go. It's not for the faint hearted. He does healing too. He can set bones. He can exorcise ghosts who have taken over your body. There's nothing that he can't do."

Before they parted company the woman gave Mae Nee the address of where the meeting with the Phaya Naak was going to take place.

CHAPTER 28

It was usually after work, in the evening, that they met, either in a bar or a Chinese restaurant or at the studio, or in Marisa's condo by the river. Then, over a glass of wine or a meal, as though they had not been apart, the conversation would carry on where it had left off. They talked about everything under the sun and argued about politics and bitched about film stars and put down other artists. They enjoyed each other's company to such an extent that during that intense initial period of involvement with one another, when no desire had yet raised its head, they seemed to share a friendship from which the world was excluded. Not that they were unaware of the terrible things that were going on all around them. In their own country the constant threat of terrorism was now at their doorstep. Two bombs had gone off in recent months, destroying a warehouse and part of a shopping mall. The economy was in a mess after the cycle of boom had come to an abrupt end. Elsewhere in the world there was war and conflict and suffering. They were conscious of all this through the papers and the magazines that they read and the television and the car radio but somehow the new found closeness that they had for one another seemed, for a time to envelop them in an invisible bubble that kept the rawness of the outside reality at bay.

When Marisa told them about the seer and how Mae Nee had learned that he was going to give a session in the city, the men's reactions were mixed. Arun said that he had never consulted anyone in his life and that he was not really interested in doing so. But Mae Nee, who was asked to pass on to them the information she had been given, explained that the man who was coming was not an ordinary fortune teller. He was a medium who went into trance and became the mouthpiece of the Naga spirit. This made Arun laugh loudly, but he admitted that he was intrigued.

"Well then you can come with me," Marisa declared. "Both of you."

"Oh no. Not me," said Don quickly. "I've seen that kind of thing up in the north-east."

But in the end he let himself be persuaded by Marisa, who told him that she would feel more secure if he went along.

"Why? Are you afraid?" he asked.

"Yes, a little. Besides, with your experience you can tell us what you think of him."

So, despite his protestations, Don joined the party that evening.

During the ride they remained silent. There was an atmosphere of shared anticipation. The traffic was light and the streets seemed unusually empty. As they crossed the bridge that took them over to Thonburi, Arun, who had been restless and fidgety since getting into the car, suddenly said to them,

"I'm not sure we should go through with this."

"It's too late to back out," Marisa told him in a tone of mock annoyance. "My God, you're complicated!"

$$\sim\!\!\!=\!\!\!\dagger\!\!\!=\!\!\!\sim$$

It took them a couple of detours down dead end streets before they found the house they were looking for. Mae Nee had been given a phone number as well as the address and when Marisa had called earlier to ask if they could attend the session the man who answered sounded suspicious and uncooperative.

"This is only for those who are sincere," he said. "It's not a show." Then, when she insisted, he gave her the directions, which turned out to be less than precise.

Marisa was still wondering what he had meant about being sincere when intuitively she recognized that they had come to the right place. They were in a narrow soi. There were a few cars parked along a tall wooden fence over which thick bougainvillea tumbled. There was a gate that looked as though a small push could have broken it. A bell hung off a beam on the right hand post.

"This is it," she declared confidently.

"But how do you know? There's no number marked anywhere," said Arun.

"You'll see," she replied as they climbed out of the car.

Before any of them had time to pull on the bell, the gate was opened by a young maid wearing a black tee shirt and a sarong, who waied them wordlessly and then immediately turned her back in order to lead them inside, even before they had told her who they were. It was as if she had been expecting their arrival that very minute.

The house was a two storey building in the style of the mansions built in the early 1900s and it was obvious from first glance that it had seen better days. Even in the dim light they could see that the paint was flaking. The steps leading up to the front door were broken. The door itself was padlocked. The shutters looked as though they would fall off their hinges at any time. A garden stood to one side of the house like a wild, dark jungle. The yard into which they stepped from the road smelt of cat's pee. The impression was that it was not a place where anyone had lived for a very long time.

The young girl led them round to the back of the house. She walked quickly ahead. The only light provided was by the streetlamp outside. Marisa almost tripped and held Arun's hand to break her fall. As she did so she felt the cold sweat on his palm and instinctively she squeezed him tighter to reassure him. She suddenly remembered a scene from one of the films she had made many years before; a ghost story set in a haunted house. For a moment it brought a smile to her face, because in it the hero had been the one to persuade the girl that all was well.

Behind the main house there was a short covered pathway, paved with bricks, that led to the servants' quarters and the kitchen. This was a low building with a tiled roof. In the two windows on either side of the doorway there shone a dim, flickering light. The girl pointed to where they were to leave their shoes and then, still without saying a word, opened the door for them.

It took a few seconds to adjust their eyes. The room, which was long and rectangular, was lit only by the candles that were lined along an altar, which consisted of a Buddharupa surrounded by vases full of flowers, bowls of rice, various dishes and fruit of all descriptions. In the four corners, as well as on the altar itself, big clumps of incense sticks were burning away and the thick perfumed smoke hit the newcomers as they entered.

Whatever ceremony that was taking place had already begun. The room was not completely full. There was still some space at the back by the door and it was here that Marisa and her friends quickly sat down on the floor like the rest of them, on the reed mat that had been laid out. A few faces turned round and one or two people nodded towards them in acknowledgment of their arrival. Marisa felt immediately uncomfortable being there, and she knew that her companions felt the same. The atmosphere was not unfriendly, but neither was it welcoming. And it was evident that they were outsiders to the group because everyone present in that room that evening was wearing black. She felt annoyed that the person she had spoken to had not told her the etiquette.

There was one person who wore white. He was seated crossed legged on a low dais in front of the altar with his back to them all and everybody's attention was on him. It was impossible to see anything of the man's face, and the only reason that they could tell that it was a male figure was because they had been told. For down to his waist there hung a length of hair that seemed to have been folded up and back over again, woven and platted together into a thick mesh. His broad back and powerful shoulders were hunched over and from the position of his elbows it looked like he was holding his hands together in prayer. For a while there was no sound in that room except the spitting of a candle flame as a moth or an insect touched it, and the occasional almost indistinct sound of a car engine, and somewhere in the distance came the moan of a ship's siren. But other than that the silence in the room seemed to buzz and hum.

Then very gently the man's voice began to be heard. It was a whisper at first, which slowly grew into a deep resonant tone, which, although not loud, filled the whole space and echoed from the four walls. He was chanting in a language which seemed both familiar and totally alien. It was not the Pali of the Buddhist scriptures, nor Sanskrit, nor Chinese and its rhythms and cadences were subtle. This went on for about a quarter of an hour, Then suddenly the man stopped in what sounded like mid sentence, clapped his hands three times then abruptly turned round towards them. This gesture made a few people gasp.

In the candlelight it was impossible to tell what age he was. His face was flat and broad, the features reminiscent of a Khmer sculpture. His eyes were closed but his mouth was moving as though he was still chanting in silence. Every now and then he would shake his head vigourously from side to side and as he did so his whole body seemed to roll with the movement. After he had done this several times a woman got up, without any prompting and quickly gathered all the candles that were burning on the altar, stuck them into a flower pot filled with sand and brought them to him. Still with eyes closed, the medium then put both his hands into the flames and held them there for a while before pulling them away and holding them up in the air for everyone, presumably, to see that there were no burn marks on them.

Now the same woman took the pot of candles and put it back on the altar, then went behind him and fetched a large metal bowl which seemed to be almost too heavy for her to carry. This she placed in front of where he was sitting and he bent down and plunged his hands into it. A collective shudder went through the assembly as if the moment they had been waiting for had arrived. The man began drawing the water up with his fingers and then letting it drop again into the bowl. It looked as though he were pulling up silvery sheets of silk and then letting them crumble down. And he went on doing this until the sound made by his motion was like that of monsoon rain falling steadily all round them. Then he stopped, opened his almond shaped eyes and very slowly gazed round staring into each person's face as he did so. On his own features there was a blankness that in another context might have been taken for indifference or even an absence of any awareness. But it was not so because his vibrant presence seemed to fill the room.

Carefully he now picked up the metal bowl and put it to his lips and from it he took a big gulp of the water. As he did so those sitting near to him bowed their heads to the floor in expectation of what they knew was about to take place. The medium now blew the water with the full force of his breath into the air. This action was repeated three times before he put the bowl down. Still crossed legged he then began to rock back and forth. His body started to twitch uncontrollably and tremble like a leaf. As it did so his eyes rolled back till the whites were clearly visible, while his tongue flicked and darted out from his lips like that of a lizard.

"The Naga is here. He has entered," said a man sitting to their right, addressing no-one in particular, and several people nodded their agreement. Marisa noticed the nervous expressions around her and the way that many of the people seemed to be moving in time to the man's rhythms.

One last stretch of the torso and suddenly the man, the Naga, had slithered off the dais and onto the floor where he lay on his belly. For a moment he was perfectly still as those around him hurriedly made way for him to move. Then with deliberate movements at first the Naga began to uncoil and gently writhe and undulate and finally to begin crossing the floor. As he passed the men and women would put their hands up to wai and bend their heads as if they were receiving a blessing. Some responded with a show of emotional devotion. One woman shouted out incoherently. A young man buried his head in his hands and wept uncontrollably. Through the room there was movement. People were craning their heads to see what was going on. Others were shifting their positions as the Naga came close to them.

Marisa, Arun, Don and Mae Nee, being at the back of the room, had not really seen what was happening once the man had come off the dais, but all of a sudden the space parted and the Naga was there in front of them, looking like a giant white python creeping towards them.

⟫⟨

Afterwards each would remember the whole event and in particular those moments of proximity to the Naga oracle quite differently. But one thing that they agreed on was that, as the Naga approached them, they could hear the sound of water flowing, like a steady gurgling stream. And also that the air suddenly smelled not of the incense that was burning but of green slime that was fetid, yet alive. As he came up to Mae Nee, she shut her eyes tight, put up her hands to shield herself and pressed her back against the wall. Don remained impassively watching the scene before him, without moving or showing any reaction. Arun, who had his hands clasped around his knees, tensed up as he felt the Naga brush over his bare feet.

Marisa was in the corner with her hands together like most of those assembled. As the Naga drew close to her he paused. His body rippled from head to toe and a hissing sound came from his lips. Marisa was not afraid, but she felt herself pulled towards him by a magnetic force, and in the next moment her face was next to his, almost touching the floor. She was looking down so she did not see his expression as he stretched his neck and put his mouth to her ear. And again all those around could hear the same hissing sound. Then he left her and continued his journey round the room, writhing and slithering, stopping here and there to do the same thing as he had done to her.

Later, when they were back home and comparing notes, they established that the performance (Don's word) had taken over half an hour. But at the time it seemed to pass in a minute. Suddenly the Naga was back in front of the dais, lying still, with his arms pinned to his side. The same woman who had held the candles for him and delivered the bowl of water now stepped up once more and poured the remaining liquid down the length of his spine. At first there was no response, but then the figure lying on the floor stirred and with laborious movements sat up. The woman helped him to his feet. Everyone could see that his clothes were all wet and bedraggled and his long hair loosened from its clips now stuck out in all directions. There was an air of collapse about him now that the ritual was over. Quickly he went onto his knees and bowed three times to the Buddharupa before being led, unsteadily, out through a side door by his helper.

Within less than a quarter of an hour they were back out in the soi in front of the house. Not a word had been exchanged between any of those who had attended the session except a brief goodnight at the gate. It seemed that everyone was eager to part company and make their way homeward.

CHAPTER 29

It was only when they had got back to the condo and Mae Nee was serving them tea that they began to discuss what had happened. Arun, in an aggressive tone, said:

"I can't believe in all that rubbish."

"What do you mean?" asked Marisa.

"Well, it was all a fake, wasn't it? I thought he was going to make some pronouncement about the future. You told me he was an oracle. And where was the healing? All I saw was a rather overweight man who needed a haircut more than I do wiggling around all over the floor."

Finding his own observation funny, Arun began to laugh. Mae Nee, who looked offended by his remarks, stopped pouring the tea and answered him.

"You don't know what you're talking about. And I saw how nervous you were, like the rest of us. And I'm sure that you heard the sound of water. That's his trademark."

"All right Mae Nee," said Arun still laughing. "I'm sorry. I didn't mean to upset you. But as for being nervous, I admit that I was, even before arriving there. I'm the anxious type. I often scare myself for no reason. And as far as the water's concerned, I think that it might have been a machine at the back piping that sound into the room."

"So you got nothing out of it?" said Marisa to him, with a slight annoyance in her voice.

"Wrong! It was a great scene. I really enjoyed it and it's given me a lot of ideas for my next work. It was the bullshit I'm referring to."

"What about you, Don? Did you think he was a fraud?"

"A fraud? No. But I told you. I've seen this kind of thing before up in the north-east. There was definitely some power. I felt it, or at least thought I did. And I don't know where it comes from or what it's all about. And I once had a dream to do with the Naga spirit. Tonight's session brought it back to me. But my old abbot used to warn us not to play around with these things. because there was so much danger of getting lost. He said that it was all just *nimitti*."

"But the man really did go into trance," Mae Nee insisted.

"Oh yes, Mae Nee. He did. But then I think he was also a bit of a showman."

"By the way, don't think you're going to get away with it," said Arun turning to Marisa and wagging his finger. "What did he whisper in your ear? Was he giving you his phone number?"

Marisa was glad that Arun had made a joke out of it because the truth was that she did not feel ready to share with them what had just happened to her. It was nothing to do with wanting to keep it a secret to her self. But she could not find the right words. She needed time to mull it over.

That night after they had left she went out onto the balcony and looked down at the river. The effect of what had happened to her was still fresh in her mind.

When the Naga had slithered towards her she felt a moment of repulsion, as though she were about to be molested and raped by this white reptile. But when he paused before her she felt that every cell in her body went into a sort of calm ecstasy and her heart wanted to cry. When she bent down she, in fact, wanted to kiss him and join herself with him. The hissing went through her as if he had penetrated her and in it she heard the words:

"Soon. Soon. Don't be frightened when the time comes. There are other journeys ahead."

She could not be certain whether the words that she had heard during the evening had come from his mouth or from her own heart. But they were so clear.

She still did not understand the message but she knew that something had changed inside her from that meeting with the Naga oracle and that her time on earth would never be the same as it was before.

PART 5

CHAPTER 30

It was difficult for Arun to make out exactly what Gaew was trying to tell him over the telephone, not only because he had just woken up but because of the crackle on the line and the sobbing that punctuated her words. From what he could make out Nong Da was missing. She had gone out to the market the previous evening and not returned.

"It's my fault. It's all my fault," said Gaew tearfully. "We had an argument and I slapped her."

"You had an argument?" It took him a few seconds to register the implication of these words. Then Arun, now fully awake, shouted down the phone. "But that means that she's speaking."

"She's been speaking for a few months."

"But why didn't you tell me?"

"Because you didn't call me to ask. This is the first time we've been in touch for ages. You just left her for me to take care of her and that's what I've been doing. I didn't think I was under any obligation to report to you, since you didn't seem interested enough to come up here and visit her yourself."

Arun immediately felt ashamed by her accusation, because it was true. He had thought that his responsibilities were over once he had persuaded Gaew to take her up north. He felt sure that Gaew would do a good job of it and that there was no need to worry about Nong Da. And the truth was that he could not handle dealing with Gaew any more. Worst of all was that, although he had insisted to Don and Marisa that he would be the one to keep in touch with Gaew about Nong Da, he had done nothing of the sort. Whenever they had asked him, he had told them that she was doing fine at the centre with Gaew. Every time that Don had volunteered to take the weekend off and go up to Chiengmai to visit Nong Da, Arun had dissuaded him, saying that Gaew would tell them when it was the right time to go, and then they would make the trip together. Nearly a year had passed.

He now felt both stupid and ashamed for having told these pointless white lies, which were a childish tactic to protect himself against any criticism of being uninterested and irresponsible. The only flimsy excuse that he could have offered was that he had been so wrapped up in his own projects over the past months that he had not noticed how quickly time had passed.

"How has she been doing?" he asked quietly.

There was a long pause at the other end.

"Well. Very well considering what she went through."

Gaew did not tell him the details.

"Have you been to the police?"

"No. That's not a good idea. She has no papers."

"Well then we'll just have to sit it out and wait."

"We?"

"You. I'm sorry. Yes. OK. I'm sorry. If you want me to go up to Chiengmai and help find her I will."

"No, it's all right. You stay there painting your pretty pictures."

With that she slammed the phone down.

⸺❖⸺

Arun called the others later the same day. He did not want to tell them over the phone what had happened, so he invited them to have dinner at his place. They had not seen each other much recently. The months had flown by. Whenever they had planned to get together, one or another of them could not make it and they knew that it would not feel right for only two of them to meet. The telephone conversations which, at the start of their friendship, were long and descriptive were now confined to short informative exchanges. Nowadays they all seemed to be constantly busy. Marisa was producing a series for television. Don had found work with an NGO called 'Clean Thailand', and Arun himself was trying to sort out the final bits and pieces before preparing to leave for France, where he had recently been offered a three months' residency in Paris.

"Is this a farewell dinner?" asked Marisa as soon as she picked up the phone.

"Partly," he answered. "My application got accepted."

"Great! Congratulations. When are you off?"

"Oh. Not for a little while."

"It'll be good to get a break from Bangkok, won't it?"

"Yes. I'm sick of it here right now. I need some fresh air. I've run out of inspiration and ideas here. I've been painting scenes of decadence and corruption for too long. I need to get a new perspective on things."

⁌ ‡ ⁍

Even though they had not seen each other for a while the three of them immediately recovered the original intimacy that had brought them close. Inevitably the subject of Nong Da soon came up. Arun confessed to them his negligence and the way he had been dishonest.

"I guess it's because you didn't have time to deal with it," said Marisa. But Don was upset that Arun had fooled them into thinking that he was in touch.

"I know. I know. And you have every right to give me a hard time," said Arun. "But I'm trying to be honest with you now. And it's a big step for me to tell you all this. Please forgive me for having been so stupid, I should have been straight with you in the first place. I don't know why I did that. It's a bad habit. I chose what I thought was the easy way out again."

"We're all like that. It's very Thai, too, not to be straightforward," said Don. "But as friends we should be simple with each other and not behave like we've always done, out of fear of hurting or disappointing, tiptoeing around the truth, Thai style. We've been so well taught to behave like that. But let's not do it from now on. That's all I ask, if we're to go on being friends. If there's something to say, however difficult it is, let's just take the risk of saying it."

"You're right. As usual," said Arun.

⁌ ‡ ⁍

"And so how is Nong Da?" asked Don, later, when the moment of tension had passed. "On the phone you said you had news of her from Gaew."

This time Arun smiled broadly like a child being given the go-ahead to tell a secret, at last.

"Well, as a matter of fact she's here. She arrived this afternoon after I called you. She borrowed some money off another girl at the centre, took the bus and made her way here. I don't know how she found this place. She must have looked in Gaew's address book or something."

"But how...?"

"Oh. And she's speaking," he added.

"What?" they both shouted. "And where is she?"

"She's in the spare room, resting. I told her that you were both coming. I think she's a little nervous of seeing us all together again."

"So she's come back. And she's talking. I was convinced that she was deaf and dumb. And how does she look?" asked Marisa excitedly.

"You wouldn't recognize her. She's beautiful. I thought so that day in the taxi. But now she's well. She's really stunning."

"And the scar?"

"That's what I find beautiful."

"I want to know what happened to her before we met her. And what made her want to speak again."

"Yes, me too," said Don who had been quietly digesting the news. "But we mustn't rush her. She'll tell us in good time."

"I just want to see her again," said Marisa.

At that moment, on queue, Nong Da appeared in the doorway.

"I'm here," she said quietly. Her voice had a northern lilt.

⁓‡⁓

During the meal they shared that evening, which went on till long after midnight, Nong Da told them her story, not once raising her eyes, speaking slowly and in a voice that trembled with emotion from time to time. She said that she wanted them to know her past so that they would not think badly about what she had done on the day of Pi O's ceremony, that they would understand that she had not been herself when she committed the ugly act. She wanted them to know the truth about her because they had been kind enough to come to her rescue. Her story was all that she could give them in return.

CHAPTER 31

Nong Da was born as Joon Saengdao. Her mother was nineteen years old when she came from Chiengkong to Bangkok to work as a domestic servant. It was the driver in the same household who made her pregnant. The man was already married and his wife, who suspected from the beginning that her husband was going after the new girl, threatened to kill both of them when she found out. So Nong Da's mother left and went to work in a squid canning factory in Klongtoey. But she had to leave the job a couple months before Nong Da was born. At the time she was sharing a room with a friend she had made at work. But when the baby came the friend asked her to leave and, having no family either in the city or back in Chiengkong, she ended up in a hostel in the Laadprao district for young unmarried mothers, run by a local women's group. All of this Nong Da learned from her mother, as she was too young to remember.

Her own memories begin when they had already left the hostel and were living in a cheap condo in the same area. By now she was nearly four and she hardly saw her mother during this period. An old 'auntie' was paid to look after her. She did not understand why until she was a little older. During the day she was taken to this auntie's place round the corner, so that her mother could sleep, and then for about an hour in the afternoon she was taken back home and it was then that they played or watched TV together. Just before it got dark her mother would shower and get dressed and make herself up to look glamourous, like the singers and the stars they watched on the TV shows, and then they would go downstairs where the auntie would be waiting again. And her mother would hug and kiss Nong Da and tell her to be a good girl before climbing on the back of a motorbike, or, if it was the rainy season, into a taxi that was waiting. Wednesday was her mother's day off. Nong Da loved the sound of that day. She knew it was somehow related to the Buddha and that it was sacred, because it meant that she was with her mother all day. Sometimes they would go shopping in the big mall on the main road, and her mother would buy her clothes and toys and jewelry to wear. And they would have a meal together and order ice cream.

This routine went on until Nong Da was eight. Then her mother got ill. The cough that Nong Da had noticed for over a month suddenly became much worse, because of the cool damp weather. For a week she had to lie in bed and send Nong Da out to the pharmacy to buy medicine for her. Then when she was feeling better she went back to work again. But she still looked tired and soon the coughing came back. One morning Nong Da found her collapsed in the bathroom. The neighbours helped to send for an ambulance, which took her to a hospital where they put a needle in her arm and gave her saline solution. But it was too late. Her mother never came round again. The doctor told her that her mother had water in her lungs and other complications which she did not understand. At the cremation she was surprised that so many people turned up. She had met some of her mother's friends over the years. But there were many men and women there who told her that they had worked with her mother in the same club. Some of them were crying.

It was at the cremation that she met Pi O for the first time. He came in a chauffeur-driven limousine and he wore a dark suit and tie. He brought with him a big wreath, which one of his assistants placed near the coffin, before the monks started their chanting.

After the ceremony somebody took her hand and led her to where he was sitting. She remembered thinking that she did not like his moustache. He reached towards her and cupped his hand under her chin and looked at her seriously.

"You're a very good looking little girl," he said. "Your mother was a good person. We were all her friends. We're all sad that she's died. But she's in heaven now. She won't suffer any more."

Up till then Nong Da had not cried. It had all seemed unreal. She had not fully understood that her mother was never going to be there again for her. But when she heard his words and felt the kindness behind them she burst into tears and he held her close to him.

Later she was put into the back of his car next to Pi O, who she was told to call Khun Ah O. She remembered how they did not speak but he kept looking at her and smiling. Just before they reached home, he said to her:

"You're too young to be alone. Will you come and live with me? I will look after you. Your mother would have liked that. She told me to look after you."

Nong Da was over the moon. Suddenly all her fears evaporated. Khun Ah O was going to look after her and protect her. The auntie must have already been told because she had Nong Da's clothes and toys all neatly packed into two suitcases, and as they said goodbye she smiled and said:

"Be a good girl." These were the very words that her mother had always used.

That evening Nong Da was driven to a big white mansion in Minburi. On arriving there she found that there were a dozen other girls staying there, all of them a little older than her. They all seemed to know that she was coming. Khun Ah O introduced her to them one by one and explained how she was to be the new member of the household. And then turning to her he said that the girls had all lost their parents too and that he was taking care of them in the same way that he was going to take care of her.

"You're all happy here, aren't you?" he asked them and they all nodded or shouted out:

"We're very happy!"

⟫⟨

The mansion, which was called Baan Ying, became Nong Da's home for the next six years. It was a building that was straight out of a movie. There was a huge electrically operated gate, decorated with elaborate dragons, above which a security camera hung. Then a driveway flanked by bushes shaped into all kinds of animals. There were big columns at the covered entrance, which led to marble floors, a big wooden staircase, sofas covered with silk, lace curtains over the windows, chandeliers, soft piped music which Khun Ah O liked to have permanently playing in all his establishments, to sooth the nerves and keep things calm. Outside, in the immaculately kept grounds, there was a swimming pool with an alabaster statue in the middle. And all around the property there was a high fence to keep out the thieves.

During that time Nong Da shared a room with a girl called Pi Noi, who was ten years old and who, from the beginning, became like an elder sister to her. Pi Noi had been there for a year. She told Nong Da that her parents were not dead but were in jail for drug dealing, and that they had not taken care of her because they were both addicts. She did not know how they were connected to Khun Ah O, but she was grateful to him for taking her in.

She was happy in Baan Ying and felt lucky to be there. And in those first months Nong Da too could not quite believe her luck. She could have been in paradise itself.

Pi Noi initiated her into the routine of the place and she soon felt at home. The sadness over the loss of her mother quickly receded into the background and she set about coping with her day to day existence, with a diligence born out of the gratitude that she felt towards Ah O. Her new life was different from what she had known in Laadprao. There she had never been expected to do anything according to a schedule. But at Baan Ying the daily rhythm was fixed and all the girls had to adhere to it or be punished by having to clean up or not being allowed to watch television. The woman in charge was called Yai Toom and she looked ancient, with grey hair tied back in a bun, wrinkled skin and bags under her eyes. It was she who decided on the punishments. Even though she was old and could not walk very well, they were scared of her when she raised her voice and cursed or threatened to tell Khun Ah what they had done. But really, most of the time, she was a kind old woman who gave them sweets and cuddled the younger ones. Under her there was a staff of six, including a cook and her niece, who also helped in the kitchen, a gardener, a woman who helped clean and who went to the market, and two drivers; all in all four women and three men who lived in a building separate from the main house.

In the morning they would be up by six thirty if it was term time and a little later during the holidays. They would bathe and dress and tidy their rooms before having breakfast. Then it was the school run in the two white vans. They all went to the same school in Minburi, where they were known as the Baan Ying girls. This created a sense of solidarity between them, so that if any of them got into trouble or a fight one of them would always be there to give support. Nong Da was nervous at first about attending a new school, but she soon felt that she belonged to a family and this gave her a sense of security that she had not known till then. Back from school and it was shower time before a period of homework, which was overseen by Yai Toom herself. Whoever finished could then go outside to play or swim or watch television before supper. And then it was lights out by eight. On weekends they were taken by May, the cook's helper, to the market or out to a shopping mall, sometimes to the local movie theatre. In the holidays they were sometimes taken to a villa resort near Pattaya, where they would spend a week by the sea.

It was strange, but Nong Da could not remember Khun Ah O being around much during this time. When she first arrived at Baan Ying she had thought that, since it was his house, she would see him every day. But she was told soon afterwards that he lived in a condo in town, that he was a very busy man. His visits were never expected. Coming back from school they might find him sitting in the kitchen, sipping tea, talking to Yai Toom. Or he would turn up on a Saturday evening and watch television for a while and chat to them. He sometimes brought tee shirts for them to share out or a case full of trainers. And he would always ask them how they were doing at school; things that an uncle would. He was usually accompanied by a young, smartly dressed middle-aged woman, who was his secretary and who they called Khun Raak. The word was that she was his girlfriend, but Nong Da herself did not think so. Khun Raak would always take pictures of them in a group, as well as separately, for the house album.

Nong Da accepted the circumstances in which she found herself, as a child might. She had landed in such a beautiful house and was being looked by such a kind uncle. She trusted what Yai Toom and the others told her; that her mother's spirit was looking after her and had blessed her with good fortune. It was like a dream. Why should she question it?

The years went by and more girls arrived at Baan Ying. Some were older but mostly they were younger. But there were never more than a dozen or so at the most, because the older ones left to make room for them. Whenever she asked where they went she was told that they were too big for Baan Ying and were now going to live in a house for older girls on the other side of Bangkok. She accepted what they told her, although she did not understand why the girls who left always seemed to just disappear without saying goodbye. And one day she happened to be outside the kitchen window during one of Khun Ah O's visits and she overheard his secretary Khun Raak saying:

"I think she's ready. Anyway he wants her tonight."

She was puzzled by this and asked Pi Noi what it meant. Pi Noi told her that she did not know, but from the way she spoke Nong Da could tell that Pi Noi was holding something back from her.

One evening, two years later, during another visit from Khun Ah O and Khun Raak, a strange thing happened. They had already gone to bed and turned the lights out when Yai Toom came into their bedroom and told Pi Noi that Khun Ah O wanted to see her downstairs. When she was gone

Nong Da lay worrying that her friend was in trouble for having failed her exams or something like that. When Pi Noi returned nearly an hour later and climbed into bed, Nong Da immediately questioned her. But Pi Noi said that she did not want to talk about it and turned her head to the wall. Then a few minutes later Nong Da heard her trying to control her sobbing.

"Pi Noi! Pi Noi! What's wrong? Are you in trouble? Are they going to punish you?" she asked, alarmed.

"No. Nothing like that. You wouldn't understand. I have to go. Tomorrow. But don't tell anyone. They'll just come and take me away while you're all at school."

"You mean to the other place, where the big girls are?"

"I guess so."

"But why do they always have to do it like this? Why can't we have a farewell party for you?"

In the darkness Nong Da waited for her friend to reply. Then after a while, Pi Noi, her voice now empty of emotion, said:

"They're taking me away because I am ready to work. There are men out there who pay good money for us virgins. Rich men who only want a girl who hasn't been touched. Khun Ah O has brought us up especially to serve them. Now my time has come. Yours will come soon enough when they think you are ripe for picking. You're a pretty girl; it may be less than two years."

Nong Da lay back in silence, confused by what she had heard. She did not want to believe Pi Noi. She could not imagine the Khun Ah O that she knew to be the kind of person who would sell her to a stranger. But she knew deep inside that it was the truth. And suddenly, in that instant, she understood everything about her mother, Khun Ah O, and Baan Ying.

"How do you feel about it?" she now asked Pi Noi.

"What choice do I have? Or any of us. They told me that this was my payment for the years they looked after me. And afterwards it was up to me. They told me that I had the chance of making good money in the business because I was good looking and fresh. They said that I could earn much more in one day than a whole month working in a factory. They've got lots of girls like us. Some even get to go abroad, to America or Europe."

She watched Pi Noi's departure early the next morning through the window. A white van with a dragon painted on the side was waiting. It had been raining in the night. The bushes were dripping and there was a mist hanging over the lawn. When they said goodbye Nong Da knew that she had to control her tears and give her friend the courage to face her uncertain future. But when she had gone Nong Da let her feelings burst through. Together with the sadness of losing someone close to her there was a sense of anger and injustice. The knowledge that they had all been tricked and betrayed sickened her and from that day on Nong Da began to plan her escape from Baan Ying. Getting away was the easy part. It was what she was going to do and where she was going to go afterwards that was the problem. She was only fourteen, with no relatives that she knew of and no friends outside Baan Ying.

Two weeks later, during the school lunch break, she slipped out of a side entrance, took the bus into Bangkok and headed for the condo where she used to live with her mother. She went and knocked on the door of the woman who used to look after her, and who she called auntie. But no one was home and she had to sit waiting on the landing for a few hours. When auntie saw her old ward she put her hand to her mouth.

"What are you doing, girl?" she said. "Why are you here?" But she already knew.

In the room which was so familiar to Nong Da she told auntie what had happened and what she had learned from Pi Noi. Auntie listened and nodded her head from time to time.

"Please can I stay with you till I find work?" begged Nong Da.

"And what work are you going to do?"

"Oh anything. I'll go and help somebody in the market. I'll be all right."

"You shouldn't have left. They were good to you, weren't they?" said auntie and there was a tiredness in her voice.

Three men dressed in security guards' uniforms came to fetch her an hour later, while she was watching television and eating a bowl of noodles that auntie had prepared. Nong Da did not protest. She understood from the expression on auntie's face that it was inevitable. The old woman pressed her hand as she walked out of the door.

That evening she was given the first of her beatings. The men took her to a corner of the garden and kicked her and beat her. It hurt so much that she could not get up, though afterwards there was hardly a sign that her body had been touched. When they threw her on the bed, one of the men said, with quiet menace:

"You're lucky. We were told not to really hurt you and to leave you alone down there. But next time watch out." Then he laughed.

Later on that same evening, Khun Ah O came into her bedroom to see her. He sat on a chair by her bed and told her how sorry he was that she had been punished.

"Try to learn from this," he said, still managing to sound like a kind uncle. "I know you're upset that Pi Noi is gone. But she's all right. And you'll see her again soon. Just be a good girl. You've got everything you need here. Why go and make trouble for yourself?"

He said much more but Nong Da was not listening because she had already decided that it was all lies.

The beating hurt her but it also strengthened her will. Overnight her character changed. She continued to obey the rules and follow the etiquette laid down. But, from being the polite and friendly girl who was always smiling and bright, she became sullen and uncooperative. Instead of playing with the others she preferred to be by herself, reading and writing in her room, which she had once shared with Pi Noi and which she now had to herself.

⇒╪⇐

Two years later, on one of his visits to Baan Ying, Khun Ah O sent for her. As usual Khun Raak hovered in the background, fetching him drinks and taking the incoming calls on the mobile phone. When the preliminaries were over, Khun Ah, with a beaming smile, said,

"How old are you now? Sixteen. A big girl."

Nong Da remembered what Pi Noi had told her on their last night together. She realized that it was now her turn.

"You've been with us for almost eight years. We've looked after you well, haven't we? Now it's time you have to do something for us. You might think that it's not a nice thing to do but it's all in the mind. And besides, you'll be following in your mother's footsteps. Her job was to make men happy. You know that, don't you? And she made them very happy. She worked for me and was well paid for it too. It's a pity she's gone. She was a good woman. I still miss her. Well now you too will be working for me and you'll earn good money to spend on whatever you like. I'm a fair, decent employer. Everyone will tell you that. I won't cheat you. You'll get a fair cut. I'll protect and look after you just as I have done while you've been here at Baan Ying. But in return you will do as you're told. Now tomorrow your new life starts. You will move from here into a house in town and you will be given your first assignment."

As Nong Da sat listening to Khun Ah, she felt an emotion rise up in her which she had never experienced before. It was hatred. And as she nodded at what he was saying, in her heart she cursed him and wished that she had the power and the means to kill the devil with the moustache, who was sitting there in front of her, pretending to be her protector when all he had ever wanted was to sell her body to a stranger.

⸙

Twenty four hours later Nong Da found herself in a house in a soi off Rama IV Road. It was a different setup from Baan Ying. The two storey building was small and modest. There was no garden. There were four other girls already there when she arrived, but no sign of Pi Noi as she was hoping. A woman showed her the room, which she had to herself. There was a television in the corner and a fridge, and the cupboard was full of dresses and shoes. Besides the woman, there were the three minders who had brought her in the dragon painted white van. They shared a room on the ground floor.

Within an hour of her arrival Nong Da was ordered to shower and get dressed. The woman came into her room and told her that she would help her with the makeup.

"You'll soon have to learn how to do this yourself, like the others do. So remember how it's done," she said grumpily.

Nong Da had only ever worn makeup for fun. But this was different. The woman did not smile or chat as she applied the foundation cream and then the rest. The only thing that she said when they were nearly finished was:

"Plenty of rouge. They like rouge on a young face."

Nong Da hardly recognized herself in the mirror. She looked more like a painted doll than a person.

The woman fetched a lime green dress from the cupboard.

"Green. They told me it had to be green, the colour of freshness."

When Nong Da put on the high heels she nearly fell over. This made the woman laugh.

"You'll soon get used to it," she cackled. "Do you want a pill? It'll keep you going through the night?"

But Nong Da shook her head.

During the drive across the river, Nong Da was nearly sick from fright. She felt as though she was drowning. They went to a place called 'Club L'Amour'. It was a building about the same size as Baan Ying. There were fairy lights hanging from the trees in front. The parking lot was full of big shiny cars. There were uniformed guards and drivers hanging about, smoking cigarettes and joking, and a couple of doormen in full livery standing by the steps to the entrance. As they drove past, all these men looked round and peered into the back, where Nong Da was sitting. They parked outside the back entrance and when the door opened she was facing Khun Raak, who greeted her, helped out and led her into a long corridor. There were doors leading off with numbers on them and from behind some of these she could hear talking and laughter. They climbed some stairs, along the side of which there was a tall window that looked down into a bar area that was dimly lit and crowded with men sitting at the tables and women serving them, who were dressed as her mother had been. A band was playing in one corner. A few couples were on the dance floor. Coloured lights flickered from a globe that hung from the ceiling. Nong Da took it all in with the keenness of a novice.

After another, shorter flight of stairs and another corridor they stopped in front of a door and Khun Raak knocked hard on it. The door was opened by a young woman holding a drink. She wore nothing but a pair of panties. Behind her at a table sat three men who nodded when Nong Da was led towards them. In a corner there was another group of men and women who were naked in a big round tub and singing along loudly to a karaoke video playing on the table next to them. They did not take any notice of her entrance. Nong Da felt disturbed by the scene but tried not to show it. Khun Raak went over to one of the men sitting at the table, leaned down and whispered something in his ear, which made him smile. It was then that she recognized one of the girls sitting in the tub. It was Pi Noi. But before she had time to even consider walking over to greet her old friend, Khun Raak was pulling her over to the man whose head was bald and whose eyes were like two slits. She stood there while he looked her up and down, nodding as he did so. Then he laughed.

"Good. Very good," he said in English.

Khun Raak now led her out again and to a room further down the corridor. This one was a plain bedroom with a bathroom adjoining. There was a TV in the corner. On the table there was a bottle of whiskey, glasses, two bottles of soda and an ice bucket. On the bed there was a pink baby doll nightie laid out. Khun Raak pointed to it and told her to put it on.

"He'll be here in a couple of minutes. Don't be nervous. He seems to be a nice man," she said before leaving.

But instead of putting it on Nong Da sat on the bed with her head in her hands, wishing that it was all a bad dream and praying that someone would come and save her. Then the door opened and the bald man appeared. He looked at her for a moment and then pointed to the nightie lying next to her and made a gesture with his hand as if to say: "Why haven't you got ready?" Nong Da shook her head and the man laughed again, as he had done earlier. He walked over to the bed, sat next to her and without any warning put his arm round her shoulder, while his other hand closed round her breast. She struggled to push him away but he was much bigger and stronger than she was. He pushed her back down onto the bed and started to kiss her face. She managed to wriggle free and rolled off the bed. She expected him to be angry but he merely laughed again.

"Come here, beautiful one," he said. "Don't be afraid. I am good. I am gentle."

She put the table between herself and the bald man, who approached her with his hands held forward, as though inviting her to fall into his embrace. As he came towards her, he smiled and made a kind of cooing sound with his mouth, which was meant to calm her down. Without thinking of what she was doing, Nong Da picked up the whiskey bottle from the table and smashed it across his face. He fell back from the blow and blood gushed out from his broken nose. But only a muffled curse came out of him.

"Oh, I'm so sorry," Nong Da was saying as she rushed over to him. "I didn't mean to hurt you." As she got near to him he grabbed her wrist and twisted it. The pain made her react and with her spare hand she thumped down hard into his groin. Now he yelled out. Nong Da jumped out of his reach and made for the door. She ran down the corridor and was about to go down the stairs when she saw Khun Raak speaking on her mobile phone and Khun Ah O coming up towards her. It was too late. There was no escape.

She stood there at the top of the stairs with her head hung like a defeated animal, all fight gone, waiting to be slaughtered. Khun Ah O put his hands gently on her shoulders as if to console her. But when she looked up he hit her hard across the mouth. She tasted blood.

"Ungrateful little bitch. That was my guest you've insulted. No. Not just insulted. You could have killed him. He's one of the richest men in Asia. He's helped me a lot. And if you had played your cards right he could have given you anything you wanted. You idiot. Now you'll have to pay." With that he walked past her.

The men who Khun Raak had called were now by her side. One of them was holding her arm tightly, as though she was a prisoner. She could not remember what he or his two companions looked like—they might even have been the same ones who had beaten her up a year before—because from that moment on and till long after it was all over her mind seemed to snap from its roots and remove itself from what was happening to her. She knew what was happening but it was as if someone else were living it. They shouted abuse at her, dragged her into a room and tore the clothes from her back and then held her down while they took turns to enter her. She felt pain and tried to scream through the hands that were held over her mouth. And then there was the sound of glass breaking and a reflection that flashed passed her eyes and her cheek had been torn open. She heard one of them say, "No work for you in this business if you don't want it." And another one was laughing. And then they sat her up. Some pills were stuffed into her mouth and she was made to swallow them down with a glug of water. She was dizzy. A woman put the green dress back on her. She was propped up on either side and taken to the white van. Then she fell unconscious.

⁕

When she woke up she did not dare to open her eyes. She knew that she was lying on a mattress on the floor with a thin sheet covering her. There was no pillow. Her head was turned to the right and her hand was touching the smooth wooden floorboard. The rain was beating a rhythm on the corrugated iron roof. A fan from her left side was blowing air gently onto her. There was the sound of a radio playing an old fashioned love song. She heard a deep throaty cough. She caught a whiff of cigarette smoke. She was still alive.

Opening her eyes she saw an old man dressed in dirty rags, sitting against cross legged against the wall, drawing on a hand rolled cheroot, watching her intently. He got up and approached her. Instinctively she turned away, but as she did so she felt pain shoot through her cheek, where they had cut her. And her whole body felt bruised.

The old man was holding a bowl of water and squeezing a wet flannel.

"I've put some medicine in it so your wound won't get infected."

He reached over and put the cloth on her face and she winced.

Later he gave her a bowl of rice soup which she could barely eat. It was still raining. She guessed that it was morning. Through the one window in the room she could see black water and the concrete columns of the expressway. They must have been in one of the rickety shacks along some canal. She did not want to speak, even to ask the old man where she was and how she got there. She did not have the strength to get up from the bed.

He did not seem to mind her silence. He knew what she wanted to ask.

"I found you under that bridge over there," he said. "Two mornings ago, or was it three? Someone dumped you, hoping that the dogs would finish you off. I was doing my rounds. I saw you lying there. Thought you were dead. I was going to walk away. There are always young people lying there with a needle in their arm or a bullet in their skull. But you moved and made a noise. I put you in my cart, the one I use to collect rubbish. You cost me a day's work, do you know that? I don't know why I've taken you. It's karma again, I suppose. I know that if I had left you there you would have died. And I didn't call an ambulance because they never come to this area. Too much bother picking up the junkies who are going to die anyway. And now it's time for me to go to work before the council team steals my rubbish."

Before he left he turned and said to her:

"Rest. No one will bother you round here. They all think I'm crazy. And by the way, I had to take your clothes off. They're in that bag in the corner. You were in a bad state. I had to clean you up. But I didn't do anything. I'm an old man, old enough to be your grandfather. I'll be back when my work's done."

He was called Loong Pae and she stayed with him for over a year. When she was well enough to move, she started to go out with him on his rounds, picking up bottles from the pavement, sifting through the garbage and the tips for anything that could be salvaged and taken to the recycling centre or sold to the merchants. Their patch was the Klongtoey Klua Naam Tai area. All they had was a cart, which they wheeled through the streets, and their bare hands.

Nong Da did not mind the filth and the smell that clung to her or the rags that she wore. Soon her hair became matted and her skin burnt from the sun and grimy with dust. People on the pavements stepped aside. But none of this mattered to her. She was no longer one of them. She had been soiled. She was like the garbage that someone had thrown out.

Loong Pae tried to coax her to talk at the beginning.

"Tell me what happened to you. Go on. I know you're not a deaf mute. You're just troubled."

But her voice felt as though it was stuck down a long tunnel.

Sometimes in the long hours Loong Pae would sit and tell her about his life, how he had been a heroin dealer and an addict, how he had been in and out of jail, how he had fallen and fallen till he reached the depths.

"But you go on. Or else you kill yourself."

One day they were putting old newspapers that they had collected into piles and tying them up. She saw a picture of Pi O standing in front of the 'Club L'Amour', giving an interview. The horror and disgust flooded back and she could hardly breathe. She read the article about how the police were raiding his establishments. She learned who he was. She noted the date of the paper. It was a month old. Loong Pae had noticed her interest and snatched it from her hand.

"Was this the man who harmed you? I've heard of him," was all he said.

A week later he came back to the shack one evening, after his usual drink at the bar on the corner, and tossed a newspaper into her lap.

"Maybe this will interest you," he said.

There were pictures of Pi O in the passenger seat of his Mercedes, taken from various angles. One bullet had hit him above the left eye, another went through the heart, and the third in his shoulder. The seat was stained with his blood, as was the driver's. The shooting took place in a carpark outside the 'Dolce Vita', one of Pi O's establishments in the Ratchada district, the previous evening at around seven p.m. The assassins had not been caught. A guard said that two men on a motorbike raced passed him and into the traffic. Both wore helmets and blue windcheaters. The bike was red. Nong

Da did not bother reading the comments and the interviews and the rest of it which filled nearly the entire edition. She sat staring at the pictures. They did not bring her any sense of triumph.

A day later Loong Pae came in and told her that the funeral was going to take place that afternoon.

"It's advertised in all the papers today. Wat Taadthong. It's just down the road."

Nong Da went to the corner and took the green dress she had once been made to wear out of the plastic bag. It was crinkled and the stains were still there. She carefully sewed up the parts that had been torn. Then she got a box of makeup that someone had thrown in a tip and applied the lipstick and the rouge (plenty of rouge, that's what they like) without using a mirror. When she was ready, without a word to Loong Pae, she put on her plastic flipflops and began walking to the temple. Loong Pae walked after her shouting:

"So how are you going to get there? You don't even know what you're going to do. You don't know this city."

She did not turn or respond to him, but kept on walking, so he had no choice but to walk with her in the white heat of the afternoon, till they got to the front gates of the temple.

"Well. I'll leave you here to go ahead and do what you have to. I've had enough trouble in my life to cope with. And I reckon I've helped you enough. We've got no more karma to run. You're on your own now." With that the old man turned on his heels and was gone.

Before finishing her story, Nong Da told them how she started to speak again. It was not something that she had any control over, she said. When she lost her voice it felt as though it had gone forever and when it came back it was as if she had never been silent. There was no decision on her part. It just happened after she had been at the centre for about four months. Living with other women who had also been through terrible things and many of whom were sick and dying made her realize that that she was not alone in her suffering and gradually helped her to come out of her darkness. But she still had no desire to communicate. Then one morning a girl younger than herself was breaking down and screaming and Nong Da went over and began to speak to her to calm her down. And from then on she started to speak. But she never told anyone her story until that evening.

"And now you know all about me," said Nong Da with a sigh. She looked tired and fragile after finishing her story.

The three of them remained silent when she had finished. Arun lit a cigarette. Marisa sat with her head cupped in her hands. Don continued to look at Nong Da, who quickly got up and took the empty dishes into the kitchen.

The jingle of Marisa's mobile phone broke the spell.

"It's Khun Chai," she said to no one in particular, when she looked at the number. "I don't want to speak to him right now."

Nevertheless she walked to a corner and held a conversation out of earshot. When she returned her face was flushed with anger.

"I have to go. Nong Da, I want to come and visit you here again tomorrow. May I?"

The young woman nodded silently.

CHAPTER 32

As Marisa drove down Sukhumvit Road, which at this hour was clear of traffic and where the only people around were those looking for a place to sleep in a doorway or under the bridge of the sky train, she kept thinking of Nong Da's words. It made her shiver to think how close she had been in her young life to suffering the same sort of fate. It was hard to believe that the Pi O that she had known had turned into such a monster. But then she reminded herself how many times she had seen people change for the worse through greed and ambition. Nong Da's story had stirred in her both anger and the sense that she wanted to do all in her power to help the victim.

She did not want to leave the others that evening. She wanted to be there and to hold Nong Da and care for her. But she knew that she could no longer put off what she had to do. Khun Chai, who she could tell was as high as a kite, had begged her to meet him in his private club on Tonglor, insisting that he needed to sort out the details of the liquidation of their company with her, in private without lawyers being present. She knew that this was partly, if not wholly, an excuse for him to see her. He had been persistently leaving messages since their separation, which she had chosen to ignore. But she realized that sooner or later she would have to see him face to face and sort out the last details with him and that evening was as good a time as any. Listening to Nong Da's story had aroused in her such strong emotions and had returned to her a sense of perspective that she had forgotten. The horror of what the young woman had been through made her own problems seem little short of ridiculous.

The club was one of Pi O's smaller establishments, called the 'Executive'; one hundred thousand baht yearly membership. There were still many cars parked outside. It had been three months since she had been there. The doorman saluted her with an exaggerated bow, then accompanied her up in the lift to the penthouse, where the hostess, standing at the entrance with her visitor's book on the table next to her, smiled and greeted Marisa before leading her inside. It had been three months since she was last there but it felt as if she had never been away. There was the panoramic view of Bangkok with the city lights twinkling below. The jazz combo playing a standard love song in the corner, the smell of perfume mingled with cigar and coffee and expensive cognac, the couples on the dance floor, single suited men drinking at the bar in the company of high class, well dressed hookers. It was a familiar scene.

Marisa looked around for Khun Chai. The hostess, anticipating her question said, apologetically.

"He's in one of the bedrooms at the back." And then she added quickly. "He's by himself."

Marisa did not want to meet him in a bedroom, there in the club or anywhere else. But she could see that she had no choice. Reluctantly she followed the hostess to a side door that opened out to a thickly carpeted corridor which led to the rooms.

She found Khun Chai in one of the suites. He was sprawled out face down on a bed. His jacket lay on the floor. A half empty glass of whiskey was by the bedside table. A soft porn video was playing on the box. Marisa had a sudden strong sense of déja vu. She waved the hostess away and then sat on the edge of the bed looking at the person she had come to see. She felt pity for him. But there was none of the dilemma as there had been a year earlier. She was not afraid any more of what he might do to himself. She was not responsible for what he chose to do. And she was no longer frightened about being alone.

She brought a wet flannel from the bathroom and wiped his face. As soon as he became conscious he tried to hold her and pull her down to him but she resisted without difficulty.

"You can have anything you want," he mumbled. "But please come back to me. I can't live without you."

Marisa shook her head. "No. You have to grow up and take care of yourself, and learn to live with all the privileges that you have and not hurt yourself. And I have to move on."

She left him on the bed with one hand rubbing his tired eyes and the other half stretched towards her. That was the last time that she ever saw Khun Chai.

CHAPTER 33

Nong Da's arrival brought the three friends back together. By offering them her story she unintentionally made their connection to one another even stronger than before. They were now the guardians who shared in being responsible for her. And in this case, the fact that the life in their care had been severely damaged made their guardianship all the more vital. Marisa saw in Nong Da a reverse reflection of herself. She had been extremely lucky; the girl tragically unlucky in her initiation. She had survived and come through to be successful, while Nong Da had been severely damaged. Marisa knew that, but for the stars or whatever mysterious force there was which decided how things happened as they did, she too might have landed up like a piece of garbage that was tossed by the roadside. Partly because of this she found that she was filled with feelings that she had never felt before; not just wanting to nurture and protect Nong Da but to be part of her future and her growth into womanhood.

As for the two men, each was affected in his own way. Arun saw in what Nong Da had been through another example of the harm that Pi O had caused by his greed and ambition. What she had suffered made him angry and frustrated that the man who was responsible for her suffering was not still alive so that he could go and confront him with his evil. He wanted to tell the world that Pi O, his uncle, was no folk hero, and that all the stuff he put out about being kind and generous and merely providing men with a simple pleasure was just a mask that hid the violence and the abuse. It was yet another example of the hypocrisy that he hated so much about Thai society. The fact that his own kin was involved made the whole episode even more bitter.

Don understood what Arun felt but he told them that he himself did not feel that he had the right to judge anybody. He admitted to them that when he was younger, to his shame, he had been to the 'Club L'Amour' and many other places owned by Pi O. In his time he had paid for women to give him pleasure. And more than once he had treated his girlfriends not as friends at all, but as shiny trophies which lost his interest once they were won. He was not blameless, but wanted to help in healing Nong Da in whatever way he could.

It was clear that all three of them now felt a commitment to Nong Da that none of them had felt for anyone else before. And so, on her arrival in Bangkok, Nong Da found herself the focus of the loving kindness of three strangers. But despite the fact that she was now speaking again it was obvious that Nong Da's recovery was far from complete. She was like a small frightened bird that had been deliberately harmed. Her expression and her movements betrayed the quiet mistrust that a victim of violence displays. From the first evening they had been talking of nothing else but how to help Nong Da to be strong again. Don thought that she still needed psychiatric help to express her hurt and anger. Only then would her wounds begin to heal. Arun disagreed, saying that she did not need to go back into her past, that what she had done at the funeral ceremony was the best statement that she could make. In its wildness there was an affirmation that no amount of analysis or psychotherapy could have produced. Marisa sat back and listened while the men, like fathers maddened by the harm that their daughter had received, debated back and forth. For her part she wanted to move Nong Da to her place immediately, but Arun insisted that she should stay with him until he left for France the next week. He wanted to make up for having been so neglectful to her before.

In the end it was Nong Da herself who decided that she would stay on in the studio until Arun left the country. Then she would move in with Marisa if it was convenient. As for psychiatric help she reassured them that she was on the way to healing and that if they were patient with her she would be soon strong enough to fend for herself and carry on with her life.

⚜

Two days after Nong Da's arrival, Gaew called Arun and told him that she was in Bangkok to fetch Nong Da back to Chiengmai. She had found out from another girl at the centre that Nong Da had borrowed money to buy a ticket for Bangkok. Arun in turn replied that the Nong Da no longer wanted to be in the north, at which point Gaew seemed no longer interested in talking to him. Then within a few minutes the door bell rang and there she was on his front step. He saw that she was highly agitated.

"Where is she? I know she's here. I have to speak to her," she said immediately, without so much as a greeting.

"She's not in right now."

"You're lying. Why are you hiding her? Do you want her for yourself? Is that it?"

Arun was startled by her words and did not know how to respond to her accusatory tone. And then suddenly everything became clear.

"Come in and see for yourself. She's not here."

Gaew said nothing now, but hung her head like a tired and defeated child. When she looked up again and when their eyes met Arun saw the truth.

"You're in love with her."

Gaew nodded. "I don't know what to do. I can't help myself. I've been going crazy looking for her all over Chiengmai."

Gaew's depleted expression reflected her words and Arun now put the pieces together in his mind and understood why their relationship had never been given a chance to take off. He was glad that he had not got himself more deeply involved with her. He saw now how disastrous it would have been. Still seeing her there in front of him he felt her utter despair touch him. He reached out and, holding the side of her arm, stepped aside and motioned for her to enter.

⁕

Marisa had taken Nong Da to a shopping mall to buy clothes and shoes. They were going to bring lunch back to Arun's studio where Don was going to join them. In the afternoon they were all to have a discussion about what Nong Da was going to do in Bangkok. At least this was what they told her. But, in fact they had already agreed among themselves that Nong Da should now carry on with her education and they wanted to persuade her to go back to college.

When Nong Da came back and saw Gaew sitting on the sofa she showed no reaction except to put the shopping bags down and to wai her. Then she picked the bags up and slipped past to her bedroom without a word. Gaew, for her part, made as if to get up when she saw the girl but Marisa gestured to her to stay seated and when Nong Da had gone she said:

"I think she's still very upset by what happened between you."

"I didn't mean to slap her. I want to tell her that I'm sorry. I lost my head. It's the first time I've done anything like that."

"But what happened?" asked Marisa who had already heard Nong Da's version. The girl told her that she did not understand why, but one day Pi Gaew started to be mean to her and say nasty things about her. Then, when she asked to go to the market with the others to help with the shopping for the centre, Pi Gaew got cross and said no, so she protested and it was then that she was slapped.

"Oh, nothing," said Gaew. "It was nothing. I was tense that day. Nothing else."

"But you hit her. After knowing what she's been through you hit her."

Gaew shrugged. At this point Arun joined in:

"She was jealous."

"Jealous? Of what?" asked Marisa.

Gaew then admitted to her what she had earlier told Arun. There was a boy, a biker, who would hang around the centre. Nong Da would go out to the corner and talk to him. When Gaew told her that she was no longer to see him, Nong Da got angry and told her it was none of her business. That's when she slapped her.

"If I wasn't in love with her I wouldn't have done that. I've had to deal with situations like that before. But this time I couldn't stop myself. It's pathetic. But I felt something for her from the beginning, when you asked me to take care of her. Now you'll think badly of me and judge me."

She was crying and Marisa went over and put her arm around her shoulder.

"We're all strange when it comes to the heart," she said.

⚜

Later, when Don arrived they all talked to Gaew and convinced her to go back to Chiengmai and to try to forget what had happened between her and Nong Da, promising that her secret would be safe with them. They were not going to report her to the authorities as she feared. She did not want to leave without seeing Nong Da, but the girl would not come out to meet her.

When she had gone they all breathed again.

"Poor Gaew," said Marisa.

"What about me?" said Arun with mock hurt.

"Oh you were never in love with her. Not really."

"It's true. But I came close."

"How painful all this love business is. And then there's the sex. Sometimes it makes me want to be a nun and forget about it all. What do you say, Don?"

"No. It doesn't help much. There's no easy way out. You can try choosing to look away from it. But it's still there. The need for tenderness and contact, I mean."

The others did not guess that afternoon that he was talking not in a general, philosophical way, but about himself. He wanted to tell them that he was beginning to feel those things towards Nong Da. But given the circumstances he thought that it was too early.

⟨⟩⟨⟩

While all of it was going on, Nong Da lay on the bed in her room watching the light playing on the ceiling. She thought of Chiengmai and the friends she had made there. She missed them, especially Mae Joi, a tribal woman from the mountains in Chiengrai who was one of the cleaners. Her husband, a drug dealer, had stolen money off a group of army men who controlled the trade in the district where they lived. When they found out they came to the house one night and shot him in front of her. Then they took her and her six year old daughter away from the village and sold the daughter to a Malay and then kept her as a slave in a house for four years. She did not even know where she was. She was raped and repeatedly beaten. She lost track of time. One day they blindfolded her, drove her in the back of a pick-up truck, then threw her into the streets. She wandered around till some people picked her up and took her to the centre in Chiengmai. Ten years later she still bore the scars from the beatings that she had endured. She never knew what happened to her daughter. This was Mae Joi's story and Nong Da drew strength from it. It taught her of the possibility of letting go of the past, however dark and evil it was.

She could hear their voices in the studio but she could not make out what they were saying. Earlier she had tiptoed out and peeped through the gap in the sliding doors and seen Pi Gaew on the sofa crying and Khun Marisa's arm around her shoulder. She was sorry that she was the cause of all the fuss. But it was not her fault. She had done nothing wrong except to talk to the boy on the bike. Pi Gaew's overreaction puzzled and frightened her. She did not want to be hit ever again in her life.

She sensed that the three of them were now talking about her. She did not even understand how she got to be involved with them, how it was that they came to be her protectors. She knew that with them she was safe, but it puzzled her why they cared what happened to her. She liked Marisa best. Arun's intensity scared her a little. Don seemed the kindest and the gentlest of the three. She already wanted him to be married to Marisa. But they were strange people, who she would never have dreamed of meeting. Now, mysteriously, they were like her family.

She was glad they were there for her but she could not help feeling that at any moment they would vanish into thin air, like ghosts, or angels. Already she knew that Khun Arun would soon be leaving. She prayed that the other two would be true to their word and look after her. The past was still a fresh nightmare, whose horror exploded into her consciousness at any moment, catching her off guard. Even that morning, in the brightly lit, clean shopping mall she found herself looking over her shoulder, wondering if there were going to be anyone from Pi O's old gang who might recognize her and drag her back to Baan Ying or worse, to the club. She did not want to be terrified any more. She wanted the fearful thoughts and the feelings of disgust that she felt towards herself to go away. It was more than being ashamed. What the men had done to her was to have covered her with filth that could not be washed off. She did not deserve love because she was a piece of used cloth.

CHAPTER 34

Nong Da could sense that Arun's imminent departure was making them miserable. It gave a heightened vividness to those last days together as though something precious was about to be lost and there was no way of stopping it. That week they saw each other as often as their lives permitted and whenever they met, usually at the studio they would talk about everything with a sense of urgency. They shared their fears, discussed big issues, gossiped about people in society, joked and argued like any other friends, except that they were acting as though they were already afraid that the bond between them would break, that everything would change when Arun had gone, that without him their friendship would be incomplete.

Nong Da sat in on most of these meetings, wide eyed, as she listened to the banter and the arguments and all the tales that fascinated and surprised her. Like a child who was allowed to sleep in her parents' bed, she was grateful to be included into their intimacy.

It was during one of their conversations that Pi O's name came up. Marisa was the one who mentioned it and Nong Da noticed immediately that they tensed up as though a tacit agreement had been broken. Up till then she had never joined in except when they asked her opinion about something. But that day she said to them, before she had the time to think; "Oh don't be afraid that I'll be upset. You can talk about him. I don't mind. He's dead now. He can't harm me any more."

Knowing that behind these brave words there were still monsters that lurked in the shadows, they nevertheless clapped and laughed and hugged her and for a moment she too felt that she was free from the past.

They had decided, to her relief, that she did not have to go back to school. She was going to take classes in English and computing and she was eventually going to be Khun Marisa's assistant. All this after Arun's departure.

When she was by herself Nong Da fantasized about the relationship between the three of them. In her mind the two men were obviously in love with Marisa, who lived up to everything that she ever thought a film star should be; beautiful, rich, elegant, generous, like a goddess whom Arun and Don worshipped. But Marisa could not be close to both of them equally and, despite what she had thought initially, she now favoured Arun, not just because he was the better looking one, with his handsome face and the long hair, but because she seemed more relaxed around him. He made her laugh, whereas Don was quiet and serious most of the time. But Nong Da herself liked Don for his gentleness and sincerity. His presence made her feel secure and warm. Once when they were out together she asked Marisa which one she preferred.

"Oh. I love them both the same. They're like my brothers," was the reply. But Nong Da did not believe her.

⟨⟩

Two days before Arun left for Paris, Nong Da was pleased to see that her intuition had been right.

That night, as always, it was taking her a long time to get to sleep. Arun was still in the studio reading. Earlier on she had helped him clean up the paint brushes and store them in the drawers. He told her that he was sad to be leaving but that he would be back sooner than she thought and then she could move back to the studio if she felt like it. In the two weeks that she had stayed there, in the spare bedroom, it had already felt like home. She had seen Marisa's place. It was as elegant as she had expected it to be. But she was nervous about moving there because at Arun's it was homely, whereas at Marisa's there were servants who had given her a funny look when Marisa told them that she was going to move in.

These thoughts were going through her head when she heard a car draw up outside. Then a door banged. Seconds later there was a loud rap on the front gate. She crept out of bed and went to the sliding door. Unfortunately she had shut it well and there was no gap to peep through. But she could make out Marisa's voice.

"I have never been so humiliated in my life," she was saying amid tears. Nong Da wanted to rush out and stop her crying. But she knew that it was not a good idea so she slid to the floor and continued her eavesdropping. She heard Marisa tell Arun how Khun Chai's family lawyer had told her to go and beg forgiveness from the auntie. (Nong Da was already familiar with these characters from the previous conversations that she had heard). The old lady was willing to drop all the legal proceedings and settle out of court, if Marisa was willing to show her that she was sincerely sorry for what she had done to Khun Chai.

"Imagine. She's been telling everyone I turned him into a junkie so I could take advantage of his wealth," she shouted at one point.

So, swallowing her pride, Marisa went to the palace on the river. She was made to wait for ages. An elderly retainer came to tell Marisa that the auntie was getting dressed. When she finally made her way slowly down the grand staircase she was accompanied by two maidservants. Marisa paid her respects by going onto the floor in front of her. Then she introduced herself.

"I know very well who you are," said the auntie. "I'm glad you came. But you have behaved very badly to our family. Chai has always been delicate. Since he was a child we've had to be careful with him. You should not have exploited his weaknesses."

Marisa did not bother to explain her side of the story or to contradict the accusations. It was clear that the auntie had already made up her mind about the matter and whatever she said would have changed nothing. So she sat and listened while the old lady lectured her on her improper behaviour. Then she told Marisa that Khun Chai was being taken to a clinic in Europe to be cured of his addiction, and that when he came back he would never have anything more to do with her. With that she made as if to get up and go back to her rooms upstairs. But she suddenly stopped and said haughtily:

"Isn't there something that you have forgotten?"

Marisa, who had hardly had a chance to speak, was puzzled until she looked over at the retainer who was carrying a silver tray on which there lay an elaborately woven wreath of flowers. A look passed between them and Marisa understood. Taking the wreath, she again went down on her knees, offered it up to the auntie and asked her to show forgiveness for whatever harm that had been done to Khun Chai. The auntie took the wreath and handed it to one of the maidservants, nodded and smiled with satisfaction. Then without another word she turned and walked back up the stairs.

When she finished there was a long silence. Nong Da expected Arun to make a comment but there was nothing. And then she heard a long sigh of satisfaction.

"Oh, that's so good. Just what I need. Who taught you to massage like that? You didn't learn it in a temple did you?" asked Marisa, whose voice was now calm and playful. Arun laughed.

Another few minutes passed. Nong Da wanted to slide the door open just a little so that she could see what they were up to. She was both excited and afraid of what she would see. Her imagination was racing ahead. But just as she could no longer control herself and her hand was already on the handle she heard Arun saying:

"I think this is as far as we go."

And then Marisa: "You're right. But it does feel nice."

"I know. It's the same for me. But it would spoil a good friendship. Let's have a drink and then I'm sending you home. Tomorrow I have to pack my bags and do a few more things."

Just before she left, Marisa said:

"I will miss you very much."

Nong Da imagined them kissing.

"You know, this is the first time I've held back from pleasure," said Arun after a long while. Then there was the sound of the door closing.

.

PART 6

CHAPTER 35

It was now two years since Don was a monk at Wat Thammacitta. The time he spent in robes living in a quiet monastery, following a path that was clearly marked out, seemed to belong to another incarnation. He did not regret his decision to leave the monkhood although every now and then, standing on a busy corner of the city with the shuddering noise level and the choking traffic fumes, he would think back to the peacefulness and simplicity of sitting by the river listening to the birdcalls.

There had been moments during his monkhood when he felt that the life of an ordained man was easy relative to the worldly existence. Once the initial hardships were overcome and the discipline a matter of habit there was no need to think about the kinds of things that people in the ordinary world had to deal with; paying the bills, looking after the children, coping with the traffic. And he had also seen how the spiritual existence could itself be a trap creating complacency and selfishness. Whenever he had these thoughts he would take them to the abbot, who would laugh and agree with him.

"Yes. We're living in luxury," he would say. "That's why now and then it's good for the ones who are getting a little fat and lazy to go out on *tudong*. The walkabout wakes them up."

Don asked his teacher several times about living the spiritual life without being a monk.

"The Buddha said it was possible," the old man replied. "But it's difficult. We get caught up in *samsara* so fast: sex, money, earning a living, responsibilities. Pretty soon we're tied up in the net."

In their final meeting, one of the things that the abbot said to him was to try to remember the lessons he had learned and apply them.

"Some people leave the monkhood and it's as though they had never practiced. They go back to their old ways as soon as they are out of the robes. Try to do good."

But at first it was hard to see where he could fit in at all, let alone do what the abbot had suggested. On returning to Bangkok he had felt yet again like a stranger in his own house. The dreams and obsessions that motivated people to do the things that they did, day in and day out, had never had much meaning for him. Now they seemed even more vapid and pointless than before. What place did he, the reformed prodigal son, have in that society except to act out the role that was expected of him and live out the rest of his days in the cocoon of comfort that his background afforded?

The sense of absurdity and pointlessness had troubled him since he was a teenager and only now, years later, did he realize that his nihilistic behaviour was a vain attempt to prick through the membrane of unreality which stifled him. His youthful defiance differed from others by the degree to which he was prepared to go. Unlike his contemporaries, who were living out their period of angst before returning to the fold, Don saw himself as a permanent outsider. The journey through the maze of drugs and alcohol had led him down into the hell which he wanted to explore; the limbo where there were no feelings or boundaries, where he played with destruction to see how far his body and mind could go. He had been in the wastelands of freedom. He had seen the darkness for himself.

The boy's death had woken him up and the monkhood had transformed him. On his return to Bangkok he could no longer remain at the fringes of society as an observer. He felt the need to participate in the life of the city and to make a contribution, however small, because he knew that he wanted a context in which to live out his days. He was not ambitious. He was guided by the abbot's injunction of doing some kind of good. In Bangkok there was a lot to be done. That much was obvious. But the trouble was that he had not finished his formal studies. There were no degrees nor any other credentials that he could show. It was too late, he felt, to go back to university.

When he went to the AIDS hospice to visit the mother of the boy he had killed, Don thought that it would be a good place to work, not merely as a penance for what he had done, but as a way of continuing the thread of the practice he had begun at the monastery. But after the week spent looking after Mae Hom he realized that he did not have the resilience needed for the job. The proximity to the dying was not a problem. As a monk he had meditated on corpses disintegrating on a slab as part of the practices the abbot encouraged to teach them non-attachment to the body. But he knew, despite seeing once and for all that the body was nothing but a bag of pus, that he had not really learned to detach his emotions. The sorrow he felt for

Mae Hom and for those around her was so raw and acute for him that it was overwhelming. He did not see how he could ever get past it and become immune to the suffering.

One afternoon, not long after Mae Hom's death, he was browsing through a newspaper and saw an advertisement placed by 'Clean Thailand', asking for applicants to work for their organization. He had already read about them in an article about the pollution and general deterioration of the infrastructure in Bangkok. They were one of the NGO's mentioned who were trying to raise the population's consciousness about these issues and finding a lot of support from the inhabitants of the capital. The candidate had to be a certain age and have a thorough knowledge of English and had to be willing to work outside normal hours.

Don had never been involved with an NGO before and he had only been vaguely aware of the issue of pollution. Like most of the city's inhabitants he had come to accept it as something to live with, like the other less attractive features of Bangkok. But the job seemed perfect for a person like himself who had no qualifications to his name, and who was too old to be taken on in any other sector. 'Clean Thailand' offered very little pay, but he calculated that, with his small private income, he could survive well enough given that his needs had become very simple.

So one morning nearly four months after arriving back in Bangkok he presented himself at their offices which were located in the Paholyotin district. And when they learned that, besides being fluent in English, he had been a monk for five years, they welcomed him with open arms, as though the angels had sent him and set him to work immediately. He soon found out why the organization was called 'Clean Thailand'. Their aim was to pressurize the government bodies into fulfilling their promises and applying the law, as well as to bring complaints to the attention of the media. They worked closely with the other NGOs who were in the same field and they had been successful with several campaigns that they had mounted. But the problem, as for all organizations working from the sideline, was money. This was why they needed someone who could communicate well in English, who could write their proposals and beg for money from the various sources overseas.

Don was happy with the work, even though he did not completely share or fully understand the politics of the couple who had founded the organization, Khun Gai and Khun Manop, who were of the generation who had been through the turmoil of the 1970s. Don had been born right in the middle of that traumatic period, in 1974, between the flowering of hope that came with the October '73 movement, and its violent suppression in 1976. He grew up vaguely aware of what had happened but the events seemed to have been pushed into the shadows. Don, like most of his age group, found it hard to identify with the passion of the previous generation. Besides, his privileged existence set him apart from the social issues. It was only when he ordained and spent five years in the backwaters of Nongkai that he learned of poverty and injustice first hand.

At the beginning when he joined the organization Khun Gai and Khun Manop were keen for him to understand the political background to their campaigns and Don was grateful to learn. They described the history of the movement to him and identified the main characters involved in the world of the NGO's. They spent a lot of time analyzing for him the contradictions in Thai society and explained to him the subtle groupings in the political arena. They were all things that Don had never had to consider.

From these conversations it was clear to him that these ex-revolutionaries still held onto an ideal which had motivated them since they were younger than he now was. And this impressed him. But at the same time it struck him that there was a certain bitterness in them, that they felt betrayed, not only by their former comrades who were now either part of the government or its keen supporters but also by the Thai people. Their memories were short and they had opted to accept the dreams of wealth that were held in front of them in the eighties and nineties, instead of carrying on the struggle for a true democracy—whatever that was. Don, who had never subscribed to any ideology or thought deeply about any of the issues that were raised, was not entirely sure that he went along with their analysis. While he admired their sincerity he could sense, behind their insistence on justice, an undercurrent of frustration and anger which coloured their vision. Unlike them he was not a crusader. And yet for all these differences he saw that what the organization was doing was sound and he was grateful to be able to support them.

Around the time of Arun's departure and Nong Da's move to Marisa's place, Don had been assigned to help a Canadian called Dr. Peter Kandy, a specialist in the field of water conservation. He was a person who was familiar with the region, having spent time as a young anthropologist doing his research thesis on the spirit cults of Thailand and Cambodia. Then after receiving his doctorate he had turned his attention to the environment and achieved international recognition for his work on the problems of managing water supply in Africa. Now, many years later and already past retirement age, he had returned at the invitation of the organization to give advice on how to clean the canal system of Bangkok and its suburbs and bring life back to the waterways. It was a campaign that they were mounting in response to the public demand that something serious should be done about the polluted waters and the cholera epidemic that had erupted the previous rainy season as a result. Don's job was to take this expert round and show him every canal that was on the map. This involved journeying to many areas of the city that were unfamiliar to Don; the Onnut district where the waterways ran alongside back alleys and skirted gigantic factory complexes and crossed marshy fields; and Thonburi with its thousands of tiny canals running off the main arteries of Bangkok Noi and Bangkok Yai. Here old wooden houses with flimsy windows, broken roof tiles and rickety balconies leaned against each other and families bathed on their front steps. And right behind these waterside dwellings there were fields and orchards that belonged far from the skyscrapers and the shopping malls. For Don it was a revelation to discover parts of his own city that he had never actually seen before. And these trips were made even richer by Dr. Kandy's ongoing commentary. His knowledge about water systems seemed inexhaustible and during these fields trips, often conducted under a blazing sun, he would explain to Don about the mangrove swamp and the water table and aquifers and hydraulic systems; all kinds of things that Don had never considered before. Like most people, he took the existence of water for granted. Dr. Kandy told Don how mysterious water itself was, how it's make up was only now being understood. He would talk about the molecular structure and the different types of water in almost poetic terms. His enthusiasm rubbed off on Don who began to read up the literature on the subject. And he also alarmed Don by sharing with him the pessimism of his prognosis.

During these months Don saw little of Nong Da and Marisa although he kept in touch every week by phone. He learnt how well Nong Da was doing and how Marisa had managed to set up her own production company. Whenever he called he would always be invited to join them for dinner, but he always made the excuse that he had too much work to do looking after Mr. Kandy. In fact, he could have easily made time to see them and it was not because he did not want to go around. Nothing would have pleased him more. But he held back because he was afraid of the strong feelings he had towards Nong Da, which he thought would be obvious to both of them. He did not want to be misread. He did not want to cause her any problems.

CHAPTER 36

Marisa had already guessed that the reason Don was avoiding seeing them was because he was in love with Nong Da. She had caught him looking at her many times with the kind of expression that she recognized straightaway as being something beyond mere fondness. She found his shyness sweet and touching and she had already thought to herself that, if Nong Da were ever to trust a man again and receive his touch, it would be with someone like Don. Nevertheless she felt immediately protective towards her charge, convincing herself that Nong Da was still too fragile to be able to cope with a relationship. The girl was now going to the classes and interacting with other young people and on the surface she seemed to be gaining a measure of confidence. But in a short space of time Marisa had already witnessed several moments when the shadows in Nong Da's heart burst out into the open with wild unpredictability. The traumas of her past revealed themselves soon after she moved in. There were temper tantrums over little misunderstandings and reactions that were out of proportion, moments of panic in a shopping mall and on one or two occasions a return to the catatonia. She did not want to see her pushed into any commitment. It was too soon for her to be involved with a man. Nong Da could so easily get hurt again.

So in the regular weekly telephone conversations with Don she never insisted on his coming to visit them but accepted his excuses gracefully. In fact, the truth was that she did not mind so much that he did not visit them, even though she missed his kind presence.

It was Arun she wanted to see again. Their brush with intimacy in his studio the night that Nong Da spied on them had left her full of questions. At the airport when they said their stiff, polite goodbyes, almost waiing, both of them had markedly avoided saying anything that would be implied as an obligation on the other. But in the way that he looked at her and smiled and nodded as he walked through the gate, she could tell that he too was communicating a sense of something unresolved between them.

As soon as he was gone she found herself thinking about him with an intensity that was surprising. She looked forward to the e-mails that he sent, written in funny English telling her how much he missed *naam pla naam prik*, the noodle stalls in the streets and even the 'perfume' of Bangkok. And she, in equally bad English, would reply with some mundane detail about what she was doing or offer him a report on Nong Da's progress. She never told him that there was nothing she wanted more than to be sitting in front of him again, listening to his complaints about the Bangkok art scene and all his gripes about what was wrong with the world and laughing with him. Or that she valued their friendship because for the first time in her life she had found a companion of the opposite sex with whom she felt relaxed, and not in some way expected to be on stage, to please and satisfy, or that the geographical distance that now separated them allowed her to realize that she had fallen in love with him. So she disguised her feelings and hid them behind the bland words of an alien language.

The e-mail served as their communication. But sometimes she would long to hear his voice and have a decent telephone conversation with him. But she did not want to overstep the invisible line that had been established.

⤺╪⤻

When she sent him an e-mail one morning saying that she was not well, it was not done with the intention of getting him to call her. She had merely stuck the information at the end of the message.

"...I am not feeling right. No energy, fevers, like flu," were the words she had used.

The next morning he called her. Later she calculated that it must have been about 2:00 in the morning in Paris.

"Have you seen a doctor? Do you have medicine? How did you catch it?"

He immediately bombarded her with accusations about the way that she did not look after herself in such a bad tempered tone that it made her laugh.

"I didn't mean to worry you," she said when he had finished. "It's probably just a virus. I'll be OK. I'm better already from hearing your voice."

She could not help but tell him how much she had been missing him and he replied that he felt the same, and that he was lonely without her. They made plans for her to fly over to meet him when the TV series was finished. But first he made her promise him to get a check-up at the clinic.

⸎

The call from Arun was the encouragement that Marisa needed to face something that she had been putting off. Marisa did not tell him that the fevers she mentioned in her e-mail had been going on for a couple of weeks and that they were not the normal high temperatures that accompanied a bout of 'flu'. Even though she slept in air-conditioning every night her bed would be covered in sweat. Several times during the day she had nearly blacked out. These were bad signs and she knew that she needed to get proper treatment. But since she was a child the thought of pain, sickness, doctors and hospitals was terrifying to her. For a while she prayed and took herbs but the symptoms persisted.

After their conversation she made an appointment for a check-up and the next morning found herself in the clinic, sitting among other women who looked as nervous as she did. There were seven of them sitting in the waiting room. It was raining outside and a child was crying. She wondered if all of them had been subjected, like her, to the physical examinations which she had found both unpleasant and painful. From their sidelong glances she knew that most of them recognized who she was, and perhaps in any other circumstance one or two might have approached her to compliment her about a movie she had made, just to make contact with a public figure. But they were all preoccupied with their own thoughts and worries that day.

Marisa already guessed what they were going to tell her even before the blood tests came back. The receptionist told her that they could have the results within an hour and that she could go and have a coffee and come back for them. But she preferred to stay and prepare herself. The palms of her hands were cold and she could hear her heart beating fast during those long minutes of waiting. She did not want to cling to any false hopes. At the same time the thought that she had a serious illness which could involve being hospitalized set her thoughts racing. She thought of how Nong Da would cope with the news if it was bad.

When Marisa heard her name called she nearly jumped out of her seat. The doctor, a middle aged man with glasses and a well rehearsed smile on his face, was looking at the computer screen as she entered his office. He greeted her and motioned her to sit down. She had hardly noticed what he looked like earlier when he had examined her. Now she could not help noticing that he was mostly bald and that he had left the few remaining strands grown long on one side in order to drape them over the shiny bald pate. She remembered a conversation she and Arun had once had about men who did this and the absurdity of it had made them laugh.

"Well, there is a problem," he said finally. "I'm sorry."

During the next few minutes Marisa found out that she had cancer of the ovaries.

"We can cure it," said the doctor confidently when he had finished explaining to her in detail, using the images on the screen at what stage her illness was. "There's nothing to worry about."

After uttering that ominous phrase he proceeded to tell her exactly what the therapy consisted of.

"I think we should begin as soon as possible," he continued. "The quicker we start the more chance we have of controlling it."

When she asked whether her hair would fall out he smiled benignly.

"Everyone is worried about that. But the answer is no. The chemo they use these days has very little side effect except for a bit of nausea. You can carry on with your life pretty much as normal."

She realized that his words were meant to give her courage and she was grateful for them. But later as she sat in the car, digesting the news that she had just received, she began to tremble violently. She wished that Arun was there to hold her in his arms.

⌒⇌⌒

The rain was stopping. The clouds were now parting to make way for shafts of golden sunlight to break through. Marisa drove in a state of heightened awareness, as though she had taken a hallucinogenic drug which now made every detail sharper and more poignant than it had ever been. The light coming after the downpour, catching the puddles and droplets that remained on the top of a zinc table of a noodle stall, struck her as absurdly beautiful. People were coming out of the shelter of doorways and folding up their umbrellas. She caught each one's expression and physical movement as though she was from an alien planet seeing this race for the first time. And her eyes feasted on the yellow and green of the taxis, which reminded her of a feeling from childhood that eluded description, and the splashes of colour coming at her from the sidewalks stirred in her old memories.

Fear made her hands tremble. But she was glad that she had taken the decision to confront the truth. The meeting with the doctor, and the official version that he presented to her, brought everything out of the shadows and into the light. She had up till then tried to retain that childlike, irrational sense of immortality, a sense that had been reinforced by being a star and an icon who was worshipped by her fans like a latter day goddess. Now the burden of having to maintain that illusion was gone once and for all.

As she made her way home that morning through the familiar streets Marisa saw, not with her eyes but with her heart, her own death as close as the motorbike that she narrowly missed. And all the while her mind held onto one thought, which was not a contradiction to this newly found insight of *annicam* and impermanence, but which was an affirmation that counterbalanced the despair and absurdity that would have otherwise overwhelmed her. The thought was simply: I want to go on living.

CHAPTER 37

Within a week of the check-up Marisa, thinly disguised behind her thick dark glasses and accompanied by Don and Nong Da returned to the clinic to receive her first dose of chemotherapy. She needed their presence and their support on this first visit in case the press or a curious admirer was going to be there to bother her. Her illness was made public knowledge within days of her visiting the clinic and once again the journalists had parked outside the condominium, waiting for whatever news they could get hold of about her. But apart from the fact that production on her TV series had to be stopped because of her deteriorating physical condition there was little else that was of interest except to the most morbid. So within days they struck camp and disappeared and the guards at the gates of the compound were left in peace. But given the national interest in the private lives of public figures, especially when they are faced with a crisis, there was always the possibility that the vultures would be circling round.

Don was glad that she had asked for his help. When Marisa rang him and told him the news, he had been shocked and then remorseful at not having called round to see how she and Nong Da were in all those months.

"I haven't been a good friend to you. I should have visited before," he told her that evening soon after he arrived.

"No. You've been busy. Besides it was partly my fault."

"Why? I don't understand."

"Dear Don. I know you're very fond of Nong Da. And I didn't really want you coming here and getting her involved with you. I thought it was too soon for her. So I let you get away with your feeble excuses, instead of telling you how much we both wanted to see you again. I'm sorry. It was stupid of me."

"No, you did right," said Don, who felt embarrassed that his feelings towards Nong Da were so transparent. "But don't worry. I'm never going to crowd her. The last thing I want to do is to hurt her."

"No. Don't you see? I think that it's beautiful that you should care for her. It's just me with my basic mistrust of life and men and my fear that, unless I'm in control, everything will go wrong. I want you to promise me that if something happens to me you will go on taking care of her."

"Of course I promise you. But you'll be well again soon." Don said these words with as much conviction as he could but he did not believe in them. And the look that Marisa threw him made him realize straightaway that he had made a mistake.

"Please! Didn't we say once that as friends we had to take the risk of being open and honest to each other? You don't need to encourage me like that. It has the opposite effect. I need to live with the truth in the time that's left to me."

⊱✦⊰

The three of them sat on the leather sofa under a large and bland abstract painting. The waiting room was in a different part of the clinic than before and had been designed to give a more informal feeling, like a corner of a hotel lobby. The smoke coloured windows looked out onto an impeccably kept Japanese garden. A pretty, neatly dressed receptionist sat behind her desk pretending to be writing. She looked up every now and then and smiled to them. The television was on, tuned to a news program, the volume turned down so low that it was hardly audible. The images were much the same as on any other day and along the bottom of the screen ran the stock market prices. None of them were really paying any attention. But there was nothing else to do, in that empty space in which the minutes seemed to stretch till eternity. And they did not want to continue talking, as they had done in the car, about how they missed Arun.

"Listen! Don't you start getting sad on me," Marisa said, showing her annoyance. "I'm glad he's not here right now as a matter of fact. He'd be fussing and making the wrong comments."

Both Don and Nong Da knew that she only half mean this. Disappointment was written all over her face when she told them that he had called to say that he would be arriving later in the week after putting everything in order, because he did not intend to finish his residency but was going to return to Bangkok for good.

"I didn't expect him to do that for my sake," she said, not trying to hide her delight at his decision.

Arun's presence that morning in the plush gloominess of those surroundings would have helped to take their minds off the matter at hand. But instead, each sat still and silent on the flowery sofa, staring at the screen with its dreary news so as to distract themselves from their emotions.

Marisa was holding Nong Da's hand and in the touch she could feel the tension they shared. The evening when she told her about the illness, Nong Da, who now called her 'mae', broke down and said,

"I lost my real mother. It was this same disease that took her and look where I landed up. I won't go on living if you die. I'd rather kill myself".

⁓✝⁓

Marisa held her tightly and told her that what she had was nowhere near to being life threatening, but Nong Da would not be consoled. It was only when Marisa promised that she could take time off her studies and accompany her to the clinic and look after her that Nong Da calmed down.

Now, as they sat side by side watching the images come and go like some shadow play, Marisa kept trying not to feel overwhelmed by all the complicated feelings she was going through. It was not just the immediate fear of the needle that they were going to stick into her vein and the poisonous medicine that they were about to inject into her system, but also her dilemma about the whole process. Within minutes she was about to receive her first treatment, and yet she knew that her scepticism about chemotherapy remained intact, despite the doctor's reassurances. But more than her doubts there was a kind of panic at the thought that she was about to cross a threshold into an unknown and basically hostile territory, even though she knew that this was a place where many women had been and survived. Ever since she suspected that she was ill, Marisa had read everything she could lay her hands on about their journey and the processes that they had been through. She had been touched by the stories of struggle and affirmation and despair and self discovery. Some of them had given her courage, others said nothing with which she could identify. But when she found out for certain that her body was being attacked, none of these roadmaps seemed relevant to her. They were other people's experiences. The journey that she had to make was her own and she had to navigate her way through the labyrinth of feelings into which the illness was leading and deal with the monsters on the way, with nothing to guide her but her own heart.

Marisa had never been so scared in her life. But at the same time she derived a quiet strength from the small hand that she was holding, and for a moment, forgetting her own predicament, she felt a deep love surge up in her for this girl who in the last months had become the closest person she had known. She turned and smiled at her, but Nong Da's eyes were fixed on the screen.

A buzzer sounded.

"Khun Marisa," the receptionist called out. "The doctor's ready for you now."

She squeezed Nong Da's hand and, getting up, she straightened her skirt, but she did not turn to either of them as she went through the door.

CHAPTER 38

It was Autumn in Paris. The dead leaves were floating down over the empty square onto the cobblestones and the cast iron benches. Reds and yellows and shades of gold that you never saw in Thailand, thought Arun, as he sat in the cafe at his usual table by the window and looked out at the scene that he knew he would probably not see again in a long time, if ever again. And he took in the hazy softness of the afternoon light which was quietly revelatory and totally distinct from the white dazzle of the tropics.

During his stay in Madrid six years earlier he had been so obsessed by the painting in the Prado that he had paid little attention to the streets and the squares. His days there had been divided between the museum, the studio and the university library. He had not allowed himself to merge with the city. In Paris it was the opposite. He had changed. He was no longer hungrily searching for direction. He had by now found his artistic path, and even though he made the obligatory tours of the famous museums and galleries which yielded their moments of inspiration, he knew that he was not at a point in his life where he was looking for anything that could be found in those places.

The residency demanded little of his time. He was expected to turn up at the studio every morning, work on his painting, and chat with other artists from Asia in the canteen before leaving. This daily routine left him many hours to explore and get to know Paris. So Arun took full advantage of the luxury of the being able to stroll along a side street, browse in a bookshop, walk along a tree lined avenue, visit an old church, stop in a café, stand on a bridge looking at the river and the boats going by; things he never did in the polluted chaos of Bangkok. It brought him fresh ideas and a sense of joy and freedom that he had not expected. He had even thought once or twice that Paris was a place where he could live and work. It felt good to be away from Bangkok. Here in this foreign land he was anonymous and he did not have to be involved in its politics and its conflicts. There was space to breath and the possibilities were beginning to open up in his mind.

But then there was Marisa, like a siren calling him across the distances. In Paris, during those long solitary walks in the sun and the rain, in the morning mist and under the stars, he thought constantly of his involvement with her. He recalled their fortuitous meeting at the temple and tried without success to understand how it had come about; whether, as he had said to them, some strange karma had thrown them together or whether it was merely coincidence, which was equally inexplicable. The empathy between them had been comfortable from the beginning and he would have been content to remain behind the barrier that separated friendship from intimacy. Even though he felt physically attracted to her, he denied it to himself throughout those first months, partly because he could not imagine that she wanted anything more from him than the friendship that he offered and partly because he was afraid of the powerful feelings that were rising in him. He had always known that he was not the kind of person who could depend on his heart to tell him what to do. He did not trust his feelings to guide him. He had always prided himself that he never let desire alone take over. Even with Gaew he had been pragmatic. It had always been easy when no real emotion had been involved, when it was a matter of attraction seeking gratification. He had been through a string of casual relationships like this.

But with Marisa it was so different that he felt he had lost all his points of reference. With her it was impossible to maintain any of the old attitudes because the emotions that he was experiencing were too strong for him. And yet when he realized that he was deeply in love with her he still held on to his last line of defence, which was a refusal to acknowledge it openly, because it would have meant crossing the threshold into a commitment which held the possibility of hurt and pain. For this was how, from the time he was a boy, he had always viewed the intimacy between a man and a woman. Watching his parents' doomed love had marked him.

Then there was the memory of that last meeting at the studio when they came close to making love. Especially during those first weeks in Paris, it stayed with him vividly and there were times when he would feel waves of physical longing wash over him. He would regret his ridiculous show of self control which was meant to show her, in such a clumsy old fashioned way, that he was an honourable man who was not guided by lust. In fact he was so surprised that evening by her response to his touch and found it too weird that the former object of his teenage fantasies was in his arms, a person of flesh and blood, that he felt overwhelmed and unable to respond spontaneously. Being away from her, he felt the intensity of suspended desire and unexpressed tenderness.

He sent her e-mails that had told her nothing about what he was doing in Paris; trite messages and little jokes, smokescreens that hid his feelings and allowed him to avoid the real issue, which was his love for her. And then came the news of her sickness.

⟨═╪═⟩

The small, scruffy café stood on a corner of a street behind a busy boulevard. He had come across it by accident on his very first morning in the city, when he was walking around the Montparnasse district where he was staying, and he had been coming back there nearly every day to have a coffee before going to the studio or a drink on the way back to his rooms. People in Bangkok had warned him that Parisians were rude and cold but the owner was a friendly woman who had been to Thailand on holiday. She had visited Bangkok, she told him soon after he began to frequent the place. She had been to Hua Hin, Chiengmai and Phuket. She communicated to him in broken English how exotic she found it all, how the food was too hot, how the people were simple and happy and kind.

That afternoon, as the light slowly faded, Arun was watching an elegantly dressed woman cross the square and pass a tramp, who raised a bottle to her and shouted out a greeting, to which she did not respond. The leaves were falling thicker now. A strong breeze was getting up. There was an hour left before he had to make his way to the airport. He had locked up his room and returned the key to the concierge and come to the cafe to enjoy his last moments in the city, having a quiet drink and observing the square that had become familiar. He sat there with the suitcase on the floor beside him. The owner was drying glasses at the counter and humming a tune to herself. The second glass of white wine that she had offered him produced a momentary rush of euphoria. But it did not take away the underlying disquiet and confusion that had been lurking around all day. He was not feeling simple, or happy or kind, but nervous about returning to Bangkok and seeing Marisa again.

He had been thinking about nothing else for days. The confirmation of her illness had shocked him and his first reaction was to rush back on the next flight. But he found that he was relieved when, during the same conversation, she provided him with the excuse not to do so by telling him to sort things out properly before leaving Paris, to inform his sponsors and the professors at the school, to make sure that they understood his reasons for leaving. Since he was breaking his contract, he had to at least explain himself to the people who invited him over, if only for the sake of decency. And then there was the studio to pack up and the canvasses to be shipped back. Then, to further reassure him, she said that she would be fine with Don and Nong Da to look after her and take her to the clinic.

"Yes. You must tie up the loose ends," she had said firmly just before saying goodbye. But immediately after their conversation he felt guilty and callous for not telling her that he would drop everything and rush back to be by her side, especially when he had been telling her and himself how much he was missing her. And he realized, from her voice, that she had guessed that he was not yet ready to be with her and to take care of her.

As a result of the phone call the last week in Paris passed by as though he were walking in a fog that would not lift and he suffered the kind of mental pain that only those who have known what it is to be consumed by doubt can truly understand. For it was doubt that was the shadow stalking him. The questions that shot up into his mind, as he paced through the old streets of the city and across its bridges and back again, were sharp reminders of his failure to be courageous and simple. And in the end, instead of doing anything that he had said he would do, and making sure, as he had promised Marisa, that everything was in order before he left, he merely drifted into an indulgent bout of self disgust, which was relieved by drinking vast quantities of the thick, cloudy pastis that numbed his mind for a while.

CHAPTER 39

The flight from Paris was packed and Arun did not manage to sleep. Having told himself to stay sober he had ended up drinking too many whiskies and his eyes were tired from watching the video movies on the impossibly small screen. It was already light when the captain told them that they were going to be in Bangkok in twenty minutes. The announcement made him lean over and look out of the window. He caught a glimpse of some buildings, a temple, a straight road and paddy fields that lay covered with water. At the sight Arun felt a mixture of elation and foreboding.

It was nearly a week after Marisa's first treatment. He did not tell the others that he was coming because he did not want them to be at the airport to meet him. He wanted a little breathing space to prepare himself and had planned to go to the studio first and unpack, shower and rest before seeing Marisa. But on the expressway, as though suddenly embarrassed by his selfishness, he changed his mind and told the taxi driver to take him to the condo by the river. There was no point in putting off any longer what he had come back to do.

There were few cars about at that hour; just the city, with its unruly skyscrapers, unfinished constructions and giant billboards spread out on either side of the carriageway. The sky was covered with thin layers of clouds that were every shade of grey. Here and there the early morning sun pierced through, catching a clump of treetops or a temple roof. But in the distance Arun could see that darker clouds were already forming. He eased his aching body back in the seat and struggled to keep awake, while the young driver, still high from the amphetamines that he used for the long hours of work, continued a non-stop monologue. He had been busy all night, he said, taking people to and from the clubs round the Rama IX district, and then later had ferried some bar girls back home. He had not stopped driving, but he wasn't complaining. Business had picked up a little recently and he was glad. The tourists were coming back, especially the Asians. Bangkok was going to be one long party again. He did not usually go to the airport, but he had dropped off a Japanese businessman. He was starting to get tired. He knew he should rest. Just before dawn he had seen an accident in which a bus had collided with a truck. Both drivers were killed. It was a bad sign. Arun was going to be his last fare before heading back to the garage.

⚒

The night porter, a new man who Arun had not seen before, eyed him suspiciously and insisted that he should phone up to the apartment first to check. But Arun told him gently that he was an old friend of Marisa and that if the porter was not sure he could accompany him in the lift. The man was apologetic and explained that there had been journalists hanging around and that the other occupants had been complaining. He had been given strict instructions not to allow them anywhere near her.

"I'm not a journalist. I've just come back from France," said Arun aware that this made no sense. But the man seemed to be satisfied with his explanation and waved him through.

Nong Da opened the door to him and showing no sign of surprise waied him. Arun could tell nothing from her face.

"Is she all right?" he asked in a low voice.

"Oh yes. It's just that she couldn't sleep all night. She was sick a couple of times. It's the medicine they gave her." She explained to him in a half whisper that Don had been there all week but had left the day before because he had to attend a conference in Ayudhya. Then she led him into the living room.

Marisa was sitting in an armchair by the window, wearing her nightgown and a pair of dark glasses. She had decided that since she could not sleep it was more comfortable to be upright with the bucket on the floor next to her, rather than getting out of bed and walking to the bathroom every time the nausea came. The doctor had told her that these symptoms would disappear in a matter of a few days and that afterwards she would, in his words, be back to normal. But it was hard to see how. Her whole body felt as though it had been invaded. Her stomach hurt from retching out the bile. Her head throbbed with pain.

While Nong Da was still asleep on the mattress in the bedroom, she had tiptoed out and made herself some lemon grass tea. Later she had seen the dawn rising over the city and the first light catch the surface of the Chao

Phraya River and she had sat watching the boats coming up the river to dock at Klongtoey. The sound of the ships' horn that morning was like a long wail that echoed the state of her heart.

When the door bell rang she guessed that it was Arun. But she did not move from her position, in case she was wrong. Despite what she had said to him in their telephone call, she had been disappointed at his failure to make an effort to be with her when she needed his support.

She could see him now in the reflection of the window, like a watery apparition. He was standing an arm's length away and looking at her with a sad smile on his lips, as if he were not sure if he was pleased to see her. She could not blame him. She had changed in such a short time. She was now a sick woman. Slowly and without turning her head, she held out her hand which he took and held with both of his.

"I'm in love with you. I can't cope with this," he said simply to their reflections, and she nodded.

"I couldn't come before..."

Now she pulled her hand away and put her index finger to her lips to silence him. Then she pointed to the river below as though the answer to his dilemmas and doubts lay down there in the dark green water. Finally, her voice cracking with emotion, she said:

"I am glad that you have come back and that you will be close by, in the same city. I am not going to be dependent on you. I want you to carry on with your life as before, and continue with your painting and all the rest of it. I only ask for your friendship. It was what we had at the beginning and it will sustain me now."

CHAPTER 40

Don looked up momentarily at the speaker who was on the podium that was twenty metres in front of him. He had almost finished his doodle of a serpent's head on the bottom of the notes that he was making. Earlier along the margin he had completed a picture of Nong Da which looked nothing like her. The speech that he was having difficulty following was being delivered by a professor of geology, who was using technical terms which Don could not understand. Behind him a large screen displayed the various images of land erosion that he was describing. It was not that Don was bored, but he felt that, during the course of that Saturday, his mind had already crammed in too much information. Besides, it seemed that every speaker who had got up had delivered more or less the same message. As he decorated the head with scales he was thinking of Nong Da and wondering how she was coping with Marisa.

He had told Peter that he was not going to attend the conference because a friend was ill and he had to help look after her. He was still slightly annoyed that Peter had insisted.

"I'm sorry, my friend," said Peter. "You have to come with me on this trip. It's really crucial. I leave in a few days and you've got to carry on here for me. I want you to know everything that's happening so that when the time comes you'll be able to say the right things and make the right decisions."

It was the first time that there had been any tension between them. In the months that they had been working together they had built up an easy-going friendship and shared bits and pieces of their private lives. Peter had talked of his divorce and his grown up children living in Canada, and Don had told him about his early life as the son of a diplomat and of later being a monk in Nongkhai. The areas of the past that both chose to leave out were understood to be the private domain that each would maintain.

On the professional level of their relationship Don could see why Peter was so well respected. He had never before seen the kind of intellectual passion that he saw in Peter's dedication to his field and gradually he had come to fall under the older man's spell. Their conversations awoke in Don the feeling that, despite Peter's basic pessimism and the gravity of the problem, there was a glimmer of hope, and that with intelligence and integrity things had a slim chance of changing for the better in the world, that there was everything to struggle for.

He understood, of course why Peter felt so strongly about this particular conference. From their first meeting he had been telling Don that he was worried about the inevitability that Bangkok would very soon be submerged under water if serious measures were not taken in time. Despite the efforts of successive governments to speed up the programs of reforestation, there was now, just as the environmentalists had predicted, a serious absence of watershed areas that could hold the rainfall. The dams that had been built on the Ping and the Pasak Rivers to control the water that flowed down from the north were near to eroding and he could not see how the system of drainage that existed in the capital would be sufficient for the kind of extreme conditions that were appearing in the last few years, due to global warming.

That year the monsoon had been unusually fierce in the whole South East Asian region, with the highest rainfall ever recorded for the month of September in Thailand. A disaster was looming. Already a few of the northern provinces had been declared as emergency zones. He had already persuaded 'Clean Thailand' to try to convince the Ministry of Waterworks, as well as the Bangkok governor's office, into taking the appropriate measures to pre-empt the catastrophe. This would involve a well coordinated effort by various ministry departments to establish a pre-emergency plan. But at some point, almost predictably, given the volatile political situation, the communications between those who should have been responsible broke down.

⋙ ✦ ⋘

The conference, held in a hotel in Ayudhya, had been organized by a United Nations Aid agency dealing with the environmental problems in South East Asia. 'Clean Thailand' was one of the local NGO's invited, along with several international agencies. Peter saw it as a last chance to tell the Thai public that the probability of a flood hitting the capital in the near future was not a question of scare mongering or the fearful predictions of some eccentric scientist, but that it was based on hard evidence which could not be ignored.

When he came to give his speech, Don, who had the task of doing the simultaneous translation, was surprised by the emotion his mentor displayed when trying to press home the point that it was no longer a matter of conjecture, that all the calculations had been made in detail, that the likelihood of the water breaking through the dam and flooding the capital was a foregone conclusion, that the only uncertainty was how much damage this would cause. Normally Peter spoke in a soft voice even when he was conveying the most frightening details of environmental disasters. But that afternoon he was shouting his message to the audience as though he wanted to wake them up and get the sense of urgency across before it was too late.

He pointed to the fact, affirmed by the meteorological office, that the weather conditions were not likely to change much within the next few weeks. The high pressure system over China colliding with the low pressure in the south had already dumped almost 200 millimetres of rain over Chiengmai province. The river waters were now surging down south. Given that the tide in the capital was soon to reach its highest level, the outcome seemed inevitable. The monkey's cheek system that was meant to drain off the excess water would be overrun within a day at the most, according to Peter.

In the press conference that followed there was pandemonium. The reporters shoved their microphones into his face, as they did to politicians, and posed their questions so fast that Peter hardly had time to answer them. Don did his best to use his body to shield him, but he did not succeed in protecting him from the onslaught. When it was all over they drove back to Bangkok in the van with the rest of the team. At the entrance to the hotel they said goodbye and wished each other well. Peter stepped forward and hugged Don saying:

"I'm sorry I have to leave. It feels like I'm abandoning a sinking ship. But I can't break my commitment. I've delayed it till the last minute already. I'm pinning my hopes on you. You've got about a month to try to convince them. And in that time if you should fail I would tell all your friends and anyone you know to leave the city if they can."

CHAPTER 41

During the days immediately after Peter's departure, Don was given the job of speaking to the media on behalf of 'Clean Thailand' about the possibility of flooding in Bangkok. As a result of the Ayudhya conference there was a sudden focus of interest on the subject which lasted a whole week. There was a feature on the main written articles in which his opinion was quoted. And several television interviews in which he tried his best to put forward all the arguments that he had absorbed from the conversations with Peter. Finally a televised round table discussion had him debating with a government official from the Department of Water Resources and an expert on flood control from the Bangkok governor's office. They both offered reassurances that the situation was under control and pointed out the measures that were to be taken if the threat was seen to be real. When Don countered with the arguments that Peter had put forward, he was accused of being an amateur who had no solid proof for his theories and that what he was claiming was irresponsible and would damage tourism and cause panic among the city dwellers. During the debate it rapidly became obvious to him that it was politically inexpedient for anybody to admit that there was a crisis at all.

Among those he spoke to in private there seemed to be a general feeling of resignation. His mother and aunts, to whom he communicated by phone his concerns, talked of the floods they had known in 1944 and then in 1983 with a certain nostalgia. They told him how they missed going round in boats to do their shopping and how they paddled to each other's houses to pay their visits. He tried to tell them that it was not going to be the same as before, when Bangkok still had waterways that functioned, that this time the volume of water was going to be greater than they had ever seen and that because of the pollution there would be an epidemic. He realized how hard it was using science and logic to convince people and warn them before the event without sounding like a madman obsessed by a dark vision. It would have been easier if he had spoken to them with the divinely inspired authority of a shaman.

In the end Don felt that he had let Peter down by not being forceful or clever enough to get the information across to the public. It seemed to him that he had not managed to persuade anyone who was not already converted to the cause. He blamed himself for even thinking that he was up to the task. But Marisa and Arun, who had watched him on television with pride and admiration, never imagining that he was capable of such forceful expression in public, told him not to be hard on himself. It was to them that he went when his fifteen minutes of fame were over, vowing that he would never again pretend to know about something about which he only had superficial knowledge handed down from others.

"They wouldn't have listened to you if you were the world's top expert. It's all about politics as always, and basic laziness. The governor's just about to retire. He's taken his cut from signing all those land deals. He doesn't want to have to do any real work now that he's on his way out," said Arun, with his usual cynicism. "You've tried your best. Now let it go."

They discussed the idea of all of them packing up and leaving Bangkok, just as Peter had urged, but they knew that it was not a serious option. Don was committed to helping organize an emergency shelter in the Klongtoey district, for those who were considered to be at most risk. And Marisa, who had already rejected Arun's suggestion of taking her to a clinic in Europe, said that she did not want to plan anything so drastic as leaving the city.

"We'll stock up and stay here and watch the waters rise," she said.

It was Nong Da who expressed what they were all feeling. She told them simply that she was terrified of what was going to come.

"I know that it will be terrible," she said. "People will die. The city will suffer. And I don't want to stay here. But where else can I go? I don't want to lose you."

PART 7

CHAPTER 42

According to the official reports, the level of sea water was going to be at its highest on October 14th, the day that Marisa was due to have her second treatment. From the beginning of the month the atmosphere in the city was tense and the talk was of nothing else. Politics and gossip and even the crash of the stock market seemed to become irrelevant in the face of what most of Bangkok's inhabitants now accepted as the inevitable impending disaster that was about to hit them. Despite the continuing reassurances from the authorities, which seemed increasingly irrelevant, many of the inhabitants living on the banks of the main river and along the canals were already piling up sandbags and unblocking whatever drainage system they had. In the stores and markets people were noticeably buying more tin food and other essentials that they could store. Bottled drinking water was already running out. Those who remembered previous floods knew that there would be a chaotic rush at the last moment. A steady exodus had begun. The airport and the bus stations were crowded with those who had decided to leave; the rich to Europe or Australia for a family holiday and the poor to their villages. But most of the inhabitants of Bangkok had no choice but to wait for what now looked like an inevitable disaster. Much of Ayudhya was already under a metre and there was no sign that the tactic to deviate the flow would work that year.

Don drew no satisfaction from seeing Peter's predictions coming true, nor that, contrary to what he had thought, people had actually taken heed of the warnings he had voiced. As the days went by he saw how the sense of danger was gripping the city, and with it the awakening of the some primal fear which no one was able to contain. It felt as if the Naga was stirring in the depths and that its power was about to burst out and envelop them all.

***

He did not see much of Marisa and Arun during those weeks because he was putting in long hours in Klongtoey, where 'Clean Thailand' and other local

NGO's had persuaded the headmistress of a secondary school to allow them to turn the building into a temporary shelter. She had chosen to ignore the circular sent round by the Ministry, saying that there was no need for extra precautions apart from closing down the school for a few days should there be flooding, because she had lost her own little sister in the cholera epidemic that accompanied the last flood. Now she acted as a director to the work which drew wholehearted support from a population who knew that they were in an area of the city that would be the first to feel the effects. There were all the logistical arrangements; food needed to be stocked, bedding put in place, a clinic set up, generators and pumps brought in and repaired if necessary. Don's job was to go round the maze of alleyways visiting the families and handing out leaflets making sure they had all the information and would be ready to leave their dwellings when the time came.

He had brought Nong Da to help him. After seeing how frightened she was by the thought of the flood, he told her that he too was afraid of what was going to happen. But instead of just feeling paralyzed by the feeling of helplessness he suggested that it was better to join in with the effort to do everything possible to minimize its devastation. He was glad that she let herself be persuaded. Together they handed out the leaflets and knocked on people's doors. At first he noticed that Nong Da was too shy to make contact and waited for him to do the talking. But within a few days he saw that she was finding her confidence and enjoying giving out advice and encouragement.

For Nong Da the knowledge that Bangkok was soon going to be flooded filled her with the same anxiety as she had known when they were driving her to the 'Club L'Amour' to her first and last assignment; the feeling that she was going to drown and be swallowed up by a huge monster. Don's words had done nothing to make her feel any better. She was surprised when he said that he too was scared. She still felt awkward with him and she sensed that he was shy of her. And she was not sure at all if she was capable of helping him when he asked her to join him. But she went along, partly because now that Arun was back she wanted to be out of the way and also because she wanted to see for herself if what Don said was true.

At first it was hard going. Even though she was born in Bangkok and had spent her early years in Laadprao she had never seen anything like the places that they visited in Klongtoey. They walked through muddy lanes and along open sewers that exuded a steamy putrid stench. They sat in shacks that seemed to have been put up in a matter of hours; bits of hardwood and corrugated iron and discarded material that had been roughly assembled. They were invited into dark, narrow rooms where rats scuttled in the corner.

During those long days Nong Da began to develop a respect for Don, as she watched the tireless energy that he was putting into helping the people in the area. She was moved by the care and the humility and tact that he showed when he was talking to them. Gradually, during the noodles that they shared in their lunch breaks and on the bus journeys and taxi rides, they began to cross the no-man's land and communicate their thoughts and feelings in a way which Nong Da found comfortable and exciting. They did not go back into the past. They talked mainly about the eccentric people they met and laughed at the funny stories that they heard.

In that harsh, ugly corner of the city she began to feel the possibility of being well. The demons came back from time to time to tell her not to hope for anything, because she was still the same unclean animal who did not deserve any happiness. But whereas before she had no means to cope with these voices, she now found that she did not take them so seriously. The place out of which they came was no longer so frighteningly all-encompassing. She had not imagined that it would be possible to trust any man again let alone to enjoy being with him. She knew that Don would never do anything to hurt her. And little by little, in a way that was hardly discernible at first, a gentle glow began to spread into her heart.

⟨⟩✚⟨⟩

She decided that she would keep her feelings for Don a secret. Even though she wanted more than anything to share them with Marisa, with all that was going on it did not seem the right time. But she could not have known that to Marisa and Arun the change in her was so obvious that they had to stop themselves from teasing her about it. They would hear her humming a song to herself in the kitchen, and noticed how she took a bit longer getting dressed in the morning. Now the evenings, which were once spent in front of the television, were dedicated to reading all the literature that Don gave her to study, and when he dropped by she would make a point of not looking in his direction. Most of all they saw how her eyes were shining with the light that could only come from one source. But they decided that she would tell them when the time was right for her.

To Marisa, Nong Da's presence in the apartment during that period before the flood, and the innocent energy that she gave off, did much to lift her sombre mood. The first session of chemotherapy and the weeks of nausea that followed had left her depressed. Her appetite was off. Her body felt tired and the uncertainty of the future weighed down on her. She could not help expressing the feelings of self pity to Arun. But she was not sure whether or not he could really cope with the intensity of her situation. For she knew that it was only the beginning of her decline.

CHAPTER 43

Two days before the full moon the sea level was rising rapidly towards its highest level. The river, swollen like an overfed python, had burst the dam at both Pasak and Saraburi. There were less than thirty hours before the two masses of water were to come together. There was no surprise when it was announced on television and the radio and on the front page of every newspaper that Bangkok was now on full flood alert. Many of the sois were now under a foot of water. But this was due to the rain which had been coming down steadily for most of the week. Lightning had struck several pylons and already there was widespread electricity failure; the telephone lines were breaking down and there was little that the already overstretched engineers could do. All of it was only a foretaste of what was about to come. The fact that all the city's inhabitants were aware of this generated both a sense of solidarity among them that no ideology could have produced, but at the same time a kind of despair that few had ever known, living in a country that had rarely suffered the kind of natural disasters that were common in the rest of the region.

The very same people who had argued with Don now spoke without conviction about the measures that had been taken by the government and the army. It was obvious that they were the scapegoats who would be accused of giving out the wrong advice and they were already covering themselves by saying that the ministers in their departments had not listened to their words. But, in the face of the imminent crisis, their suggestions about what the inhabitants of the capital should do to protect themselves sounded pathetically late in coming. And besides, nobody in the city was concerned any more about who to blame. The political context was as tired as yesterday's B movie.

In those last two days everybody was busy making sure that the preparations they were making against the coming flood would be sufficient. Where possible the whole household had been moved to the upper floors where families would now share sleeping space and cook their meals on the balconies. Cars had been cranked up onto newly constructed wooden platforms. Boats that had not been used since the last time Bangkok flooded were brought out from storage and repaired. The ones who had not believed that it would happen were now rushing round trying to buy sacks, sandbags and pumps, all of which had trebled in price if they were available at all. And while the rain bucketed down on the tiles and rooftops and plastic awnings, the black water pushing up from the drains brought with it the armies of cockroaches who now found themselves homeless. And so the city was gradually and visibly returning to its swampy roots. Those who had faith lit their joss-sticks and candles, remembering the Naga. But they knew in their hearts that it was too late for their prayers.

⤙✦⤚

It took all her theatrical skills for Marisa to persuade the doctor to give her an earlier appointment than the one originally fixed. The first treatment had left her feeling frail and the fevers were still bothering her at night. She needed his reassurance that it was normal for her to be feeling so low and that the therapy would eventually yield good results. The doctor had told her to call him any time that she wanted, if she was feeling unwell. But when she spoke to his secretary, she was told that there was no appointment till the end of the month. The hesitation in the girl's voice made Marisa wonder if she was being told the truth. She guessed that, like all those who had the means to go elsewhere, the doctor was planning to abandon the city. When she demanded to speak to him personally there was a long silence. Finally he came on the phone and told her that the second treatment could wait, having previously insisted that the timing was crucial, and that the success of the therapy depended on it. Besides, he said, he did not want her to travel across the city in the rain, since her immunity was low after the first dose of chemo.

All of it sounded reasonable, but she did not trust him. It was the smooth voice and the all too ready answers that did not ring true. And the thought that he, a doctor, was about to leave Bangkok at a time when his skills were most needed made her angry. With as much command as she could muster, she told him that she insisted on seeing him before he went away and left him with no doubt that he would have to comply.

She drove herself to the clinic that morning. Don and Nong Da were now camping out at the centre in Klongtoey, where the local inhabitants were already coming in with their cloth bundles and their bedding. They had no choice but to help with the organization and were not able to take time off. She had told them that she did not mind going alone, and that, in fact, it was important for her to do so because it would give her more courage to be unaccompanied and independent. The effects of the chemo would not kick in until a few days later. That was when she would need them all to give her support.

She had also told them that she did not want Arun to accompany her that morning. They had been arguing for the past few days over his reluctance to go to the studio and make sure that the paintings were going to be safe. She guessed the reason for his stubbornness, but she did not express this to him. The past two weeks of being constantly by each other's side had not been easy. She could see how he was struggling to be caring and attentive to her, but how hard it was for him to cope with the reality of being with a sick person. They had not made love. And she knew that, although his love for her was genuine, he was scared of coming into physical intimacy with someone who was as ill as she was. He told her that he did not want to leave her alone in the apartment but she knew that it was not true, that he wanted to be back in his own place, preparing another canvas. She could not make him understand that she did not feel threatened by this.

The doctor was especially friendly. He examined Marisa and asked her how she had coped with the first treatment. When she told him that she had been sick for almost two weeks he merely raised his eyebrows. She was sure that this expression of surprise was not quite genuine. The appointment lasted no more than half an hour. At the end of it she asked him where he was going and he said that he was flying to India to do a Yoga course with his guru.

"I am very stressed out with the work right now," he told her. "I need a break."

When she left she had the feeling that she would not be seeing him again.

Except for a few private cars and motorbikes carving their way through the puddles the streets were ominously empty that morning. No roar of buses, no noisy tuk-tuks. In fact there was hardly any activity. The pavements that were usually thick with stalls selling fake products to the tourists were bare. In the covered market near the condo the trestle tables were piled up in a corner next to discarded boxes and damp newspapers. Bottles and plastic containers floated in the puddles by the roadside. A smell of rotting vegetation hung in the air. Under the bridges, beggars and stray dogs huddled in the mud. The sky was still the colour of sepia and there was no sign that the rain was going to stop.

Arun had been standing in a doorway shivering for half an hour peering at the desolate scene. The call-a-cab service had closed down that day and he had walked out to find a taxi on the road, but it seemed that the drivers, like everyone else, were not bothering to work. The umbrella had not kept him from getting soaked and he was on the point of giving up and running back to the condo, when an old songtaew taxi that looked as though it would hardly make the journey came cruising towards him. He could barely believe it when it stopped and the driver rolled his window down, and asked him where he was going. As he climbed in he felt a sense of relief. He did not mind that the seat was torn and smelt of piss and sweat or that the driver insisted on more than three times the usual fare to take him there and back.

"I'm not even going to let you bargain with me today," he told Arun. "You're lucky I happen to be going by. You won't get anyone else taking you. What are you doing out in the streets anyway? Everyone else is at home praying." He laughed.

As he sat looking out through the curtain of rain, Arun cursed himself for not having taken Don's advice. As usual he had dithered and left things too late. He should have gone to the studio a week earlier to make sure that the paintings were safely packed and stored. But he had been annoyed at his friend's certainty and jealous of the way that Marisa had listened to him like some prophet. Delaying the task at hand was his way of affirming his own doubts. In their arguments, which were brief and unpleasant, he insisted that Peter Kandy had made the wrong calculations, that all the talk of flooding was exaggerated and unnecessarily alarmist, that the panic that gripped the city was typical of the herd mentality that Bangkokians regularly displayed. He did not really believe any of this and now he felt ridiculous for having been so obnoxious and cynical. His childish show of defiance and stubbornness had backfired and in the process he had again managed to let Marisa down. Although she had insisted that she preferred to go to the clinic alone, he felt that he should have gone with her. But time was fast running out and he knew that if he did not go to the studio that day the paintings would be lost.

The soi was under a foot of water. The songtaew was high enough of the ground to clear it but Arun had to first offer the driver another hundred baht before he agreed to turn into it and wait for him. Outside the entrance to the studio Arun's neighbours, wearing rubber boots and plastic macs were trying to unblock a drain. It looked like a pointless exercise. He took off his shoes, folded up his trousers, stepped into the water and waded past them waving as he did so. From their expressions he could tell that something was wrong.

Inside he saw that the water had already seeped in from the garden at the back and there was a pool along the outside wall that would inevitably cover the whole area before long. Fortunately the paintings, which were all on the other side of the studio, were still dry. He had been thinking of taking the ones he felt were the best over to Marisa's apartment. But when he stood there in front of them all he knew that he would have to take the rest of the day to decide which these were. Besides he knew that there was a risk of getting them wet when he took them out to the taxi.

Sensing that he was running out of time, Arun burst into action with frantic energy and began to lift those that were hanging on the wall off the hooks and stack them on top of a cupboard in the corner. Then he found an old bedspread which he threw over them. The rest that were leaning in the far corner he took through into the spare room where Nong Da had slept. Next he dragged in the dining table and put it on top of the bed and placed the paintings one by one on top of this improvised platform. By the time he finished the sweat was soaking through his shirt. Then he took an overnight bag from his own room and threw into it some clothes and underwear. Then he knelt down opened the drawer of the bedside table and brought out a cigar box in which he kept things that had been precious to him since he was a boy; old photos, his father's watch, shells. He was about to put it into the bag when he stopped, sat on the bed, and realized all of a sudden that he was about to remove these things because he was going to lose them if he left them behind. And he thought about the paintings and a feeling of desperation overwhelmed him. Before closing up the studio Arun looked round one last time quickly as though to make sure that he would remember his home.

The driver started the engine as soon as he saw him coming.

"One more minute and I wouldn't have waited for you. I told my wife I wouldn't be long. She'll be worried about me," he said as he revved the motor.

Just at that moment the jingle of Arun's mobile phone sounded.

It was Marisa.

"I'm stuck. The car's stalled. It must be the water. It won't start. I won't make it without your help."

CHAPTER 44

Marisa found shelter under a section of the expressway near Rama IX intersection. She had chosen the route thinking that it was the quickest way back home and the one to be less likely to be under water. But now she wished that she had taken the usual road that she knew. Standing in the middle of the road she had tried several times to wave down the few vehicles that passed her on the way towards the toll gate, which was about a kilometre further up the road. But either they did not see her or thought better of stopping to take a stranger. Discouraged and soaked through to her skin she had retreated under the concrete. As she waited eagerly for Arun to arrive she tried not to be afraid. She had given him the directions and he had told her to stay put, and that he would be there soon. But the feeling of collapse was palpable and enhanced by the bleakness of the surroundings. The shop houses across from where she stood were all shut up and barred. The electricity lines gave off a sizzling sound as though they were about to explode. Water poured down from the expressway above and the road in front of her, where her car now stood, looked like a fast flowing stream. She noticed also that there was a group of people who were huddled together about fifty metres from where she was standing. She could not make out how many they were or whether they were other motorists stranded like her or drug addicts who used such areas as their home. From out of the corner of her eye she thought that she caught sight of one of them pointing over in her direction. Already she calculated that if they approached her she would give them all that she had in her handbag; the wallet which contained about three thousand baht and her credit cards, her mobile phone. They would surely let her keep the medicine.

The condo by the river felt far away, in another country that was warm and secure. Her friends were scattered all over the city. It now seemed like tempting fate to set out by herself in such conditions. She should have insisted on Arun accompanying her. But it was too late to regret. She had to trust that he would turn up in her hour of need. There was no way of walking across the city. She was too tired to make a move in any direction. Her head was pounding. Her back ached from standing around for so long. Trust and wait. That was what faith was, Don had once told her.

She was thinking of these words and the other things he had said in the same conversation and trying to remember why they were talking about it at all, when, as if it had lost all of its strength, her body began to sag and slowly sink down onto the ground. She lay gazing up at the grey pitted surface of the concrete underbelly of the expressway that now seemed high above her. Her hair and her back and her bare legs felt the contact with the warm slimy surface onto which she had crumpled and she could smell the bitter green odour of piss and shit and mud that now enveloped her. Unable to move she closed her eyes. Lying there in the dirt and hearing the rain splatter down onto the pools that seemed to surround her on all sides, it crossed her mind that if Arun did not come soon to find her she could die right there under the expressway. But there was no fear attached to this thought, which surprised her. And then, just as she thought she heard voices coming in her direction, something happened to her which she had never known. It was as if, after a whole lifetime of struggling and trying to keep everything under control, she finally surrendered, and in that moment she felt a radiant peacefulness flood her heart. The voices were nearer now and behind them in the background there was another, deeper sound, like a rumbling that was shaking the earth beneath her.

CHAPTER 45

The evacuation of the government ministries to Nakorn Rajasima had been completed. There was no precise moment when it was officially declared that Bangkok was a city under flood. It would, in any case, have been a superfluous announcement. The warnings had long ceased to make much impression on the inhabitants who had been watching, like impotent witnesses, the failure of one tactic after another to stop the disaster which many considered avoidable if the proper measures had been taken when the first signs appeared. Now they could only hope that they had done enough to save themselves and their loved ones. Already as a result of the relentless rain, Bangkok was looking like a floating metropolis. The sandbags and the hastily constructed barriers had been inundated in the first wave that surged up through the drains and spilled over the banks of the river and the canals. There was not one street or soi or market place that was not immersed. Lawns had become lakes. Street children surfed off the steps of shopping malls. Plastic bags and polystyrene containers bobbed their way through the city. The only cemented surface left that was not below water was the expressway but even there it looked more like an elevated river than a carriageway. Yet for all this most people knew that this was merely the benign phase of the deluge. It was calculated that the water level would exceed two metres before the day was out.

Only the diehard optimists still clung onto the belief that nothing more drastic was going to happen, that their prayers had been answered, that the city would be spared. They reassured themselves that natural catastrophes were rare for Thailand, not like in Bangladesh or the Philippines or all the other places in Asia that were hit every year by earthquakes and typhoons and all the violence that nature could muster. We Thais were lucky people, they said. The flood would only last a few days. It would be nowhere as severe as the doom mongers had predicted. We could cope. We would adapt to the circumstances. We were good at that. There was no need to worry. The water would soon recede and life would return to normal.

But the wishful thinking turned to defeat and hysteria, when some time during the early morning of the 15th October, the tide reached its highest level and the sea joined with the Chao Phraya River. It was a union that awakened the full force of the element. Even while the people of Bangkok slept there was the sound of a deep rumble followed by a roar such as no one had ever heard in the city before, like a hungry monster waking up in the depths and eager to display its destructive power. And when it finally burst onto the city, everything was uprooted and pulled along and battered into a pulp. Trees, lampposts, cars and trucks were carried along like toys. The houses that were not rock solid were broken up and their inhabitants, if they had not been evacuated already, sucked out and plunged into the swirling fury with no hope of survival.

That initial onslaught lasted no more than a couple of hours, but during it almost fifteen thousand drowned and over two million were made homeless. By the time the rushing torrent calmed down, Bangkok had been transformed into a place that was unrecognizable to its inhabitants. Through the windows of the upper stories to which they had retreated, they saw a spectacle that was grotesque and macabre. The brown swirl that looked treacherously dangerous was thick with the debris and the detritus of the metropolis, normally seen only in the stagnant backwaters; dead dogs with bloated bellies, bits of furniture, wooden planks from a wall, giant billboards. And among all of it corpses of men, women and children and even newly born who had been sucked down and then thrown up to the surface again. They no longer looked human but resembled strange creatures that had risen from the silt bed. Even those in their tall condos who were watching from their balconies could see clearly the horror below, like some hallucination floating up towards them.

As expected, the flood, which would very quickly be called 'The Great Flood' hit the poor areas most. Not only the flimsy shacks in the slums, but also the two story shophouses that had been built on the cheap, were swept aside as soon as the deluge began. But for those who had watched their friends and relatives washed away in those first terrifying hours, there was no time to mourn. In the days that followed, survival was the most urgent issue. The evacuation program by helicopter that was put into effect and the rescue operation mounted with the aid of foreign agencies were suitably effective but not sufficient. Unlike other countries in the region, Thailand had little experience of how to deal with a large scale natural disaster. The original plan was to set up a temporary shelter using army tents. But these were not enough to house the people left homeless. In the end the inhabitants who were left behind had to rely on their own determination and inventiveness. The disaster and the collective grief strengthened the sense of solidarity. Those who could do so shared what they had with their neighbours. Boats were used communally. Kitchens were set up to distribute food and water to those who, for one reason or another, were now without the means to look after themselves.

But these long days of insecurity took their toll. The sense of tragedy was intense and the mood was one of despair. Within a week, five thousand more were to die from the epidemics that rapidly followed. This time it was not only the poor who were hit. The lack of clean water and sanitation brought along hepatitis, cholera, typhoid to add to the pneumonia and flu to which almost everybody succumbed at one point or another. The diseases that overran the city during those fragile times did not discriminate between wealth or class.

⇒‡⇐

Bangkok was under water for over a month. During this time there was total collapse of the infrastructure; no electricity and hence no communication except by mobile phone and only then while the batteries lasted. Fridges did not work, so food could not be stored. The ill could not be taken to hospital because there was no health service. People who died in their beds were wrapped up in cloth and lowered into the water to join the rotting corpses that were already floating on the surface. And, little by little, the city reverted to the mangrove swamp that it had once been. Reptiles that had almost all disappeared in recent years crawled out of their secret layers. Abandoned palaces and ambassadorial residences, solid office buildings and empty shopping malls all became home to the iguanas, pythons, and monitor lizards that could be seen climbing and sliding through the broken windows and up the steps. In the evening there was the cacophony of the bullfrogs and during the day the squawking of the crows and magpies that had come to feed on the carnage.

At the end of the third week the water finally began to subside. Then, one bright morning, when the sky was the colour of sapphire, it was all gone. What remained was a thick layer of sludge, a metre high in some of the lowest areas. It was greeny grey with a marbled texture and within it and sticking out of its shiny surface were the corpses of humans and beasts and all that had been broken and mangled; the weird bas relief of destruction that the flood had sculpted. Before the authorities rushed in with their army of bulldozers and trucks, the survivors could only stare in disbelief, knowing that the image would stay in their minds for as long as they lived.

The damage was incalculable. Figures of hundreds of billions of baht were quoted but these were more to do with the economy than the reality that now faced the great majority of people in Bangkok, who had lost everything they had. What was sure was that it was going to take years to start again and rebuild and restore. The task looked so daunting in those early days after the Great Flood that there was strong talk of moving the capital altogether and starting again, further down the coast, where there was no river and no risk of another flood.

CHAPTER 46

Don and Nong Da were worried when they could not get through to Marisa. They had begged her not to go by herself, to insist on Arun accompanying her or else to postpone the appointment for a later date. After the third attempt Don called Arun. He had not wanted to, because he was angry at his friend for being so caught up in his own dilemmas that he could not see that it was not a matter of choice, but a necessity, for him to be at Marisa's side. He could not understand how Arun could profess to love and yet behave so selfishly and he could not help but judge him for being so weak and unreliable. They had not spoken since the last time he and Nong Da visited the condo for dinner. It was to be their last meal together before he and Nong Da moved into Klongtoey. But what should have been a happy reunion turned out to be a bad tempered affair with Arun, who was drunk, picking holes in what Marisa was saying and arguing that the flood was going to be much less severe than people (meaning Don) were thinking. He could remember the last one, he told them, being like a glorified water festival. He had gone out on a boat with his sister Ladda to the market and they had water fights with the other children.

Don remembered that evening not so much because of Arun's behaviour but because, during the course of it, while the others were in the kitchen, he told Marisa that he was in love with Nong Da. It was both a confession and a way of asking her permission. He saw how protective she was and he did not want to make a move which she might disapprove. When Marisa heard his declaration she frowned.

"I am happy for both of you. I know that Nong Da feels for you too. But you must be careful. You know how damaged she is. You must be kind and patient. Otherwise you will destroy her."

"But you'll give us your blessing."

"Of course. As though you need it!"

On the day of the flood, Don had to redial four times before Arun answered.

"I'm sorry. I heard it ring. But I think my battery's going. I can hardly hear you now," Arun was shouting over the sound of an engine.

"Where are you? Are you with Marisa?"

"No. That's the problem. I'm in a songtaew. I've been to the studio. She called me. Her car's broken down. She's somewhere on Rama IX but she gave me bad directions. And the taxi driver is refusing to take me. Says it's too far out of his way. Says he's got to get home. I don't know what to do."

Don stopped himself from saying the obvious. From the tone of Arun's voice he knew that he did not have to rub it in.

"There's no way I can get out of here," he said. "All the streets around me are already flooded. There are only boats being used."

"It's OK. It's OK. I'll find a way," Arun said without conviction. And then the signal was cut off.

When he finished his conversation with Don, Arun turned to the driver and once again pleaded with him.

"I've got to get to her. She will die." As soon as the words were out of his mouth he felt the truth of them and suddenly he shivered with panic. He even thought of knocking the driver out and grabbing the wheel and hijacking the vehicle.

"Do you think you're the only one in this city shitting himself right now?" the man was shouting at him. "What about all the other people who are trying to get to their loved ones, who don't have nice comfortable safe places to go to? What about me! I have a wife and children. Any other day I'd be glad to help you. But we're all about to drown. Can't you see?"

With that he gestured for Arun to get out of his cab and refused the payment offered.

⚬╾╂╼⚬

Arun had been walking for nearly an hour. He did not feel tired and he was hardly aware of the rain. There was only one thought in his mind and it gave him the strange, trance-like energy that only the religiously possessed and the manic have. From their windows people saw a wild eyed man, with a shoe in each hand and long wet dishevelled hair nearly down to his waist and clothes that clung to him, moving swiftly along the empty, rain-drenched streets as though he was floating.

He chanted her name like a mantra and with every step he felt nearer to her. He knew that she was waiting and holding out. He would soon reach her.

Then from behind him came a sound that made him stop and turn and in a split second he sensed the danger. There was a derelict half finished building to his left that was covered in graffiti. Without thinking, he ran into it and up a flight of steps then another and another till there were no more steps.

Now he was in a vast room. Along one long wall there were motorbikes neatly parked in a row. Their owners paid him no attention because they were all leaning outside the window with their backs to him.

"Here it comes," one girl shouted. And just then the building felt as though it was going to be swept away.

CHAPTER 47

Marisa did not die in the flood. But the morning that she waited for Arun to come was the beginning of her death. As she lay under the expressway the three derelicts who had been watching her walked to where she was and carried her across the street to a shophouse that they had broken into a few days earlier when the owners had abandoned it. They took her up to a room which must have been used for storage and laid her on a sheet of cardboard on the floor. There were two men with long matted hair, beards and the dark grimy skin of those who had been living in the streets. They wore rags that hung off their thin, bony bodies. She saw track marks on their arms. The woman looked stronger than either of them, although her face, with the hollow expression and the dark rings, showed all the signs of terminal addiction. She was small with short spiky hair and she wore a dress with flowers printed on it.

The three of them stood over her and spoke to each other in a dialect that Marisa could not understand. It was a mix of Thai and Khmer and she guessed that they were from Surin. One of the men emptied out her bag. Coins and a packet of mints rolled onto the lino. He extracted the money from her wallet and held it up in the air, waving it around before sharing it out with his companions. Next he took out her identity card and handed it to the woman, who scrutinized it for a while before uttering some words of recognition. Marisa heard her name spoken, and then the name of a film she had once made; 'The Fallen Woman'. They talked again over her prone body; this time their voices had more urgency. She thought for a moment that they were going to kill her. Then the two men got up and left, never to come back.

When they had gone the woman went to a far corner of the room and came back with a pa kama. She then asked Marisa, in Thai if she could sit up. Marisa shook her head and said that she had no strength left. The woman took the wet blouse off her and reached behind to unhook her bra and then pulled the trousers off her waist. Then using the pa kama she carefully dried her hair and her body. When she had finished she handed the pa kama to Marisa and said;

"Here. Cover yourself. It's all I've got."

It was not long after this when the flood water crashed through the ground floor of the shophouse and while it did the woman lay down next to Marisa and closed her eyes. They held each other tightly like two animals in a storm while the building shook and swayed and the rain poured in through the window.

Marisa was delirious with fever. The woman produced a bottle of water from somewhere and held it for her to drink. Days turned into night. Rats scuttled through the room. A bird screamed at dawn. Smoke the colour of sweet metal drifted over. She heard the woman singing a love song. She saw her mother sitting in the far corner. Her body was burning. Fire on the water. The Naga rising from the depths. Then the rain stopped. Light poured in. The woman was giving her more water and speaking to her, telling her to sit up. There was another voice. It was a man's, saying:

"Prepare your things. Come to where we can reach you." It came through a loudspeaker and it was repeating the same message over and over again.

"Get up. You must try. They're coming to save you." The woman was dragging her to her feet.

They took her by boat and transferred her to a rescue helicopter. She was taken to a hospital in Petchburi, where she stayed for three weeks with tubes in her arms through which medicines dripped. She thought constantly of the woman who had helped her and whose eyes now haunted her and whose name she would never know. The night that she died she remembered the words of the Naga oracle she had once visited with her friends and she understood them clearly. She was not afraid and she was as sure as she had ever been about anything that she was about to embark on a new journey.

CHAPTER 48

It was two months after the flood. The weather was dry and the sky clear. There was a breeze blowing off the Chao Phraya. The early morning air was fresh. There were few boats on the river itself, none of the bustle of the water buses or the loud longtails, and the big cruisers that used to take the tourists up to Ayudhya and back were no longer operating. Normal life—that is, the activities that took place before the flood—had not resumed. Nevertheless, all along the river bank there were signs that some kind of reconstruction was taking place, evidenced by the bags of cement piled high, and the cranes and the logs that were ready to replace those that had been destroyed. But all over the city, despite the government's efforts to pump up enthusiasm for the new Bangkok that was now going to be built, a truly modern metropolis that was going to be green and clean and free from slums and poverty and dirt, people were still going about in a kind of shocked apathy, like patients recovering from a major operation, glad to have survived but hurting and knowing that it was going to take years before the wounds healed.

It was Nong Da who remembered that Marisa had once said that she wanted her ashes scattered on the river when she died. They had hired a small boat at the landing near the condo and were now nearing the landing pier under Saphan Put bridge, in sight of the Temple of Dawn. Their destination was Wat Prayoon where they were going to hold the tamboon ceremony for Marisa. It was her favourite temple in the city. As a little girl she had once lived in the district and her mother used to take her to see the turtles that were in the temple grounds. She had often talked of taking them all there, but it never happened.

The ashes they took in a small celadon urn were not the remains of her body, because she had already been cremated in the temple near the hospital in Petchburi, where she had died along with a thousand other people who had been evacuated there. Since no relative or friend had been present, the people in charge of the ovens there had not bothered to put them aside. So the three of them, who never found out exactly what happened to their beloved friend and who had in the end accepted that she had perished, had instead taken her favourite dress, some photographs that she liked, a small painting that Arun had given her and put these things into a bonfire in the garden of the studio. These were the ashes that they scattered into the river that morning. And they said a prayer for her and threw in the roses they had brought from the market at Paak Klong Talaad.

At Wat Prayoon, which was near the river, the clean up was still in progress, as in every other part of the city. The old kutis that dated back to the reign of Rama 3rd had all been destroyed. The frescos in the main Vihara were beyond repair. The turtle garden was still full of broken branches and debris. The turtles had all disappeared. Phra Ieng, who took them round to the sala where the ceremony was to take place, explained how they had all sheltered on the top floor of the temple school, along with many of the locals and how hard it had been during that month, living on top of one another. A woman had given birth but lost her baby and they had to throw it onto the water.

It was a simple ceremony. Nong Da placed the photograph of Marisa by the altar and each of them lit a candle and a joss-stick. Then four monks chanted for her. Had it been under any other circumstance the occasion would have been a very public affair attended, no doubt, by the celebrities of Bangkok. But her death was one among so many that it had gone by unnoticed and unmentioned in the newspapers. Only years later would people remember that she was no longer around and wonder where she had gone. The monks had been doing the same ceremony for the families who had lost one or more of their members. They offered no words of comfort to those who came to mourn. Grief linked them all together. Only time would heal.

CHAPTER 49

Less than a week later Arun was packing up once more and preparing to leave for Paris. The studio was to be repaired. Ladda, with whom he had made peace, was going to take it over and use it as a guest residence for visiting performers who did not like staying in hotels. There was little for him to do except to take care of some details. He stood in front of the tall mirror that was in the room that Nong Da had once stayed in, uncertain whether to leave it as part of the furniture or put it the store room in the garden. In it he saw a figure he hardly recognized. Instead of the long ponytail his hair was now cropped short. And it had turned noticeably grey. His body had lost a lot of weight and the clothes hung off it untidily. He knew why these outer transformations had taken place.

He was glad that he had remained for the ceremony. At first, when Don and Nong Da suggested it, he had hesitated. Losing Marisa was still too painful, he told them, and he did not know if he could cope with it. Besides, they knew that he did not believe in the afterlife or reincarnation. What difference would it make to Marisa, nor to how he was feeling, to listen to some monks chanting? It was all too late. But in the end he postponed his journey and went along with them, because deep within him he knew that he needed some kind of closure to what had happened, if he was to carry on with his life at all.

During the two months after the flood, he had been in a state of inner torment that had battered and almost destroyed him, just as the waters had nearly wrecked the city for good. When one morning he finally came to terms with the fact that Marisa had died alone somewhere in the city, he went numb, as though all the blood had drained from his system. There were no tears. He remained in the apartment for days unable to feel anything in his heart, immobile, watching the sunset and the sunrise in the seat where Marisa used to sit watching the river and he did not care whether he lived or died.

Afterwards the demons came to him in full force; the grief and the remorse, the guilt and shame of not reaching her that day, of having failed to love her in the way that he might have, if he had not been so caught up in his own mess. There were times that he hated himself so much that he wished that he had drowned when he was on his way to find her.

He went over and over the details of the way he had landed up in that derelict building covered with graffiti, and was looked after by a biker gang who then later took him by boat back to the condo. And he tried to fathom out if there was a reason why his life had been spared while others, which were probably more deserving, more honest and innocent, had been taken so casually. The injustice of it all felt like a physical weight that crushed him. And the realization that he had lost the one love of his life broke his heart.

⌐‡⌐

He had expected nothing from the ceremony but a sense of completion, of having performed a ritual that was part of the culture into which he had been born. He put his hands together and listened to the familiar rhythms and the words of the ancient language. The thought of Marisa brought tears to his eyes once again. He wished that she were there so that he could ask her to forgive him for not having been able to look after her, for being a coward and an idiot. He could not pray as the others were doing. What was the point? She had gone from him, from them all. It was merely wishful thinking to believe that there was any continuation.

At that moment her photograph fell off the altar. Nong Da rushed to put it back where it was.

At the end of the ceremony, as the monks filed past on their way back to their quarters, the senior one who was assistant to the abbot turned to the three of them and said, pointing to Marisa's picture;

"It happens sometimes when the link is a strong one."

Arun remembered those words as he finished packing and it struck him that perhaps that was what continuation meant: a link that could not be severed by death, that transcended space and time. For he knew that Marisa would live on in his heart wherever he went, that everything that he did from then on would relate in some way to her.

⌐‡⌐

Later, as the plane took off and climbed towards its cruising level, Arun felt a sense of release that he had not known for a long time. The sky was cloudless and deep purple, the colour of the skin of an eggplant. In it the stars pulsed and there was the crescent of a new moon. An unfamiliar optimism began to well up in his heart. Paris! The idea of starting again. He knew that there was a chance of finding healing there in the old streets and parks and cafés and rooms where he had no past.

He looked down at the lights of the city that were now rapidly receding. The buildings were still visible and the familiar avenues and the temples came into view for the last time. And then there was a brief glimpse of the river. The sight produced a pang of longing and melancholy. He was leaving the city that had trapped him for so long in its shadows, but which was, nevertheless, his birthplace. He did not know when he would return, if ever.

In front of him and all around him there was a wide, bright, open space as big as the sky itself. It was too early to say for sure that he could see what he was going to do next in his life. All he knew was that the terrible flood had washed away the obstacles that he had created to resist the pain of being alive. The loss of Marisa had freed him from the fear and the doubt which had kept him so self-obsessed and closed off since he was a child. He had only known a pain as deep as that once before and it was when he had lost his mother. After that he could not open to life, because there was always the possibility that his love would be snatched away from him. Now, having lost Marisa, his worst fear had come true. There was nothing left to lose. And in those weeks of grieving he had come to see that he could either kill himself or take the risk of beginning again.

That he chose to begin again was an act of trust. At thirty eight years old, he was only just beginning to understand the meaning of this word. He had never been near to grasping its implications, until his heart had been ripped open through grief. Now he saw it as the essential quality that had always been lacking in him; the trust that had no conditions, but was an affirmation of the force and beauty and sacredness of life, despite the pain and the suffering that were its essential ingredients. He knew that he would never be able to explain this to others, not just because he was clumsy with words, but because each person had to come to this simple realization through a personal journey. He had reached this point thanks to Marisa and now, in the stirrings of the new creativity that he could sense within him, he saw that he would consecrate his paintings, and all that he was going to do for the remainder of his time, to her. And as the plane turned away from the city and set its nose towards the west, Arun, who never prayed with any conviction, offered up a prayer of thanks.

CHAPTER 50

When they said their awkward goodbyes at the airport there was an air of finality. Don knew that a phase in their lives was closing. During their last days together, they had been sharing their thoughts with the same openness that they had once done. They went over old ground and reminisced about what they been through together. They talked about Marisa in the past tense but her presence during these conversations was taken for granted. They knew how she would have reacted to the things that they said.

In their last meeting at the studio, before going to the airport, Arun had asked for Don to forgive him and to give him his blessing for the journey he was about to take and the new life he was about to embark on.

"I'm not a monk any more," Don laughed.

"Yes, you are," said Arun. "You never stopped being a monk. It's nothing to do with wearing a robe. You said that once yourself. Marisa and I always joked that you probably would have been an abbot if you had stayed up in Nongkhai."

"But you never believed in these things."

"I know. Still I need your forgiveness. And Marisa's too."

"It's better if you forgive yourself."

"I know. I'm trying to. But I need your help. Please do this for me. Out of friendship."

In the end Don agreed, even though he felt embarrassed at the request. He took a bowl of water and poured some wax from a candle into it chanting a stanza from the Metta Sutta as he did so. Then he took a rose from a newly planted bush in the garden and dipped it into the bowl and sprinkled the water onto Arun's bowed head. As he did so, he prayed with all his heart that his friend would find the peace that had eluded him.

A month later Don himself was kneeling on the floor of the vihara of Wat Thammacitta, in front of the golden Buddharupa, receiving a blessing. Nong Da was next to him and his mother and his aunt, who had come over from Chiengmai, were behind. There were villagers who had known Don when he was Phra Boontam sitting further back and his ex fellow monks were on the dais to the right of the altar. Above them the old fan whirred as it revolved. It was a hot day. The dry season had begun early.

The abbot had just finished giving a short, ironic speech which had made them all laugh. He told them how he had completely failed in his own attempt at being in the world, how difficult it was for two people to be committed to one another and how he did not understand why anyone should choose the secular life at all. Given all the pitfalls, it was the most foolhardy thing to do, for it only brought problems and conflict. But he did not want to discourage anyone from doing so, he said, if they were brave enough and sure enough of their capacity for suffering.

To those present, most of whom were familiar with his style, which became more barbed as the years went by, the abbot's talk was taken as another instance of his mischievous humour. They knew that his playful dig was harmless fun. But they were unaware that earlier in the kuti, when Don had been summoned to visit him without Nong Da, the old monk had gently tried to persuade Don to return to the monastery and ordain once more.

"The life out there can't satisfy you for long," he said. "You're the spiritual type. I saw you during those five years. I know who you are. There's nothing there for you. You'll have children to take care of and all those worldly responsibilities and there'll be no time for yourself. It'll get you down. And then, when you have to part from them or if you lose them like all those people did in the flood, you'll suffer terribly."

There was no malice in his words, but as Don listened he suddenly caught a glimpse of the abbot as a young man who had just arrived at the monastery, relieved to have fled the everyday life of the householder. He loved his former teacher no less for trying to undermine him. Just before their meeting came to an end, the abbot took his hand and shook it softly.

"I'm getting old," he said. "The monastery needs to be cared for. I need someone like you to take over this place. I always thought when you went away that you needed to finish off some karma before deciding to return. I was waiting for you. I never imagined you would come back in order to say goodbye again."

Don saw the sadness in the old man's eyes. But there was nothing he could do about it.

After the ceremony, before leaving the monastery, he walked alone to the bank of the Mekong with bags full of left-over food to feed the fish. The river was still that afternoon. There was hardly a ripple on the glassy surface on which the sunlight danced. On the sandbank in the middle, two huge cranes were standing still, like sculptures. In the distance, against the backdrop of the thick trees on the opposite bank Don could see men in their thin wooden boats casting their nets. The idyllic scene was so different from the slums of Bangkok to which he was returning. It was good to be reminded that a simpler way of life still existed, away from the hard pavements of the city, and to see the wild greenery again. It would probably be their last break from the city for some time. Nong Da had enrolled in a nursing college and would be kept busy for the next few years. And he had now been made one of the directors of 'Clean Thailand', which, given the tasks that faced them, meant that he would be committed to being in Bangkok.

He stood for a while in the sala where he had once sat and meditated and noticed that, in contrast to the freshness of the scenery that spread out in front of him, everything looked dilapidated and in need of serious repair, as did the rest of the monastery. In the time that he had been away the buildings seemed to have been left to decay. Roof tiles were missing, the paintwork was cracked, the vegetable garden that had once been so well tended by the lay supporters now overgrown with weeds. He understood the abbot's concerns.

In spite of the awkward reunion with his old teacher, he was glad that they had decided to come all the way up to Wat Thammacitta to do the tamboon. To his mother it was a strange choice, which she put down to his habitual need to surprise her. They could have gone to any temple in Bangkok to perform the ceremony, she said. Why did he have to go all the way back to Nongkhai, especially when it was only a formality? And in a way she was right. There was no reason to make the long trek from Bangkok. But when he discussed it with Nong Da, she guessed straightaway that he wanted to do it in the place where he had been ordained. He did not have to explain to her his motives. Nor could he have done so in any intelligible way. There was no sentimentality or nostalgia. He merely felt that it was right to come there, to make merit for all the people who had perished in the flood.

As he stood there in the small sala he felt a gratitude towards the monastery and its abbot. The five years he had spent there and all the practices had allowed him to glimpse the possibility of peace and redemption and the power of the compassionate heart. He learned that he no longer had to destroy. And for a while it seemed that the disciplined regularity of the spiritual life within the confines of those faded walls, among others who could not find their place in the world, had been perfect for him.

He recalled the irresistible force that had pushed him back into the world. He did not understand at the time what happened to make him leave, except that it was to do with the strange dream that he had in which he became possessed by the Naga. A dream which he still could not properly decipher and yet which, at the time, had disturbed him so deeply that he had to step out of the path he was on and take a different journey, back into his past and into the unknown.

Don saw now why the abbot had made no effort to dissuade him from disrobing, but even encouraged him to go back into the world. Having been a gambler, he was betting that Don would quickly become disillusioned with the worldly existence beyond the monastery walls and return to the monkhood ready to resume his vows and his commitment to the Dhamma. Perhaps, Don thought, this had been the abbot's own journey. And he saw how close he had been to repeating it, as he remembered how many times during those years in the noisy chaos of the city, he had been tempted to come back to the monastery and start again on the well trodden path which, if he persisted on it and managed not to fall into the traps along the way, would perhaps have led him eventually to the ocean of peace that was the destination of all good Buddhists.

If he had not met Nong Da, the abbot's gamble may have paid off. Even now, as he felt again the peacefulness of the surroundings and the spaciousness of being far from the crowds and the frenetic bustle of Bangkok, Don could appreciate the attraction that such a life offered. But through the love that he had found for her he decided to stay in the world and not to retreat from it.

Standing there watching the light and the wide expanse of water he could sense the presence within him of the Naga, the mysterious spirit of nature that lay behind all the things that man tried and failed to dominate.

By returning to the monastery he understood, intuitively, that what moved him to leave was the reawakening in him of the force of curiosity, the primal energy which, in his confusion and guilt, he had lost for a long time. The Naga spirit left him no choice but to flow on and face what he had done and to take the step of finding out if the things he had experienced in the quietude of monastic life would serve in the absurd theatre of daily interchange, if the transformations that he thought he had undergone were real or merely another level of self delusion.

⚬━✦━⚬

Nong Da's voice pulled him out of his thoughts. She had been standing behind him for a long time, watching him. He heard her voice call him.

"It's time to leave. They're waiting to take us to the station," she said as she approached the sala. "What are you doing here, looking so sad like that? Are you missing the peace you had here?"

She was smiling broadly at him. He knew that she saw into his heart and he smiled back at her.

"Would you ever live here, in the north-east?" he asked her.

"It's too quiet. It scares me a little. I prefer the streets and the markets. But I will be with you wherever you want to be."

⚬━✦━⚬

Don stretched out on the top bunk, savouring the delicious feeling of riding the night train. He was glad that they had found berths on the sleeper. The villagers had told him that it would be crowded. People who had left Bangkok to escape from the flood were still returning to the capital. Through the parted curtain he could see the countryside, bathed in the light of the moon, flashing by; villages, fields and forests and distant hills, shadow and liquid light melting into one another. He had just leaned over to check that Nong Da, in the lower bunk, was asleep and now he too felt the tiredness begin to come over him. It had been a long hot day. He listened to the pleasant rhythm of the engine; *tung-gaw chang-mai tung-gaw chang, tung-gaw chang-mai tung-gaw chang*—the rhyme that he had learned as a child, which had always amused and comforted him. As he lay there and entered the floating in-between state before losing consciousness, his body rocked by the steady jolt of the train winding its way southward to the capital, Don's mind drifted back and forth like a tide that brought up thoughts and images of his friends Arun and Marisa, of the flood and the people in Klongtoey that he had come to know, until everything was mixed up into one vast tableau, out of which, for a second, a pattern would emerge, only to disappear again in the next instant. And then in this swirl of colourful impressions Nong Da's smile loomed out and spread through the breadth of his consciousness, as if the whole vast ocean was giving a blessing. And just as sleep overtook him he felt a simple, warm happiness well up in his heart and he knew that the journey ahead which he was about to share with her would be as rich and unpredictable as both of them could imagine.

Glossary of Thai Terms

Achaan: Teacher.

Ah: Uncle. The younger brother of the father.

Annicam: Impermanence, one of the four marks of existence according to Buddhist teachings.

Bodhi: Wisdom. The Buddha achieved his Enlightenment under a Bodhi tree.

Brahmacharya: sexual abstinence.

Buddharupa: Image of the Buddha

Dhamma: The teachings of the Buddha.

Dukkha: Suffering, another mark of earthly existence.

Farang: Foreigner, foreign.

Isan: The north-easterly area of Thailand.

Karma: Action which has consequences. It has come to take on the meaning of fate.

Khun: Mr. or Mrs., a polite term of address.

Klong: Canal.

Kuti: A monk's dwelling.

Laakmueng: The city's foundation stone.

Luang Pi: Holy Brother. This is how lay men and women often address a monk.

Mae: Mother.

Mae Ping: The river that runs through the northern town of Chiengmai.

Mawlum: Folk songs from the North-east.

Maw Ya: A herbalist, a healer.

Metta karuna: Loving compassion.

Momrajawong: The great grandson or granddaughter of a king.

Nong: Younger sister. Also a term of endearment.

Ngo Heng: A popular method of reading a person's physiognomy (Chinese in origin).

October 14th, 1973: A popular uprising led by students which toppled the military government.

Pa kama: Traditional Thai dress.

Pali: The ancient classical language in which the Buddhist Suttas were written.

Phaya Naak: The Thai term for the Naga.

Phra: A monk. Holy.

Pi: Elder brother or sister. Another term of endearment.

Preta: Ghost. There are many types of ghosts in Thailand.

Samadhi: Concentration.

Sala: A hall in a temple or a public place.

Silpakorn: The Fine Arts Department in Bangkok.

Soi: A lane leading off the main road.

Songtaew: Cheap communal taxis with two rows of seats.

Suan Lumpini: The main park in Bangkok.

Tamboon: Merit-making ceremony.

Tuk-tuk: Three-wheeled passenger carrying motorbike taxis common in Bangkok.

Tung-gaw chang-mai tung-gaw chang: Arrive-ok, not arrive-ok.

Wai: The formal greeting and sign of showing respect by putting the palms together and bowing your head

Wat: A temple.